Henri Le Caron

Twenty-Five Years in the Secret Service

The Recollections of a Spy. Sixth Edition

Henri Le Caron

Twenty-Five Years in the Secret Service
The Recollections of a Spy. Sixth Edition

ISBN/EAN: 9783337406363

Printed in Europe, USA, Canada, Australia, Japan

Cover: Foto ©Andreas Hilbeck / pixelio.de

More available books at **www.hansebooks.com**

Yours truly,
H. Le Caron

TWENTY-FIVE YEARS

IN

THE SECRET SERVICE

The Recollections of a Spy

BY

MAJOR HENRI LE CARON

With Portraits and Facsimiles

"No citizen has a right to consider himself as belonging to himself; but all ought to regard themselves as belonging to the State, inasmuch as each is a part of the State; and care for the part naturally looks to care for the whole."
—ARISTOTLE.

Sixth  Edition

LONDON
WILLIAM HEINEMANN
1892

INTRODUCTION.

It has seemed good in the sight of many people that I should place on record, in some permanent and acceptable form, the story of my eventful life. And so I am about to write a book. The task is a daring one—perhaps the most daring of the many strange and unlooked-for incidents which have marked my career of adventure. I approach it with no light heart, but rather with a keen appreciation of all its difficulties.

To cater, and cater successfully, for the reading public of this *fin de siècle* period is an undertaking which fairly taxes all the powers of resource and experience of the most brilliant writers of our time. And I am in no sense a practised writer, much less a professional *littérateur*. I have spent my life working at too high a pressure, and in too excited an atmosphere, to allow of my qualifying in any way for the rôle of author.

Nor am I handicapped in this way alone. I am, unfortunately for my purpose, deprived of the most important of collaborators a writer ever called to his aid—the play of imagination. For me there is no such thing as romance to be indulged in here. The truth, the whole truth, and nothing but the truth is what I have set myself to tell regarding all those matters with which I shall deal. There are many things, of course, to which I may not refer; but with respect to those upon which I feel at liberty to touch, one unalterable characteristic will apply all through, and that will be the absolute truthfulness of the record.

This may seem strange language coming from one who, for over a quarter of a century, has played a double part, and who to-day is not one whit ashamed of any single act done in that capacity. Men's lives, however, are not to be judged by the outward show and the visible suggestion, but rather by the inward sentiments and promptings which accept conscience at once as the inspirer of action and arbiter of fate. It is hard, I know, to expect people in this cold prosaic age of ours to fully understand how a man like myself should, of his own free will, have entered upon a life such as I have led, with such pureness of motive and absence of selfish instinct as to entitle me to-day to claim acceptance at the bar of public opinion as an honest and a truthful man.

Yet such is my claim. When years ago, as these subsequent pages will show, I was first brought into contact with Fenian affairs, no fell purpose, no material consideration prompted me to work against the revolutionary plotters. A young man, proud of his native land and full of patriotic loyalty to its traditions, I had no desire, no intention to do aught but frustrate the schemes of my country's foes. When, later on, I took my place in the ranks of England's defenders, the same condition of mind prevailed, though the conditions of service varied.

And so the situation has remained all through. Forced by a variety of circumstances to play a part I never sought, but to which, for conscientious motives, I not unwillingly adapted myself, I can admit no shame and plead no regret. By my action lives have been saved, communities have been benefited, and right and justice allowed to triumph, to the confusion of law-breakers and would-be murderers. And in this recollection I have my consolation and my reward. Little else indeed is left me in the shape of either the one or the other. There is a popular fiction, I know,

which associates with my work fabulous payments
and frequent rewards. Would that it had been
so. Then would the play of memory be all the
sweeter for me. But, alas! the facts were all the
other way. As I will show later, in the Secret
Service of England there is ever present danger,
and constantly recurring difficulty, but of recom-
pense, a particularly scant supply.

TWENTY-FIVE YEARS IN THE SECRET SERVICE.

I.

Of my early youth little that is very interesting or exciting can be told. A faded entry in the aged records of the ancient borough of Colchester evidences the fact that a certain Thomas Beach, to wit myself, came into this world some fifty and one years ago, on the 26th day of September 1841. My parents were English, as the American would phrase it, "from far away back," my grandfather tracing his lineage through many generations in the county of Berkshire. The second son of a family of thirteen, I fear I proved a sore trial to a careful father and affectionate mother, by my erratic methods and the varied outbursts of my wild exuberant nature. My earliest recollection is of the teetotal principle on which we were all brought up, and the absence of strong drink from all our household feasts. The point is a trivial one, but not unworthy of note, as it supplies the key to some of my successes in later life, in keeping clear of danger

A

where the efforts to curb my impulsive nature resulted in increasing bitterness of spirit on my part every day. In eleven months it was conceded on both sides that the continuation of the arrangement was distinctly undesirable, and so I was free once more. A short residence with my parents followed; but the old promptings to wander afar were too strong for me, and once more, for the third and last time, I broke away, and reached London at last, in the month of May 1857.

Through the kindness of relatives. employment was secured for me in a leading business house ; but my stay there was of short duration. With my usual facility for doing everything wrong at this period of my existence, I happened to accidentally set fire to the premises, and was politely told that after this my services could not be properly appreciated. I was not long out of employment, and strangely enough, through the agency of one of the gentlemen whose house had suffered through my carelessness, I was later on enabled to obtain a much better situation than I had held in their house.

From London I subsequently made my way to Bath, and from Bath to Bristol, always in search of change, though everywhere doing well. When in Bristol, however, I was struck down with fever, and reduced to a penniless condition.

Then came the idea of returning to London, which I duly carried out, walking all the way. My foolhardiness proved almost fatal, for ere I got to the metropolis, my illness came back upon me, and I was scarce able to crawl to St. Bartholomew's Hospital in search of relief.

My stay at St. Bartholomew's was not a very long one. Horrified at the terrible death of a patient lying next to me, and fearful that, if I remained, something equally horrible might be my fate, I managed to obtain possession of my clothes and to leave the institution. Thoughts of home and mother decided my return to Colchester, and thither I immediately proceeded to make my way on foot. Again the fever attacked me, and once more I had to seek the friendly shelter of an hospital, this time taking refuge in the Colchester and East Essex Institution. Here I remained till I was permanently recovered, after which I entered the service of Mr. William Baber of the town. However, my efforts to lead a sober conventional life were all in vain. The wild longing for change came back in renewed strength, and in a little while I had left London altogether behind and journeyed to Paris *viâ* Havre.

II.

I AM amused as I look back now upon the utter recklessness and daring of this proceeding of mine. I knew not a soul in France ; of the language, not a word was familiar ; and yet somehow the longing to get away from England and to try my luck on a new soil was irresistible. One place was as good as another to me, and Paris seemed rather more familiar than the other few centres of activity with the names of which I was then acquainted. And so to Paris I went. It was my good fortune to hit upon an hotel kept by an Englishwoman in the Faubourg St. Honoré, and here I tarried for a time while my little stock of money lasted. This was not by any means a long period, and soon I found myself reduced once more to a condition of penury, having in the interval gained little but an acquaintance with the principal thoroughfares and their shops, and a slight knowledge of the language, to which latter I was helped in no inconsiderable degree by a wonderfully retentive memory.

Things were at a very low ebb for me indeed, when help came from an entirely unexpected quarter. Happening one Sunday to pass by the

English Church in the Rue d'Aguesseau, of which,
by the way, the Rev. Dr. Forbes was at that time
chaplain, I was attracted by the music of the service then proceeding, and entered the little unpre-
tentious place of worship. Here I joined heartily
in the service, with the order and details of which
I was perfectly familiar, having already sung in
the choir of my native town. My singing and
generally strange appearance attracted the attention of a member of the church, with whom I
formed an acquaintance. We left the church
together—not however before I had promised
my assistance in the choir—and at his request I
breakfasted with my English friend at one of the
crêmeries in the Faubourg. Now, as then, a
respected citizen of Paris, I am happy to number
this countryman among the truest and most
steadfast of my friends.

We passed the day together, attending the
remaining two services at the church, and in the
hours we spent in each other's company I told
him my history and my needs. Warm-hearted
and impulsive, he immediately suggested that I
should vacate my room and share his lodging,
even going the length of advancing me money to
enable me to do so. Before a week had passed,
he had capped his goodness by securing a situation
for me; and I found myself at length comfortably

installed in the house of Withers, *à la Suis-sesse*, 52 Faubourg St. Honoré. Through his influence also I became a paid member of the church choir, and in a very short time I was the recipient of the friendship and confidence of Dr. Forbes and his wife, from both of whom I received very many kindnesses. Thanks to them, I was very soon enabled to better my position, and to change to the house of Arthur & Co., where matters improved for me in every way. There then succeeded some of the happiest days of my life. Freed from care and anxiety, with all the necessaries of life at my control, and a fund of boyish spirits and perfect health, I was without a trouble or a dark hour, happy and contented in my daily task.

So the weeks and months came and went without discovering any change in my position, till an unlooked-for incident once more brought the wild mad thirst for change and excitement back to me, and sounded the death-knell of my quiet life. On the 9th April 1861, the shot was fired at Fort Sumpter which inaugurated the war of the Rebellion of the United States. That shot echoed all over the world, but in no place was the effect more keenly marked than in the American colony in Paris, which even in these early days was a very numerous one.

Arthur's, the place of business of which I speak, was one of the most favoured of the American resorts, and here the excitement raged at fever heat, as little by little the news came over the sea. Those were not the days of the cable, flashing the news of success or defeat simultaneously with its occurrence, and picturing in vivid phrase and description every incident and climax of warfare, till almost the figures move before us, and our eyes and ears are deadened by the smoke and sound of shot. The tidings came in snatches, and the absence of completeness and detail only served to give the greater impetus to discussion and imagination.

There was no more excited student of the situation than myself; and very soon, of course, I was fired with the idea of playing a part in the scenes which I was following with such enthusiasm and zest. Friends and associates, many of them American, were leaving on every hand for the seat of war; and at last, throwing care and discretion to the winds, I took the plunge and embarked on the *Great Eastern* on her first voyage to New York.

I reached that city in good time, and without delay enlisted in the Northern Army, in company with several of my American associates from Paris. In connection with my enlistment there occurred a circumstance, trivial in itself at the moment, yet fraught with the most important consequences in regard to my after-life. This was the taking to myself of a new name and a new nationality. I had no thought of remaining in America for any length of time— at the outset, indeed, I only enlisted for three months, the period for which recruits were sought—and, regarding the whole proceeding more in the light of a good joke than anything else, I came to the conclusion that I should not cause anxiety to my parents by disclosing my position, and decided to sustain the joke by playing the part of a Frenchman and calling myself Henri le Caron. So came into existence that name and character which, in after years, proved to be such a marvellous source of protection and success to me personally, and of such continued service to my native country, whose citizenship I had, by my proceeding, to resign.

As subsequent events proved, however, I was not to carry out my original idea of returning. The three months came and went, and many more followed in their wake, till five years had passed and left me still in the United States' service. The life suited me. I made many friends ; soldiering was a pleasant experience ; and I was particularly fortunate in escaping its many mishaps. I had no care for the morrow, and, happily for me. I found my morrows to bring little if any care to me. Only on one occasion was I seriously wounded. This was when, during an engagement near Woodbury, Tennessee, I had my horse killed under me by a shell, my companion killed at my side, and myself wounded by a splinter from the explosive, which laid me up for about a month.

Interesting and animated as was my career as a soldier, I must not delay to deal with it too fully in detail, but must hurry on to that subsequent life of mine in America, which possesses the greatest interest for the public at large. I shall, however, before leaving it, run over very shortly the different stages of my soldiering experience. The facts may be interesting to the many people in this country and America who are familiar with the history of the American war of the Rebellion. I enlisted as a private soldier on August 7, 1861, in the 8th Pennsylvanian Reserves, changing therefrom to the Anderson Cavalry, commanded by Colonel William J. Palmer. Here I remained for a year and ten months, serving through the Peninsula campaign of the army of the Potomac, including the battles of Four Oaks, South Mountain, Antietam, and Williamsport, all of which were

fought under the command of General George B.
MacClellan.

In October 1862, I joined, with my regiment,
the Western Army, under General William S.
Rosencranz, and participated in the advance from
Louisville, Nashville, and Murfreesboro', including
the engagements at Tullahoma and Winchester,
and ending with the capture of Chattanooga and
Chicamanga in September of the same year. The
failure of Rosencranz at Chicamanga closed his
career. He was succeeded by General George
H. Thomas, who remained in command up to
the end of my service in the army. By this
time I had obtained a warrant as a non-
commissioned officer, and was principally engaged in scouting duty. On the command in
which I served being ordered to the relief of
General Burnside at Knoxville, I left Chattanooga, then in a state of siege and semi-famine,
and reaching Knoxville, I took part during the
whole of the winter of 1863 in the East Tennessee campaign against the rebel General Long-
street, my engagements including Strawberry
Plain, Mossy Creek, and Dandridge. I was fortunate enough to be recommended for a commission
in 1864, and, after my examination before a military board, was gazetted Second Lieutenant in
the United States Army in the month of July of

that year. For the next twelve months I was exclusively employed in scouting duty, in charge of a mounted company, serving in this capacity under General Lovel L. Rousseau in West Tennessee. In December 1864, being attached to General Stedman's division of the Army of the Cumberland, I was present at the battle of Nashville, and took part in all the engagements through Tennessee and Alabama, being promoted in the course of them to the rank of First Lieutenant.

During 1865 I was appointed upon detached service of various descriptions, filling amongst other positions those of Acting Assistant-Adjutant-General and Regimental Adjutant. At the close of the war I joined the veteran organisations of the Army of the Cumberland, and the Grand Army of the Republic, and held the appointment therein of Vice-Commander and Post-Surgeon, ranking as Major.

Long ere this I had, of course, given up all idea of returning to France, and had communicated my whereabouts and position to my parents, much to their anxiety and dismay.

Tragedy and comedy blended together in strange fellowship in our experiences of those days; and, as I write, a couple of amusing examples of this occur to me. It was in 1865, when engaged on scouting duty in connection with the

guerilla warfare carried on by irregular bands of
Southerners, that I received the following order:—

"HEAD-QUARTERS, THIRD SUB-DISTRICT, MIDDLE TENNESSEE,
"ACTING ASSISTANT-ADJUTANT-GENERAL'S OFFICE,
"KINGSTON SPRINGS, TENN., *May* 17, 1865.

"SIR.—The following despatch has been received:—

"NASHVILLE, *May* 16. 1865.

"Brig.-Gen. Thompson.

"In accordance with orders heretofore published of the
Major-Gen. Commanding Dept. of Cumberland, Champ Fer-
gusson and his gang of cut-throats having refused to surrender,
are denounced as outlaws, and the military forces of this district will deal with and treat him accordingly.

"By Command of Major-Gen. Rousseau,

"(Signed) H. C. WHITTEMORE,

"Capt. and A.A.A.G."

This, of course, meant sudden death to any of
the band who might come within range of our
rifles. The men, indeed, were nothing less than
murderers and robbers, carrying on their devilish
work under the plea of fighting for Southern independence. It was not long before an opportunity was afforded me of coming in contact with
a specimen of the class, and it is on this meeting
that one of my anecdotes will turn.

A few days after, when riding ahead of my
troop, in company with a couple of my men, in
order to "prospect" the country, with a view to
finding suitable accommodation for our wants, I
came to a well-built farmhouse a few miles from

the Duck River. As we approached the front, my attention was attracted by an armed man, in the well-known butter-nut grey uniform of the enemy, escaping from the back in a very hasty and suspicious manner. Reading his true character in a moment, I shouted to him to halt, at the same time directing my troopers to "head him off" right and left. Disregarding our cries, he started off in hot haste, while we pursued him in equally hurried fashion. The chase was a hard and a stern one, his flight being only broken for a moment to allow of his discharging his carbine at me. Not desiring to kill him, I saved my powder, and in the end ran him to earth, and stunned him with a blow from the butt-end of my revolver.

When my companions arrived, we proceeded to examine our prisoner, and found, on stripping him of his grey covering, that underneath he wore the unmistakable blue coat of our own regiment, with the plain indication of a corporal's stripes having been torn therefrom. As we had a few days previously discovered the stripped, bullet-riddled body of a brave corporal of ours, who had been murdered by some of these scoundrels, we at once concluded that this was one of his assassins, and my troop, coming up at this point, dealt him scant mercy, and filled his body with their bullets ere consciousness returned. A search of his pockets revealed his identity, his pocket-book containing some two hundred dollars in bills, and an oath of allegiance to the U.S. Government, which he had doubtless used many times to save his wretched life. The following is a *facsimile* of the original document, which I have kept through all these years—the stains being those of the man's blood :—

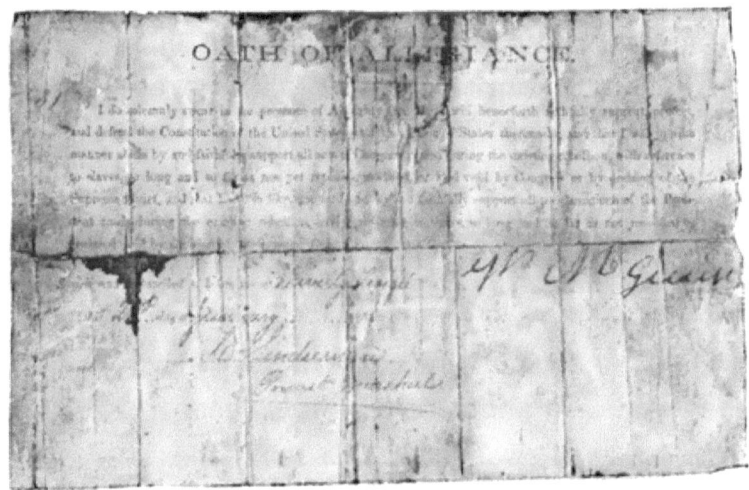

Making our way back to the house, we discovered two weeping women, and half-a-dozen small children. A single question elicited the fact that the elder of the two was the mother, while subsequent inquiries proved that the dead man was the notorious William M. Guin, a nephew of ex-U.S. Senator Guin, of California, and one

of the leaders of as notorious a gang of cut-throats
as ever operated in the South-West. Our custom
was to burn the houses of any persons found
harbouring these guerillas, but the heartrending
entreaties of the wretched women and children
caused me to leave them unmolested. Some
time afterwards, when peace was finally declared,
I was quartered at Waverley, in the same vicinity, and often met the unfortunate mother,
who knew me as "the man who killed her boy,"
though, as she told me, she never blamed me,
having often warned her son that he would come
to a bad end.

And now for the other side of the picture.
During these operations, my men were principally
mounted on horses captured from the citizens,
who were invariably rebels; and as our habit
was to take every available animal when found,
the methods adopted to hide them in caves,
ravines, and swamps were sometimes very remarkable. Upon one of my expeditions at the
time, in the direction of Vernon, on the Duck
River, I came across a fine black horse, which I
speedily confiscated to the use of "Uncle Sam."
My prize, however, did not long remain in my
possession, for in a few days my quarters were
invaded by a deputation of the fair sex, who presented me with the following amusing appeal :—

I.

" We write in good spirits to you,
  For our glad expectations we hope to find true,
  That you'll act as a gentleman always should do,
  And with a request from the ladies comply
  Which a fame would attain you that never should die ;
  While we'll think of you ever with kindness sincere,
  And say of you what it would please you to hear,
  And wish for you always a life long and free
  From grief and visitation that sometimes will be.

II.

" Now, what must you do these good wishes to gain,
  And make us rejoice that we asked not in vain ?
  Well, a something 'twill be a great boon to obtain
  To us who now ask—and a kindness most true
  And most earnestly wished for—but to you
  It will be what they tell us a victory is—
  Quite easy to " Grant," and we hope you'll grant this.

III.

" We once (not long since) had a favourite here,
  Obedient and gentle, deservedly dear ;
  He was patient, obeying our will without force,
  And he seemed like a friend, though he was but a horse.
  How much we esteemed him we never can say,
  And Dixie we named him.   You took him away !
  And sadly and truly we've missed him since then—
  Oh, captain, do give us poor Dixie again.
  If you have conquered *one* Dixie, be generous here ;
  Return us the other we all count so dear,
  And we'll say Captain Le Caron (and hold it so too)
  Is the very best soldier that ever wore blue.
  Your country is famed both in prose and in song ;
  To its sons truth and justice are said to belong—

Good principle, honour, with bravery too;
Prove now to us, captain, that this is quite true.
Let us have our old friend—you have better by scores,
But to us none so dear can e'er stand at our doors;
None other can seem half so good or so wise,
So worthy our care as he was in our eyes.
You *must* be enlightened, be generous too;
Give us back our poor Dixie,
Do, captain, please do.
Just say we may have him, that welcome word say,
And your petitioners will evermore pray.

> " MARY BARR.
> " CYNTHIA BARR.
> " POLLY HASSELL.
> " MARY L. G., *a sympathiser.*

"VERNON, TENNESSEE,
    "*July* 1865.

" To Captain Le Caron."

I naturally pursued the only course which a
soldier could, and surrendered the horse. Strange
to say, one of my lieutenants afterwards surrendered his affections and future happiness to one
of these fair damsels, and still lives with her as
his wife, surrounded by a charming family, away
out in central Kansas.

III.

IN the midst of all my soldiering, I wooed and
won my wife. She is the principal legacy left
me of those old campaigning days of mine, as

bonny a wife and as sympathetic and valuable a
helpmate as ever husband was blessed with in this
world. Many years have gone by since we first
met away in Tennessee, where she, a bright-eyed
daring horsewoman, and I, a happy-go-lucky
cavalry officer, scampered the plains together in
pleasant company. Little thought either of us
then what the future years held in store. Yet
when these years came, and with them the
anxious moments, the uncertain intervals, and
the perilous hours, none was more brave, more
sympathetic than she. Carrying the secret of
my life close locked up in that courageous heart
of hers, helping me when need be, silent when
nought could be done, she proved as faithful an
ally and as perfect a foil as ever man placed like
me could have been given by Heaven. A look,
a gasp, a frightened movement, an uncertain turn
might have betrayed me, and all would have been
lost ; a jealous action, a curious impulse, and she
might have wrecked my life ; a letter misplaced, a
drawer left open, a communication miscarried, and
my end was certain. But those things were not
to be. Brave, affectionate, and fearless, frequently
beseeching me to end this terrible career in which
each moment of the coming hours was charged
with danger if not death, she tended her family
lovingly, and faced the world with a countenance

which gave no sign, but a caution which never slumbered.

I had not to wait for these later years, however, to prove her readiness and resource. These had been shown me long ere marriage was dreamt of by either of us, and when, in one of the most exciting episodes of my military career, she gave me my freedom and my life. For our wooing was not without its romance. Our first meeting was quite a casual one. An officer in charge of a party of thirty, engaged in scouting duty, I stopped my little troop one night, in the winter of 1862, at a house some fifteen miles from Nashville, Tennessee, in order to rest our horses and prepare our supper. We selected the house, and stopped there without any prearrangement. This, however, was in no way extraordinary. It was quite the common practice to stop *en route* and buy hospitality from the residents. The house was the property of my wife's uncle, and here she lived. While our supper was being prepared, we chatted agreeably together, and the time swept pleasantly along. We were in fancied security, and gave no thought to immediate danger. In a moment, however, all was confusion. The house was suddenly surrounded by a band of irregular troops, calling themselves Confederates, but in reality nothing more or less than marauders, and soon the fortunes of war were turned against us.

Half my little command, fortunately, escaped, owing to their being with the horses at the time of the enemy's approach, and so enabled to take to flight. The other half, however, with myself, were not so fortunate. We were in the house, surprised, and immediately taken prisoners. A large log smoke-house was improvised for a prison, and in this my comrades and myself were placed, tortured with indignation and hunger, as the riotous sounds which followed proclaimed to us that our captors were partaking of the supper which had been originally intended for ourselves. Our position altogether was anything but a happy one. Death was very near. Irregular troops like those with whom we had to deal seldom gave quarter. If we escaped immediate death, it would be only to be brought within the Southern line to be condemned to a living death in prison.

We sat and pondered ; and as the probabilities of the future loomed heavily and darkly before us, the sounds of revelry in the adjoining house gradually died away. Our captors, filled with the good things provided for us, gradually dropped to sleep, and soon nothing was heard but the measured movement and breathing of the guard stationed at our door. In a little time, however, there was perfect silence, and our watchful ears detected the absence of our sentry's person. Curious but silent we anxiously waited, and soon heard the withdrawal of the bolt by some unknown hand. Opening the door, we found the pathway clear. My brave Tennessee girl, finding the gang of irregulars all steeped in heavy slumber, had decoyed our guard away on pretence of his obtaining supper, and returning, had unbolted our prison-house, prepared to face the consequences when the sleeping ruffians awoke. Through her action our safety was assured, and after walking fifteen miles, we reached camp in the morning to join our comrades, who had given us up for lost.

This happened on Christmas Eve 1862; and it was not until April 1864—sixteen months afterwards—that I again met the girl who had done so much for me, and who was subsequently to become my wife.

The house in which these exciting events had taken place had meantime been totally destroyed by the ravages of war, and she was now living with her aunt in Nashville itself. I was stationed in camp, there awaiting my examination before a board of officers for further promotion, and here occurred the most eventful engagement in which I ever took part, where, conquering yet conquered, I ignored all the articles of war and subscribed to those of marriage, entering into a treaty of peace freighted with the happiest of results.

IV.

THE war was now over and done, a thing of the past. I was situated in Nashville with my wife and family, and with my savings, happy in the enjoyment of the moment, and the pleasant reminiscences of the past. Henri le Caron, the agent of the British Government in the camps of American Fenianism, did not exist, and I had not the shadow of a conception as to what the future held in store for me. The future indeed troubled me not one whit. Looking back, as I do now, upon all that has happened since then, I am filled with astonishment as great and sincere as that which affected the world when I first told my story in its disjointed way before the Special Commission. It may be that I am somewhat of a fatalist—I know not what I may be called—but my ideas, strengthened by the experience of my life, are very clear on one point. We may be free agents to a certain extent; but, nevertheless, for some wise purpose matters are arranged for us. We are impelled by some unknown force to carry out, not of our own volition or possible design, the work of this life, indicated by a combination of circumstances, to which unconsciously we adapt ourselves. In such a manner did I become connected with Fenianism and the Irish Party in America. For I never sought Fenianism; Fenianism rather came to me.

I use the phrase Fenianism as one that is familiar, and requires no explanation from me. All the world must surely know by this that almost from time out of mind there has existed in America a body of discontented and rebellious Irish known as Fenians, who, working in harmony with so-called Nationalists in this country, seek the repeal of the Union between Great Britain and Ireland. It will, however, be necessary for me to say something about the position of Fenianism at this time—I speak, of course, of the year 1865—in order that what follows may be quite clearly understood.

Fenianism at this period was in a rather bad way. Its adherents in America and Ireland were divided into two hostile camps, and its most recent effort had been of a very poor and depressing character. In fact, the division of forces had been brought about by the failure of this selfsame effort, an attempt at the emancipation of Ireland, which is known as "the '65 movement." It was organised by the Fenians in Ireland and America, under the direction of James Stephens; and for the purpose of its development very many officers and men crossed to Ireland from American soil. The attempted rising, however, proved, like almost all Fenian efforts, a fiasco. It was found that Stephens had wofully misrepresented the state of affairs at home, both as regards preparation and enthusiasm; and those who had come from America returned to their homes, disgusted and indignant at the way in which they had been sold.

In the result disaffection quickly spread, and the organisation in America broke up into hostile camps, the majority, under the leadership of Colonel W. R. Roberts, revolting from the leadership of Stephens and Mahoney, and declaring their belief that "no direct invasion or armed insurrection in Ireland would ever be successful in establishing an Irish Republic upon Irish soil, and setting her once more in her proper place as a nation amongst the nations of the earth." Not content, however, with the situation, the seceders met in convention in September 1865 in Cincinnati, and formed themselves into what was known for the next eventful five years of its existence as the Senate Wing of the Fenian Brotherhood. They scoffed at the idea of invading Ireland successfully, but by no means advocated a policy of inaction. They simply sought to change the base of operations. "The invasion of Canada" became their cry; and with this as their programme they succeeded in gaining the allegiance of some thousands of the disaffected Irish, whose support was attracted by the familiar device of a *de facto* civil and military Irish Government upon paper, framed upon the model of the United States. A good deal of money was subscribed, and with funds so obtained ammunition was purchased and shipped along the Canadian border.

The methods of obtaining money were many and varied, but none was more successful than the issue of Fenian bonds. The following is a reproduction of a twenty-dollar bond in my pos-

session. These bonds were given in exchange for ready money to the many simple souls who believed in the possibility of an Irish republic, and who were quite ready to part with their

little all, in the belief that later on, when their
country was "a nation once again," they would
be repaid with interest. Very many of the
persons displaying this credulity were Irish girls
in service in the States, and thus came into vogue
the sneering reference to the agitation being
financed by the servant-girls of New York.

A curious feature of the intended invasion
was the publicity given to the design, and, more
remarkable still, the action, or rather want of
action, of the United States Government in
regard to it. This latter, indeed, was the subject
of very angry comment at the time on the part
of Englishmen resident in the States. It certainly seemed strange, and passing all compre-
hension, that the United States Government,
although in full possession of the facts, and quite
peaceful in its relations with England, could have
permitted the organisation of a raid upon a portion of English possessions without movement
or demur on their part of any kind whatever.
Yet such is the deplorable fact. From the commencement of the preparations till five days after
the Fenians had crossed at Black Rock, the
government of President Andrew Johnson did
nothing whatever to prevent this band of marauders
from carrying out their much-talked-of invasion.

Let it not be thought that I exaggerate or draw

on my imagination. I do not. If evidence in
support of my statement be needed, it is to be
found in the speeches made from public platforms,
in open meetings, fully reported throughout the
country at the time.

It was during this period that I was brought
into close acquaintance with Fenianism and its
workings. Strangely enough, it was my army
associations which formed the medium. Through
an old companion-in-arms, the man O'Neill mentioned above, by whose side I had served and
fought, I learnt, at first casually, and in broken
conversation, what was transpiring in the circles
of the conspiracy. Indignant as I was at learning
what was being done against the interest of my
native country, I knew not how to circumvent
the operations of the conspirators, and did nothing
publicly in the matter. Without my own knowledge, however, I was to become one of the instruments for upsetting all these schemes. Writing as I regularly did to my father, I mentioned
simply by way of startling news the facts I learned
from O'Neill. My letters, written in the careless
spirit of a wanderer's notes, were destined to become political despatches of an important character. Without reference to me, my father made
immediate and effective use of them. Startled
and dismayed at the tidings I conveyed, he, true

Briton that he was, could not keep the information to himself, but handed over my letters immediately to John Gurdon Rebow, the sitting member for Colchester.

Mr. Rebow, fully concurring with my father as to the importance of my news, proposed that he should, without delay, communicate with the Government of the day, to which my father agreed. In this way my first connection with the Government was brought about. So keenly alive to the position of affairs did the Home Secretary show himself, that he, as I learnt subsequently, in the most earnest way requested my father to correspond with me on the subject, and to arrange for my transmitting through him to the Government every detail with which I could become acquainted. This I did, and continued so doing until the raid into Canada had been attempted, and attended with failure.

V.

BEFORE proceeding further, I had perhaps better give some idea of what the raid was like. The details should prove of interest, if for no other purpose than that of contrast with those of the second attempted invasion, of which I shall have to speak more fully later on. This, which was the first invasion of Canada by the Fenian orga-

nisation, took place upon the morning of the
1st of June 1866. As I have already stated, the
design had been flourished in the face of government and people for six months previously. All
this time active preparations were proceeding,
and thousands of stands of arms, together with
millions of rounds of ammunition, had been purchased from the United States Government and
located at different points along the Canadian
border; while during the spring of the year,
military companies, armed and uniformed as
Irish Fenian soldiers, were drilled week by week
in many of the large cities of the United States.

No opposition was offered to the proceedings;
indeed, John F. Finerty, the editor of the *Chicago Citizen*, in a public speech made by him
at Chicago so late as February 5, 1886, declared
with great glee that Andrew Johnson, the then
President of the United States, openly en-
couraged the movement for the purpose of turning it to political account in the settlement of
the Alabama claims. Be the blame whose it
may, however, the result was not unsatisfactory.
The attempt proved a complete failure. The
Fenians were driven out of Canada, sixty of them
killed and two hundred taken prisoners, with the
loss of but six lives in the Canadian ranks. All
the same, however, the unsatisfactory condition

of things I speak of existed, while, to make matters worse, not a single one of the defeated invaders was called to account by the United States for the violation of the Neutrality Laws.

The whole affair, viewed from any but an imaginative Fenian standpoint, was of a ludicrous character. The time for the operation was chosen by the Fenian Secretary for War, General T. W. Sweeny, then commanding the 16th United States Infantry stationed at Nashville, Tennessee. A particular route had been selected, but when the amount of funds came to be questioned, the original idea of carrying the men by steamer to Goodrich, Canada, had to be abandoned for the less romantic but more economical process of crossing the Niagara River in flat boats with a steam tug called into requisition. Under the command of General John O'Neill, and a number of other gentlemen of high-sounding ranks, and distinctly Irish patronymics, the raid actually came off on the morning of the 1st of June, when about 3 A.M. some 600 or 800 Irish patriots, full of whisky and thirsting for glory, were quietly towed across the Niagara River to a point on the Canadian side called Waterloo!

At 4 A.M. the Irish flag was planted on British soil by Colonel Owen Starr, commanding the contingent from Kentucky, one of the first to

land. Unfortunately no Canadian troops were
in the vicinity, and O'Neill's command, which
had by the next day decreased to some 500,
marched upon and captured Fort Erie, containing a small detachment of the Welland battery.
Matters, however, were not long allowed to go
in favour of the invaders. In a very little time
the 22nd Battalion of Volunteers of Toronto—a
splendid band of citizen-soldiers—appeared upon
the scene, and at Ridgeway, a few miles inland,
there occurred a fair stand-up fight, in which the
Fenians in the end got the worst of the day's
work. Ridgeway has frequently since been
claimed by the Fenian orators as a glorious
victory, but without justification. It is true that
at first, flushed with their almost bloodless victory at Fort Erie, the Fenians advanced fiercely
upon their opponents, and for the moment
repulsed them; but in the end the Canadians
triumphed, and succeeded in putting the invaders
to flight, driving them back to Fort Erie a
frenzied, ungovernable mob, only too thankful to
be taken as prisoners by the United States war
steamer *Michigan*, and protected from total annihi-
lation at the hands of the, by this time, thoroughly
aroused and wrathful Canadian citizens.

The following extracts from the official report
made by General O'Neill to Colonel William R.

c

Roberts, President of the Fenian Brotherhood, though very highly coloured, admits the defeat :—

"Here truth compels me to make an admission I would fain have kept from the public. Some of the men who crossed over with us the night before (*i.e.*, the morning of the 1st of June) managed to leave the command during the day, and re-crossed to Buffalo, while others remained in houses around the fort marauding. (Real Irish patriots these!) This I record to their lasting disgrace.

"On account of this shameful desertion, and the fact that arms had been sent out for 800 men, I had to destroy 300 stand to prevent them from falling into the hands of the enemy. . . .

"At this time I could not depend upon more than 500 men, one-tenth of the reputed number of the enemy, which I knew was surrounding me—rather a critical position.

"Thus situated, and not knowing what was going on elsewhere, I decided that the best course was to return to Fort Erie and ascertain if crossings had been made at other points ; and, if so, I was content to sacrifice myself and my noble little command for the sake of leaving the way open.

"I returned to the old fort (Erie), and about six o'clock sent word to Captain W. J. Hynes, and his friends at Buffalo, that the enemy would surround me with 5000 men before morning, fully provided with artillery ; that my little command, which had by this time considerably decreased, could not hold out long ; but that, if a movement was going on elsewhere, I was perfectly willing to make the old fort a slaughter-pen, which I knew would be the case the next day if I remained.

"Previous to this time, some of the officers and men, realising the danger of their position, availed themselves of the small boats and re-crossed the river ; but the greater portion of them— 317, including officers—remained until 2 A.M., June 3rd, when all, except a few wounded men, went safely on board a large scow attached to a tug-boat, and were hauled into American waters.

" Here they were hailed by the United States steamer, which fired across their bows and demanded their surrender. With this request we complied, not because we feared the twelve-pounders or the still more powerful guns of the *Michigan,* but because we respected the authority of the United States."!!!

Thus fought the Irish patriots of 1866. Thus ended the first Fenian raid upon Canada. Not a glorious achievement, by any means. Quite the reverse, in fact. Even the leader of the expedition himself has to subscribe to failure and defeat. And yet there have been, and are to-day, men who boast of all this as a glorious victory, and proudly vaunt the statement that they were present at and participated in it.

Lucky it was that the movement was thus defeated at its very start. If it had not, the consequences might have been very different indeed. The news of the temporary victory at Fort Erie had a wonderful effect, and by the 7th of June not less than 30,000 men had assembled in and around Buffalo. The defeat of their comrades, however, and the tardy issue of Andrew Johnson's proclamation enforcing the Neutrality Laws, left them no opening, and so the whole affair fizzled out in the most undignified manner. Undignified indeed it was for all parties concerned. The prisoners were, without a single exception,

released on their own recognisances, and sent
home by the United States authorities; while the
arms seized by the United States Government,
through General Meade, commanding in Buffalo,
were returned to the Fenian organisation, only to
be used for the same purpose some four years
later.

VI.

MEANTIME the conditions of peace, in purely
American matters, had set in, and the army was
reduced to a nominal footing. I took advantage
of the state of affairs to settle down to a civilian
style of life. The first question that called for
thought and care was my future vocation in life.
The father of a family, it became necessary for
me to look out for some means of obtaining a
settled income. Acting under the advice of an
old comrade, now a Senator of Illinois, I finally
determined to study medicine, and set to work in
this direction without delay.

While so engaged, I paid my first visit to
Europe in the autumn or "fall" of 1867, and
once more met my father and mother in the flesh.
My letters regarding Fenian matters were naturally a topic of interesting conversation between
us, and my father with much pride showed me
the written acknowledgments he had received

for his action in the matter. Poor old father! Never was Briton prouder than he of the service he had been enabled to do his country—services unpaid and as purely patriotic as ever English-man rendered. No payment was ever made—none was asked or expected—for whatever little good I had been enabled to accomplish up to this time. Matters, however, were now to develop in a new and unexpected way. Mr. Rebow expressed a desire to see me, and, accompanied by my father, I visited him at his seat, Wyvenhoe Park. He subsequently visited me on several occasions at my father's house, and had many chats on the all-absorbing topic of Fenianism. Learning from me that the organisation was still prosperous and meant mischief—my friend O'Neill having succeeded Colonel Roberts as president— he gained my consent to enter into personal com-munication with the English Government. In a few days I received through him an official com-munication requesting me to attend at 50 Harley Street. To Harley Street I went, and there met two officials, by whom a proposition was made that I should become a paid agent of the Govern-ment, and that on my return to the United States I should ally myself to the Fenian organisation, in order to play the *rôle* of spy in the rebel ranks. I knew that this proposal was coming. I had

thought over the whole matter carefully, and I
had come to the conclusion that I would consent,
which I did.   My adventurous nature prompted
me to sympathy with the idea; my British instincts made me a willing worker from a sense of
right, and my past success promised good things
for the future.

I returned, therefore, to the States in the
Government service; and, taking advantage of
an early meeting with O'Neill in New York, I
proffered him my services as a military man in
case of active warfare.   O'Neill, delighted at the
idea, promised me a position in the near future,
and I returned to my home in the West, pledged
to help the cause there meantime.*

And now a few words as to O'Neill.   Taking
the prominent part he did in Fenian affairs at
this time, he certainly proved a very interesting
personality.   General O'Neill, Irish by birth, was
born on the 8th of March 1834, in the town of
Drumgallon, parish of Clontifret, Co. Monaghan.
He emigrated when young with his family to the
United States, and settled at Elizabeth, New
Jersey.   Enlisting in the 2nd U.S. Cavalry as a

---

* I was not the only member of the family fighting for Queen and
country then.   Two others of my brothers entered the army at home.
One is to-day a commissioned officer in South Africa; the other, poor
fellow, left his bones to whiten on the battlefield of Tel-el-Kebir.

private soldier in 1857, he was engaged in fighting Indians in the Far West for some three years. Upon the breaking out of the War of the Rebellion, he was commissioned as lieutenant in the 5th Indiana Cavalry. From this he received promotion in the 15th U.S. Coloured Infantry, with which regiment he continued to the end of the war. Resigning his command at the conclusion of hostilities, he commenced business as a United States Claim Agent in Nashville, Tennessee, where, it will be remembered, I was stationed with my regiment for a long time after the cessation of active operations.

When freed from the discipline of his military service, O'Neill—ardent Fenian that he was—threw himself heart and soul into the Irish rebel movement in the States. He raised and commanded the Tennessee contingent in the movement upon Canada in 1866, taking command of the entire expedition by reason of his seniority of rank and his proved knowledge of military tactics. I have already quoted his report of the termination of this "invasion."

At the Cleveland Convention of September 1867, he was elected a senator of the Fenian Brotherhood; and on the 31st of December 1867, owing to the resignation of Colonel W. R. Roberts, he was elected President of the Brotherhood.

In personal appearance O'Neill was a very fine-looking man. Nature had dealt kindly with him. Within a couple of inches of six feet in height, possessing a fine physique and a distinctive Celtic face, he combined an undoubted military bearing with a rich sonorous voice, which lent to his presence a certain persuasive charm. He had one fault, however—a fault which developed to the extremest point when he attained the presidency of the Fenian Brotherhood. This was his egotism. He was the most egotistical soul I ever met in the whole course of my life. In his belief, the Irish cause lived, moved, and had its being in John O'Neill; and this absurd self-love contributed to many disasters, which a more even-headed leader would never have brought about.

VII.

ON my return to my Western home, I lost no time in commencing my double life. I organised a Fenian "circle" or camp in Lockport, Illinois, and took the position of "centre" or commander of it, thus becoming the medium for receiving all official reports and documents issued by O'Neill, the contents of which documents were, of course, communicated by me to the Home Government. I went to work with a will, and was soon in the very thick of the conspiracy, organised a military company for the Irish Republican Army, and eventually attended the Springfield Convention in the position of a delegate.

While so engaged, I entered the Chicago Medical College, and commenced my medical studies in earnest. I was much assisted in this direction by the kindly help of an old friend, Dr. Bacon, who had been attached to my regiment in war times as surgeon. He was then surgeon to the Illinois State Penitentiary, and through him I obtained the position created at this time of Hospital Steward, or, in other words, Resident Medical Officer in that institution. There was a comfortable salary attached to the office, which I found to be in every sense a useful post. Although, as matters turned out, I was only to spend some few months there, I gained even in this short time a vast amount of experience in almost every branch of medical study.

Life, indeed, in the Illinois Penitentiary gave me experience in many ways. It brought me for the first time into direct contact with many of the evils which then affected official administration. Things, of course, are different now, though it must be confessed still anything but perfect; but when compared with the usages of olden times, the shortcomings of the present

system are of no account whatever. At the time
of which I speak, money could accomplish everything, from the obtaining of luxuries in prison
to the purchase of pardon and freedom itself.
Everything connected with the prison administration was rotten to the core. Corruption
was in every place. The penitentiary contained
some fifteen hundred prisoners, and the whole
management of affairs affecting these men was
vested in three Commissioners, as they were
styled, whose proceedings were of the most
flagrant and jobbing character. So great did the
scandals of their doings become at one period,
that one of the three had to abscond; but so
demoralised was the condition of affairs that no
attempt was made to arrest and bring him back.
These three men had no object save that of
gaining money. They were the proprietors of
a general shop inside the prison, from which the
prisoners purchased luxuries at usurious rates;
and the work of the prisoners themselves was let
out to contractors, who paid heavily for the privi-
lege of remaining undisturbed in their monopoly.
Everything was turned to money. In one case
I knew of a prisoner, failing to win his cause on
appeal, and having thereby to undergo a period
of seven years' imprisonment, being offered his
release for a sum of 10,000 dollars, which offer he

refused, stating in the most business-like way that he would only give 7000. This was not considered satisfactory, and so the negotiations fell through.

No popular idea of prison life now indulged in at all fits in with the actual condition of affairs five-and-twenty years ago. Money was useful for the purpose of commerce in the Commissioners' interest, and therefore was allowed free circulation amongst those confined. Those who could afford it, and whose cases were not finally decided —appeals were constantly being heard — were allowed to board at the Governor's table, to wear their own clothes, and in every way conduct themselves as if in a private house. In those days the prisoners were not shaved—they wore their hair and whiskers as they pleased. Those who could not afford to live the lives of gentlemen had the store to go to for petty luxuries; and so, no matter how matters turned, the Commissioners were the gainers. The Governor, or Warden, as he was called, was their nominee, dependent upon them for office; and everything was governed by their wishes and desires.

In such a vast assembly of criminals there were many whose characters and careers formed subjects for very interesting study to me. I was fortunate in being connected with the prison at a time when some more than usually clever and

facile scoundrels were temporarily resident there.
Towering head and shoulders over the whole
crowd was that king of forgers, Colonel Cross,
perhaps the most daring, successful, and expert
penman of our time.   About forty years of age at
this period, a man of fine commanding presence,
splendid diction, and gentlemanly demeanour,
Cross attracted me from the first day I was
brought into contact with him.   The son of one
of the most prominent Episcopalian clergymen in
the United States, he was possessed of a wide
classical education, and discoursed with intelligence and wondrous fluency on theology, medicine, and every kind of science.

He was no ordinary criminal.   Even in prison
he commanded admiration from his fellows, and
I was often amazed to see how respectful were
the salutations accorded him as he moved
about.   He boasted, I learned afterwards with
truth, that he had never robbed a poor man ;
and, strange being that he was, he had borne
almost all the cost of the education of his
brother's children.   Indeed, at the time I met
him, he was educating in the most expensive
manner a poor little girl whom, in a moment of
generous caprice, he had adopted as his daughter.

When I was first brought into contact with
him, Cross had his case before the courts on

appeal, and, pending the decision, he was living in the most expensive way in prison, boarding at the Governor's table, dressing in the most fashionable way, and smoking the best of cigars. Having no work to do, he interested himself in the affairs of his fellow-prisoners; and so clever and capable was he, and so great a knowledge of law did he possess, that he succeeded in preparing the cases of many of them for appeal in such a way as to allow of their regaining their liberty.

I had not been in the prison very long before he appealed to me to take him as my assistant in the hospital; and attracted by the man as I was, I acceded to his request, to discover subsequently that I had a most valuable attendant, whose knowledge of medicine was both extensive and practical.

VIII.

THE career of Cross would supply material for a most exciting novel. He always went in for "big things," as he phrased it. Nothing troubled him more than the fact that he was then undergoing punishment for a small affair which he contemptuously referred to as being too paltry altogether for association with him. Perhaps the "biggest thing" he ever did was the forgery of a cheque for £80,000 in Liverpool, and his escape

with the booty.   Like many other talented criminals, if he had but turned his ability to proper
account, he would undoubtedly have won a place
and name in the foremost ranks of honest men
to-day.   He planned his enterprises with the
most consummate care, and worked them out for
months before reaching the final stage.   An illus-
tration of his method was very well afforded by his
forgery on the Park National Bank of New York.

Determining to commit a forgery on this bank,
he set to work to obtain the needful introduction
and guarantee for his accomplice, who should
eventually present the forged cheque.   He, by
the way, never presented a forged cheque himself—this was always the work of an accomplice.
In order, therefore, to obtain the introduction to
the bank, he opened some business with a certain
firm of brokers in Wall Street who happened to
" deposit" at the particular bank in question.   In
this way he ran up an account for a respectable
sum, to obtain the repayment for which he one
day went to the office in Wall Street accompanied
by one Simmons, the accomplice in the future
forgery.   The cheque—a draft for twelve hundred
dollars—was duly drawn, when Cross asked his
friend Simmons to go to the bank to cash it,
requesting in a free-and-easy way that the broker
might send one of his clerks with him to identify

Simmons, he being a stranger. No suspicion was indulged in—there was no ground for such, and the request was willingly complied with. Simmons, coached by Cross beforehand, had a hundred-dollar bill in his pocket, the use for which will be apparent in a moment. When the clerk and he reached the bank, the necessary introduction took place ; and in reply to the usual question how he wished the money, Simmons replied, " In hundred-dollar bills." As the clerk counted the notes, Simmons drew his bill out of his pocket, and mixing all up as he stood aside to check his payment, he recalled the clerk's attention by the announcement that he had given him thirteen instead of twelve bills. The clerk indignantly protested he had made no mistake. Simmons, playing the *rôle* of honest man, became distressed, the manager was appealed to, one of the notes eventually received back, and Simmons retired, the recipient of most fulsome thanks, his character and reputation fully established in the minds of the banking officials. Of course the clerk was one hundred dollars to the good at the end of the day, but Simmons' claim to honesty in no way suffered by the fact, as no one for a moment thought of a plot.

Content to lose the hundred-dollar bill, in the promise of things to come, Cross continued his legitimate traffic with the brokers, Simmons, on the most friendly terms at the bank, cashing the cheques, which increased in amount as the time passed. Months had passed, and nothing of an illegal nature had been attempted, when at the end of the fifth month a genuine cheque for thirty dollars was by Cross changed to 30,000, and cashed by Simmons without the slightest hesitation or suspicion at the bank, both Cross and he escaping with the booty.

Many and varied as were Cross's tricks with his pen, none was more daring or successful than that which led to his escape from Sing-Sing Prison, that famous home of criminals in New York. Obtaining through outside agency a printed and properly headed sheet of note-paper and envelope from the Governor of the States' Office at Albany, he actually forged the order for his own release, had it posted formally from Albany, and, on its receipt, obtained his freedom without provoking the slightest suspicion or inquiry.

I am glad to say that Colonel Cross still lives, and is now working out an honest existence under another name in the north-west of America.

My life at the Illinois Penitentiary was crowded with incidents, and little leisure was left me. Where real sickness did not exist, shamming and malingering in their most ingenious phases were

resorted to. I was amazed at the talent brought
to bear upon their attempts to escape work by
those with whom I had to deal. Some of the
methods adopted were simply marvellous in their
conception and execution. A more quick-witted
lot of men it has never been my fate to meet.
Every twist and turn of daily life was subordinated
to the needs of the trickster, and not one single
daily incident seemed to be without its possibility
of application, either to assist in the attempt to
shirk work or to escape from imprisonment altogether. Nothing in this way impressed me more
than the case of a man known as Joe Devine,
an eminent hotel sneak thief, some two-and-thirty
years of age, and of very distinguished appearance.

It happened that one afternoon about five
o'clock a negro prisoner died of consumption.
It was the practice to bury the dead immediately
the coffin was made ready ; but, owing to the fact
that the coffin in this case was not ready till after
the prison gates had been locked for the night,
the burial had to be postponed till the following
morning.

Under the circumstances, I arranged that the
coffin with the body enclosed should remain for
the night in the prison bath-room. This Joe
Devine of whom I speak happened to be in
charge of the bath-room at this period, and it

D

therefore became his duty to see that proper
arrangements were made for the disposal of the
coffin for the night. Early the next morning, as
was customary, Devine and some of his fellow-
prisoners were allowed out of their cells some
little time before the others, in order to prepare
the bath-room and other places for their use.
With assistance Devine unscrewed the coffin,
took the dead negro out, and concealed himself
in his place, not, however, before he had worn
down the thread of the screws in the lid, so that
they could be thrust out with a heavy push from
the inside. The time for the funeral arrived in
due course, and the coffin was removed in a little
cart accompanied by two prisoners whose time
was nearly expired, and who were therefore trusted
outside the gates of the prison (being known by
the name of "trusties"), together with the clergyman of the jail.

Nothing happened till the grave was reached,
when Devine, presumably concluding that it would
be dangerous to remain longer where he was,
burst the lid of the coffin and jumped out, immediately starting off at a run. The clergyman and
" trusties " being too horrified to offer any resist-
ance, he escaped without molestation. The first
I heard of the matter was on the return of the
clergyman and the "trusties" with the news that

the man had come to life ; but, as they explained
in their horrified way, he was white, not a nigger!
The roll was called, and Devine was missing; so
we concluded he was the white man in question.
We then set to work to find the corpse of the poor
negro. For two hours the prisoners searched up
and down without any result. Eventually, however, the body was discovered underneath a pile
of towels in one of the box-seats of the bath-room,
the corpse being doubled up in two, the head and
feet meeting, in order to permit of its being concealed in its narrow hiding-place.

Another escape equally effective, for the moment
at least, was that of a man known as Bill Forester,
a notorious bank robber, and one of the suspected
murderers of Nathan the Jew, whose death in
New York created a profound interest at the
time. Forester, fortunately for himself, selected
as his medium of exit one of the many boxes
employed by Mack & Co., contractors for shoe-
making, who employed some four hundred of the
convicts. Surrounded and hedged in between
boots and shoes, in one of the large boxes used
for their transport, Forester passed through the
prison gates in one of Mack's vans, and not
till he had got a distance of a mile and a half
from the jail did he venture to emerge from his
hiding-place. His liberty, however, proved to

be only of a temporary character, for, caught in another State a little later, the enterprising burglar was again arrested, and carried back to the Penitentiary to complete his term of imprisonment.

His method had many imitations. None was more novel or disastrous than that employed by a fellow-convict whose name I cannot at the moment recall. This poor fellow hit upon the ingenious idea of getting out of durance vile inside a load of horse-manure, and when the load was half-way packed, he lay at full length with a breathing space arranged, while the remainder of the loading was completed. His intention, of course, was to be freed from his uncomfortable position within an hour, when the manure would be discharged at the quay adjoining the prison. To his horror, however, he discovered, when the cart reached the quay, that a gang of fellow-convicts were engaged unloading a boat under the charge of armed wardens or sentries. To attempt escape meant instant death, and there he lay for hours with the heavy weight of the upper portion of the cart's load pressing upon him. Six o'clock came and with it the return of the men and sentries to prison. Through the long weary hours of the night the poor fellow lay, unable now to move from the consequences of his continued prostration in the manure; and

when the morning arrived he was found but too
willing a captive. He was immediately placed
under my charge, but his recovery proved by no
means a rapid affair.

IX.

In the midst of all these exciting incidents of
prison life, I received a telegram from O'Neill
in New York, as follows: "Come at once, you
are needed for work." To comply was to surrender my pleasant and interesting position, and
to lose for the moment all chance of pursuing my
medical study. On the other hand, however,
the opportunity of doing good service to my
native land presented itself. I did not hesitate.
Communicating immediately with the "Warden"
or Governor, I resigned my position, much to
his disgust. He sought an explanation. I could
give none. He offered an increased salary. I
was unable to explain why even this could
not tempt me, and so I left in a way which
was misunderstood, and under circumstances
which, by the very reason for their existence,
could not be appreciated.

Hurrying to New York, I soon presented
myself in person to O'Neill at the headquarters
of the Fenian Brotherhood, then situated in
the mansion at 10 West Fourth Street. Here

I found the President of the Brotherhood, surrounded by his staff of officials, transacting the duties of their various positions with all the pomp and ceremony usually associated with the representatives of the greatest nations on earth. I was not long left in suspense as to what was required of me. Commissioned at the very

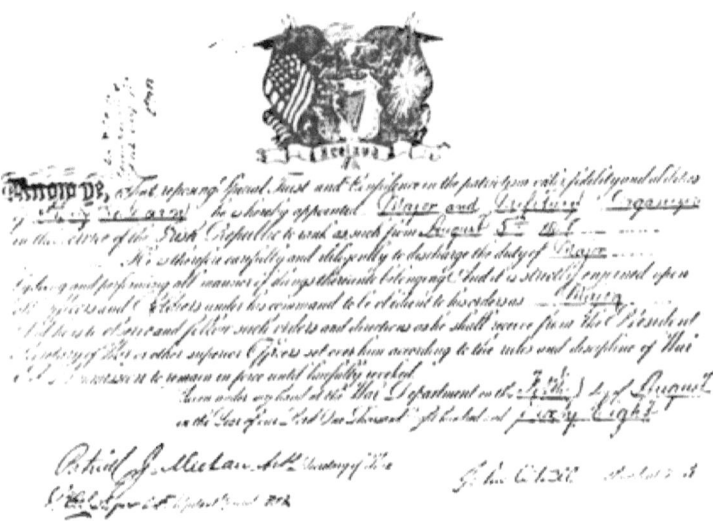

outset as Major and Military Organiser of the Irish Republican Army (at a salary of sixty dollars per month, with seven dollars per day expenses), I was instructed to proceed to the Eastern States in company with a civil organiser, in order to visit and reorganise the different military bodies attached to the rebel society. To my unhappy amazement, I learned that I was, while engaged on this work, to address public meetings in support of the cause, and my miserable feelings were accentuated by O'Neill's desire that I should accompany him, the very evening of my arrival, to a large demonstration being held at Williamsburg, a suburb of Brooklyn. I was in a regular mess, for if called on to speak—as I feared—I should be found absolutely ignorant of Irish affairs. There was nothing for it, however, but to keep a brave face, for I had undertaken my work, and in its lexicon there was no such word as fail.

The evening came, and with it our trip to Williamsburg. On arrival there, in the company of O'Neill and some brother officers, I found several thousands of persons assembled. We were greeted with the greatest enthusiasm, and given the seats of honour to the right and left of the chairman. My position was a very unhappy one. I was in a state of excessive excitement, for I greatly feared what was coming. Seated as I was next to O'Neill, I could hear him tell the chairman on whom to call, and how to describe the speakers; and, as each pause took place between the speeches, I hung with nervous dread on O'Neill's words, fearing my name would be the next. The meeting proceeded apace; some four or five of my companions had already spoken, and I was beginning to think that, after all, the

evil hour was postponed, and that for this night
at least I was safe. Not so, however. All but
O'Neill and myself had spoken, when, to my
painful surprise, I heard the General call upon
the chairman to announce Major Le Caron. The
moment was fraught with danger; my pulses
throbbed with maddening sensation; my heart
seemed to stop its beating; my brain was on fire,
and failure stared me in the face. With an almost
superhuman effort I collected myself, and as the
chairman announced me as Major M'Caron,
tickled by the error into which he had fallen, and
the vast cheat I was playing upon the whole of
them, I rose equal to the occasion, to be received
with the most enthusiastic of plaudits.

The hour was very late, and I took advantage
of the circumstance. Proud and happy as I was
at being with them that evening, and taking part
in such a magnificent demonstration, they could
not, I said, expect me to detain them long at
so advanced an hour. All had been said that
could be said upon the subject nearest and dearest
to their hearts. (Applause.) If what I had experienced that night was indicative of the spirit
of patriotism of the Irish in America—(tremendous
cheering)—then indeed there could be no fears
for the result. (Renewed plaudits.) And now I
would sit down. They were all impatiently wait-

ing, I knew, to hear the stirring words of the
gallant hero of Ridgeway, General O'Neill —
(thunders of applause)—and I would, in conclusion, simply beg of them as lovers of liberty and
motherland—(excited cheering)—to place at the
disposal of General O'Neill the means (cash)
necessary to carry out the great work on which
he was engaged. This work, I was confident,
would result in the success of our holy cause, and
the liberation of dear old Ireland from the thral-
dom of the tyrant's rule, which had blighted and
ruined her for seven hundred years.

These last words worked my hearers up to the
highest pitch of enthusiasm, and amidst their
excited shouts and cheers I resumed my seat,
with the comforting reflection that if it took so
little as this to arouse the Irish people, I could
play my *rôle* with but little difficulty. And as
time passed on, and my experience widened, the
justice of the reflection was fully assured. With
a little practice and scarce any labour, save that
necessitated by the use of a pair of scissors
and some paste, I succeeded in hoodwinking the
poor and deluded, together with the unprincipled,
blatant, professional Irish patriots.

Before, however, starting on my travels as
organiser, I had an experience which went far to
justify all I had previously thought and heard as

regards the part played by Andrew Johnson in connection with the first Canadian raid. I recall the incident as important, as showing to what extremes American political exigencies have carried men in catering for the Irish vote in America. About American politics generally I shall have something to say later on ; but as this matter fits in chronologically here, I think it better to deal with it now. Johnson, it must be remembered, was not by any means a man above suspicion. In 1868, so great was the disaffection with his administration of the Presidency, that he was impeached, though unsuccessfully, by the Senate.

It was in this year—1868—that, at O'Neill's request, I accompanied him to the White House to have an interview with Johnson. O'Neill and he had been personal friends from '62, when Johnson had acted as Military Governor in Tennessee. The precise object of our visit was the securing of Johnson's influence in the return of the arms to the Fenian Brotherhood, previously seized by the American Government. It will be remembered that I mentioned, some pages back, that every gun taken by the United States Government, after the first raid in 1866, was returned to the Fenian organisation by this government under a promise, only made to be broken, that they should not be used in any unlawful enterprise; and in consideration of certain worthless bonds.

Our reception at the White House was a cordial one, O'Neill's distinctly so. During the conversation the President used some remarkable words. So strange did they sound in my ears, that they impressed themselves upon my memory, and are even now fresh in my recollection.

"General," said Johnson, addressing O'Neill, "your people unfairly blame me a good deal for the part I took in stopping your first movement. Now I want you to understand that my sympathies are entirely with you, and anything which lies in my power I am willing to do to assist you. But you must remember that I gave you five full days before issuing any proclamation stopping you. What, in God's name, more did you want? If you could not get there in five days, by God, you could never get there; and then, as President, I was compelled to enforce the Neutrality Laws, or be denounced on every side."

Such was the language used, such the position assumed, and such the apology tendered to the Fenian leader of 1868 by the President of the United States Government. Can any comment of mine point the moral and adorn the tale of all this better than the incident itself can do when left in its naked and startling significance? I think not.

X.

I ENTERED with a will upon my duties as travelling organiser, and was alike successful in winning the confidence of almost every Fenian with whom I was brought into contact, and in obtaining the most important information and details for the Home Government. Matters had meantime proceeded apace, so that when the Philadelphia Convention of 1868 was held, O'Neill's determination to invade Canada a second time was ratified without a dissentient voice. I was now promoted to the rank of Inspector-General, and was from time to time sent along the Canadian border to locate the arms and ammunition. The situation was becoming critical where British interests were concerned; and, in order to grapple with the pressure of the moment, I was placed in direct communication with Lord Monck, then Governor-General of Canada. I paid a visit to Ottawa, and when there, planned a system of daily communication with the Chief Commissioner of Police in Canada, Judge J. G. M'Micken, with whom, from this date to the total disruption of the Fenian organisation in 1870, I acted in concert and in the most perfect harmony.

I cannot speak too highly of the treatment I

received at Judge M'Micken's hands. Comparatively young in years as I was then, distinctly youthful in Secret Service experience, I found him ever ready and willing to help me, meeting me at a moment's notice, placing everything at my disposal, and watching over my safety and my interests with a fatherly care which I shall ever recall with thoughts of the keenest appreciation. Equally pleasant and agreeable was my connection with the Home Government. Many changes had taken place since my visit to England, and those with whom I had first had communication had disappeared from this work to give place to Mr. Anderson, with whom alone I had to deal from this time forward. I shall have a good deal to say about Mr. Anderson further on, and therefore I shall only delay here to repeat what I have said above, that with England as with Canada my connection was of the most satisfactory and pleasant character.

XI.

IT was during the autumn of 1868 that, in the course of my travels on behalf of the organisation, I first met Alexander Sullivan. Alexander Sullivan is a well-known man to-day, but if by any chance his identity has to be marked, little

else need be mentioned beyond the words, " The
Cronin affair." He was a young man then, but
then as now he was the same Alexander Sullivan,
clever, unscrupulous, careful only of himself, sub-
ordinating everything to his personal ambition,
using Irish politics as a stepping-stone to advancement in American affairs, and reckless who or
what suffered if but he did succeed.

The " Arch Fiend " of Irish American politics,
as he has been dubbed, and the alleged chief conspirator in the brutal murder of Dr. Cronin, is no
ordinary man ; he is an individual with a history,
and that not by any means a creditable one. The
son of a British pensioner, born in Canada some
forty-five years ago, he left that country under a
cloud, and settled down in Detroit, where he
started a boot-and-shoe store in the Bresler
Block, Michigan Avenue. On the night of the
12th May 1868 a fire totally destroyed his shop
and its contents. The occurrence had its suspicious features, and Sullivan was arrested on a
charge of arson. Although the over-insurance
of his goods and other questionable proceedings
were proved at the trial, he gained his liberty
through an alibi, sustained by the evidence of
Margaret Buchanan, a teacher in the public
school of Detroit, who afterwards became his
wife. A man, as I have said, of stirring ambi-

ALEXANDER SULLIVAN

tion, he had from the outset of his career
in Detroit taken a prominent part in political
affairs, and his status as an Irish leader (he was
then a State "Centre" for Michigan) lent his
position and views a certain importance. He
took an active part in the then pending national
campaign upon the side and in the interests of
General Grant and Schyler Colfax, who in that
year were nominated as the respective Republican
candidates for President and Vice-President of
the republic.

It was at this time that Sullivan commenced
his political tricks in the manipulation of the Irish
vote in American party interests, and it was in
consequence of his action in this respect that I
was first brought into contact with him. Previous to this date, the Irish vote had been almost
exclusively Democratic; but, from the loud and
frequent complaints which reached headquarters,
Sullivan was found to be using his influence in
the organisation for political purposes, and seeking to bring about a change of policy in the
organisation itself, which threatened a serious
schism amongst our members.

I was despatched by the President to Detroit
in order to investigate the case, and if possible
settle the difficulty. I found ample proof of
Sullivan's guilt of the charges alleged against

him, and, after repeated interviews between us, he agreed that the best thing he could do would be to hand in his resignation as State "Centre" of the Brotherhood, which he accordingly did. My intercourse with him at this time left no doubt on my mind as to his great ability. His line of defence was an exceedingly clever one, and is well worth recording here, as showing how in these early days Sullivan had carefully mapped out his policy in regard to Irish affairs, and their connection with American matters. He contended that, in all he had done, he had had the best interests of Ireland at heart. He did not, he said, consider that the Irish people in America had ever occupied the position in the body politic to which they were fairly entitled. The Irish vote, argued he, had been hitherto solidly cast for the Democratic party. Only a division of that vote would cause them to be a potent power in politics. With that position and influence to which they were entitled assured to them, they could make terms with the American Government for the cause of Ireland.

The history of the past twenty years shows how cleverly Sullivan worked out these views of his, and gained acceptance for them at the hands of his fellow-patriots. The pity of it is, however, that in the result Ireland has gained not at all, while Irish patriots like Sullivan and Egan have filled their pockets and reaped their harvests in Chili and elsewhere.

Sullivan's immediate reward was his appointment as United States Collector of Internal Revenue at Santa Fé, New Mexico. His resignation of his official position in the Brotherhood had come too late; his work bore fruit in the Presidential election, the vote was split, and so he earned his wage. It is worthy of note that this was the first time the Irish vote was split, and that Sullivan was the primary cause of it. Ever since the vote has so remained, to the advantage of the Irish leaders of both sides, who, in the scramble for office, barter the adhesion of their followers in the public market-place.

Santa Fé, however, did not hold Sullivan long. His shady methods compelled him to make an inglorious exit; and so he was to be found in the year 1873 working with his wife, *née* Buchanan, in a reporting capacity on Chicago newspapers.

Here for the present, however, I must leave Sullivan. I have dealt thus fully with the man at this early stage, because of the strange influence he from this time forth wielded over Irish politics in America; and in order to properly represent his character, I have somewhat anticipated events in his life which are far ahead of the

E

time with which I am at present dealing. I have done so advisedly, for Sullivan will play a large part in the chapters to which I must now proceed. Where his personality will not thrust itself upon the scene, his shadow will darken every act and incident. From this time onward, for a period of twenty years, I used the man as my dupe. Feeding his vanity, assisting his ambition, helping him in the hundred and odd ways in which it was possible for me to do, I gained his friendship and his confidence to such an extent, that no man in the whole course of my career in the Secret Service proved a more valuable, albeit an unconscious, ally than he.

XII.

BEFORE continuing my narrative, I will stop to relate one of the few cases in which I was forced into a very narrow place, and faced with the near possibility of complete exposure. The incident is useful as illustrating the dangers by which I was surrounded, and the requirements of the position in which I was placed. At a council of war held in Troy House, Troy, New York, in the month of November 1868, I came in contact with John Roche, well known as one of the shining lights of Irish nationality in that city.

Roche was one of those hypercritical and over-suspicious individuals who were constantly recognising British detectives in every stranger whom they met. He had been, I discovered, originally a resident of Montreal, and as I had been instructed by O'Neill to visit and study the enemy's country, I indicated to Roche my desire of ascertaining the names of a few reliable brothers whom I could visit. The truth was that the Canadian Government were at this time particularly anxious to find out the extent of the organisation which they knew existed in several of their large cities, notably Montreal, Kingstown, and Toronto; and I thought this a good opportunity of getting some useful hints.

Roche furnished me with the names of several leading members. Unluckily for me, I foolishly wrote the particulars down in a note-book in his presence. The act, in his opinion, was a suspicious one. He watched me closely, and evidently conceived the idea that my patriotism was of a very incautious character, if not worse. On the eighth of the following month, at the Annual Convention held in the Masonic Hall, Philadelphia, to which he was a delegate, I found his suspicions solidified in the form of a set of charges against me, imputing carelessness, dangerous conduct, and suspicious acts. My friends, and they were legion, together with myself, indignantly denied the allegations, and virtuously demanded an inquiry, which was granted, and a committee was appointed to lay the charges. Roche was duly heard, injured innocence was largely *en evidence* on my part, and very quickly a unanimous verdict was reported back to the Convention, asserting that the charges were scandalous and without the slightest foundation, it being fully demonstrated by the following letter that I was authorised to visit and acquaint myself with the other side, as I represented to Roche :—

> "HEAD-QUARTERS FENIAN BROTHERHOOD,
> "No. 10 WEST FOURTH STREET,
> "NEW YORK, *October* 23, 1868.

"P. O. Box 5141.
  "HENRY LE CARON,
    "Care of Capt. T. O'Hagan,
      "Ogdensburg, N.Y.

"DEAR SIR AND BROTHER,—Yours of the 20th and 21st came duly to hand and are perfectly satisfactory.

"I think it better not to commence equalising goods just yet ; I will write you again on the matter.

"It would be highly beneficial to us for you to avail yourself of every opportunity to study the country on both sides of the line for future emergencies.

"Everything here is going on satisfactorily.

> "Yours fraternally,
> "JOHN O'NEILL,
> "*Pres. F.B.*"

I did not, however, deem it prudent to let matters rest even here, feeling that my ultimate success in the interests of the Government depended upon absolute confidence on the part of the ruling powers. Accordingly I sat down and immediately wrote out my resignation as an officer of the Irish Republican Army, giving this want of confidence as my reason, and couching my letter in indignant terms. As I hoped and anticipated, my letter brought the following welcome response, which placed me on a surer footing than ever, and brought me into even more confidential relations with the head of the organisation than I had hitherto enjoyed :—

"WAR DEPARTMENT, FENIAN BROTHERHOOD,
"No. 10 WEST FOURTH STREET,
"NEW YORK, *December* 29, 1868.

"P. O. Box 5141,
"Major H. LE CARON,
"Box 1004,
"Chicago, Ill.

"MAJOR,—Your letter tendering your resignation as an officer of the I.R.A. came duly to hand, but I delayed answering until such time as I could submit it to the President, who was out of town, as without his instructions I could give you nothing definite in reply. He now directs me to say that it is his wish you should remain an officer of the organisation, and that if you require a leave of absence for a month or more, you can have it. He further says he hopes it will not be long before the opportunity you refer to may be granted. Your services have been thoroughly appreciated both by him and the officials of both Departments, civil and military, there-

fore you should not notice the inuendoes or taunts of parties
who cannot value your services.   If the officers of the organisation who have been vilified and calumniated were to resign
on that account, some of its best officers would not now be at
their post.   The 'Patriot's meed is bitter;' they must bear
with much, even from those who should be the first to defend
and sustain them.

"Personally, I would advise you to act on the suggestions
of the President, and hope you will.

"The President will write you in a few days.   Whatever
course you may decide upon pursuing in this matter, you shall
always carry with you the best wishes of

"Your friend and brother,

"J. WHITEHEAD BYRON,

"*Col. & A.A.G., F.B.*"

I got thus safely out of my awkward position,
and learnt one good lesson.   I never kept a
pocket-book again.

XIII.

THE Annual Convention to which I have made
reference in connection with the Roche incident
took place in Philadelphia, "the city of brotherly
love," in the month of December 1868.   It was
made the occasion of an immense demonstration,
no less than 6000 armed and uniformed Fenian
soldiers parading the streets.   The convention
itself was numerically a large one, and was attended by over 400 properly qualified delegates.
The proceedings were of the usual kind.   Brag

and bluster were the order of the day. The determination to invade Canada once more was still
upheld by the vote of the assembly, and the
position of O'Neill and his colleagues was as
fixed and satisfactory as ever—that of myself, of
course, being included in this reference.

The report of the envoy to the sister organisation in Ireland—Daniel Sullivan, Secretary of
Civil Affairs—was an interesting document, and
contained full details of the Clerkenwell Explosion
of the previous year. This was the attempt to
blow up Clerkenwell Prison which Mr. Parnell
subsequently described in reply to Mr. Gladstone
—the old Mr. Gladstone, I mean, not the new
one—as "a practical joke." It was, however, as
we in Philadelphia were to learn, anything but a
practical joke. It was rather as cool and carefully
planned a scheme as ever Fenianism indulged in
to spite the British Government. If the attempt
failed to accomplish all that was expected of it, it
was yet very fruitful in drawing from Mr. Gladstone a confession about its effect being "to bring
the Irish question within the range of practical
politics," which has ever since proved the most
effective and popular argument advanced on
behalf of dynamite in the United States.

About this time, John Boyle O'Reilly, a very
well-known Irishman, late editor of the *Boston*

Pilot, a poet and novelist, and author of a
delightfully written novel, "Moondyne," the
material for which was obtained during his confinement in Australia as a Fenian prisoner, first
arrived in New York, having succeeded in
making his escape from the convict settlement at
Freemantle. With his appearance came the idea
of rescuing his fellow-prisoners. The proposal,
first mooted in uncertainty, was eventually taken
up with the greatest enthusiasm, and carried to
a most successful conclusion. For the purpose a
whaler was chartered by the organisation and
fitted out at New Bedford, Massachusetts, with
the ostensible object of whaling in the South
Seas, but, in reality, for bringing the convicts off
from Australia. The boat was partially manned
by trusted men of the organisation, though, to
keep up the deception, a certain number of well-
known whalers' men went to make up the crew.
On arrival at Australia, some of the most trusted
Fenians were landed with instructions to open up
communication with the convicts, while the vessel
cruised about on the high seas. It was not
anticipated that the task set the men left on shore
would be a difficult one, because the convicts
were hired out as labourers during the day, and
communication with them was not by any means
a trying matter. As affairs turned out, it was

quite easy. The men from the whaler, however, had not been landed more than a day or two, when they found that they were not the only persons arranging the convicts' rescue. Two men— M'Carthy and Gray—were already at work in this direction, having been sent out by the Supreme Council of the Fenian Brotherhood in Ireland, at the instigation, as he claimed to me subsequently, of Patrick Egan. M'Carthy and Gray had, it appeared, already established communications with the convicts; and so, in order to expedite matters, the two sections of rescuers joined forces. On a given day, the plot was carried to a successful termination, and the rescued men were placed on board the whaler, which immediately set out for the States. Although an armed cruiser was immediately despatched to stop it, and some firing took place, the whaler succeeded in getting out of Australian waters and on the high seas in safety.

XIV.

THE year 1869 saw O'Neill still at the helm of Fenian affairs, and large sums of money rolling in to the coffers of the organisation; although, as always the case with Irish movements, dissensions reigned within the ranks. The Stephens section, now presided over by John Savage, who had

succeeded John O'Mahony, was constantly
attacking the Senate wing, and many and bitter
were the feuds which raged. In my position as
Inspector-General of the Irish Republican Army,
I was fully engaged in my old work of inspecting
the companies, and directing the location of arms
along the Canadian country for coming active
operations. In this way I distributed fifteen
thousand stands of arms and almost three million
rounds of ammunition in the care of the many
trusted men stationed between Ogdensburg and
St. Albans. Some thousands of these guns were
breech-loaders, which had been re-modelled from
United States Government "Springfields" at
the arms factory, leased, and "run" by the
organisation at Trenton, New Jersey. The depôt
from which the bulk were packed and shipped
was "Quinn and Nolan's" of Albany. Quinn
was a United States Congressman and Senator of
the Fenian Brotherhood; and Nolan, that very
Mayor Nolan so prominently mentioned by Mr.
Parnell in his evidence as one of the eminently
conservative (!) gentlemen who received him in
America. Constantly the recipient of compli-
ments for the admirable way in which I discharged
my duty, I was now promoted to the office of
Assistant Adjutant-General, with the rank of
Colonel; and my new position enabled me not

only to become possessed of the originals of every document, plan of proposed campaign, &c., but also specimens of the Fenian army commissions and uniforms of the time, which of course I conveyed to the officials of the Canadian Government.

Successful as I was in evading detection through all this work, those assisting me in my Secret Service capacity were not always destined to share in my good luck. This was particularly the case on one occasion. I was at the time shipping arms at Malone, N.Y., and attended, on behalf of the Canadian Government, by one of the staff of men placed at my disposal for the purposes of immediate communication and the transit of any documents requiring secrecy and despatch, as well as for personal protection, should such prove necessary. This man, John C. Rose, was one of the most faithful and trusted servants of the Canadian administration, and for months he followed me along the whole border. Though stopping at the same hotels, and in constant communication with me, no suspicion was aroused, until his identity was disclosed by a visitor from the seat of Government at Ottawa to G. J. Mannix, the head-centre of that Gibraltar of Fenianism, Malone. Men were immediately set to watch him without my knowledge, and the fact of his being found always in my wake on my visits to and return from several towns led to the belief that he was spying upon my actions. A few nights after this belief had been formed, poor Rose, on his return from sending a despatch from the post-office, was waylaid, robbed, and brutally beaten, and subsequently brought back to the hotel in as sorry a plight as I ever saw. I was immediately advised by my Fenian friends as to the dangerous character of this mutual enemy of ours, as he was termed ; and though shocked and embittered by the treatment accorded to the poor devoted fellow, I had, for politic reasons, to applaud their cowardly assault, and to denounce my brave friend, who was bearing all his sufferings in silence and with a splendid spirit. For months poor Rose was quite prostrated, and through this act of my brother Fenians, I was deprived of the services and co-operation of as faithful and capable an ally as ever was given me.

In the winter of 1869, the Fenian Senate announced the completion of the arrangements for the invasion ; and in the month of December the Ninth Annual Convention was called in New York. In connection with this convention, I was called upon to perform a little act which served to more closely knit the bonds of friendship between O'Neill and myself, and, if possible, to obtain for me an even larger share of his confidence than I had hitherto enjoyed. O'Neill, as was customary in Irish revolutionary circles, had, in his capacity of leader, been making free with the funds of the organisation. In a word, he had been spending for personal purposes monies received from the circles or camps. Professor Brophy, the Treasurer, one of the few honest deluded Irish patriots of the time, refused to cook the accounts in order to cover the President's delinquencies. The books had to be submitted to the Convention, and O'Neill was in a frightful difficulty. In his embarrassment he came to me, and, to my surprise, made a clean breast of the whole matter. The opportunity was too good a one to be lost. I advanced the money, and took his note of hand, thus saving his reputation before the Convention.

Need I say that money was never repaid me. Surely not! The only memento which I have of my dollars is O'Neill's note of hand, which, as a curiosity, I have preserved to this date. It is certainly an interesting document, so I give it here.

"NEW YORK, *April* 19, 1870.

"$364, 41/100.

"Received from Colonel H. le Caron, three hundred and sixty-four dollars and 41/100, borrowed money, to be returned whenever demanded.

"JOHN O'NEILL.
"*Pres. F.B.*"

A council of war followed, and all was now activity. In view of active operations in Canada, all monies were called in, and orders were issued from head-quarters to have in readiness all the military organisations. The final order was issued in April as follows :—

" Head-Quarters Fenian Brotherhood,
" No. 10 West Fourth Street,
"New York, *February* 10, 1870.
" P.O. Box 5141.

" *To the Military Officers of the Fenian Brotherhood.*

" Brothers,—You have, no doubt, ere this received general orders No. 1 from General Michael Kerwin, Secretary of War, F.B. (head-quarters, No. 50 North 12th Street, Philadelphia, Penna). *A strict compliance with the requirements thereof is hereby imperatively demanded.* The success or failure of our holy cause now depends upon the prompt and energetic performance of the duties incumbent upon each and all of us, and upon none does the responsibility rest so heavily as upon the military officers of the F.B.

" Brothers, if you be so situated that business or family duties will prevent you from getting your commands in readiness for *active and immediate service*, you will please forward your resignations to the Secretary of War *at once*, and at the same time send on the names of persons suitable to take your places. If you are thoroughly in earnest, you will not hesitate to give your assistance to those who may be appointed to fill the vacancies created by your voluntary withdrawal from the positions to which you have been commissioned.

" Your duty, if circumstances permit, will be to get your men in readiness at the earliest practicable moment. If you should resign, this duty will devolve upon your successors. If there are any arms, ammunition, or military clothing within your knowledge which can be forwarded to certain points, to be named hereafter, so inform the Secretary of War, whom you will address in reply to this circular, and he will, on receipt of your communications, forward *private instructions* with regard to your respective commands.

"Pay no attention to what may appear upon the surface or in newspapers. We mean fight—speedy fight—*and nothing else, thigin thu?* *

"Officers receiving copies of Military Oath with this circular will sign the same in presence of witness, and return to the Secretary of War.

"Ascertain and report how many of your men can and will furnish their own transportation, and in the meantime try and persuade all of them to save enough for that purpose. Military men should not forget that the civic circles have supplied the means wherewith to provide breech-loaders, ammunition, &c. &c. Their liberality in these regards will, to a limited extent, relieve them from the responsibility of advancing the means of transportation. They will not, however, hesitate to co-operate with the military branch of the F.B. in this matter.

" *Preserve the utmost secrecy with regard to this circular, and reply at once.* Delay, and you are guilty of neglect of duty!

"Yours fraternally,

"JOHN O'NEILL,
" President Fenian Brotherhood.

"HEAD-QUARTERS, WAR DEPARTMENT, F.B.,
"DECKERTOWN, SUSSEX COUNTY, N.J.,
" April 28, 1870.

" General Orders.
" No..........

" Commanding officers of regiments, companies, and detachments will hold their respective commands in readiness to move at a moment's notice.

---

* The Irish for "Do you understand?"

" Officers of circles having no military organisations attached will immediately take the necessary steps to organise the military of their neighbourhoods, and forward to this office the names of officers selected, so that they may be commissioned.

" Commanding officers of companies will get as many men as possible ready to move at once, leaving to the civic officers the task of collecting and forwarding—if possible within twenty-four hours thereafter—those who may not be able to move with the first detachments.

" Officers and men must avoid the use of uniforms or any insignia that would distinguish them.

" Officers must not be recognised by military titles, and officers or men must not speak of Fenian matters while *en route*.

" Take no man who is a loafer or a habitual drunkard.

" Take no man who has not seen service, or who has not sufficient character to ensure his good behaviour *en route* and in presence of the enemy.

" Any arms, uniforms, or war material remaining in the hands of circles *must be immediately* packed and forwarded to the points designated in circular of February 19, 1870.

" Hold no communications with any person not authorised from these head-quarters. All letters relating to military matters must be addressed to M. Kerwin, Deckertown, Sussex County, New Jersey.

" Let no consideration prevent a prompt compliance with this order.

" M. KERWIN,

" *Brig.-Gen. and Sec. of War.*

" Approved,

" JOHN O'NEILL,

" *President Fenian Brotherhood.*

" H. le Caron,

     " *Col. and Adj.-General.*"

XV.

At this time I was out West, and receiving a telegram from O'Neill, directing me to meet him in Buffalo, I hurried thither without delay. I reached that city only to find that O'Neill had ordered an immediate movement on Canada, and that, as he phrased it, "no power on earth could stop it." This condition of things startled and surprised me. His determination in the way of immediate action was opposed to the decision of the last council of war, and my chiefs in Canada would, I feared, be quite unprepared. I at once telegraphed the authorities at Ottawa, and was soon in personal communication with their trusted agents in Buffalo. Fortunately, as matters turned out, the plan of action was the same as decided upon at the last council of war, the full details of which the authorities possessed; and so the situation was not so complex as I had at first feared.

The next few days were busy ones. All military commanders were ordered to report at given points with their commands; instructions were issued for the placement of arms by the following Tuesday, at rendezvous near the line at Franklin and Malone, and I was appointed Adjutant-

General with the rank of Brigadier-General. We had quick promotion and brave ranks in the Fenian army!

On Saturday, April 22, 1870, O'Neill and I left Buffalo for St. Albans, he full of enthusiasm and the belief that the Canadians would be taken entirely by surprise, I laughing to myself at his coming discomfiture. We arrived at Milton, Vermont, at daylight on the following morning, to find that everything was proceeding most satisfactorily. Prompt action had been taken by those in charge of the munitions of war, and by the following Tuesday morning sufficient war material for our army was ready at the appointed places.

This second and last invasion of Canada differed in many respects from that of 1866. Then the raid was loudly advertised for months before it actually took place. This time everything was different. Secrecy (as it was supposed) covered every move and intention. Had not the Canadian authorities been fully advised, the results, under the circumstances, would have been undoubtedly serious. There was another important feature about this second raid, and that was its preparedness. Matters in connection with the first affair had been of a very happy-go-lucky character. Now the services of a number of ex-military men of undoubted ability had been

secured, and war material for at least twelve
thousand men was actually on the ground.

O'Neill's ideas may be set forth in very few
words. The chief object he had in view was to
obtain possession of Canada, not as the permanent seat of an Irish republic, but as the
only vulnerable point of attack—the base for
operations against England. His theory was
that the Fenians needed the ports and shipyards
of the Dominion from which they could despatch
privateers to prey upon English shipping. By
the possession of territory he anticipated they
could claim and obtain the rights of belligerents
from the United States. In this event he held
the promise of many men, eminent on the side of
both North and South during the War of Rebellion, to enroll themselves under the Irish banner,
and to command expeditions which it was fondly
hoped and expected would wrest Ireland from
the hands of the oppressor.

His plan was to get across the boundary line
without delay, and then to intrench himself at
a point where his small contingent would form
the nucleus round which a large army and un-
limited support would rally from the United
States. Buffalo, Malone, and Franklin were the
three points from which attacks were to be made
However, " the best laid schemes of mice and

men gang aft aglee." O'Neill expected 1000 ·
men to meet him at Franklin on the night of
Tuesday, April 25, 1870. The history of 1866
repeated itself. As was the case then, so now,
only a quarter of the number presented themselves. By the following morning only 500
had mustered. Every hour's delay added to the
danger of failure and collapse ; and so he feared
to postpone the arrangements any longer. I
viewed the situation with a good deal of equa-
nimity, for on the previous night all my trusty
messengers had departed, carrying full details
as to the time, exact points of crossing, numbers,
place of operations, &c., to the enemy's lines.

At eleven o'clock on Wednesday, O'Neill left
the Franklin Hotel to place himself at the head
of the Fenian army, not without hope and confidence, yet struggling with the disappointing fact
that one-half his men had not arrived. His
chief anxiety appeared to be that the Canadians
would not give him a chance to fight. He mis-
apprehended the situation on this score, however,
as subsequent events showed.

Hubbard's Farm, the Fenian camp and rendezvous, was situated about half a mile from Franklin,
and here all the available "invaders" were mustered. Arranging them in line, O'Neill addressed
them as follows :—

"Soldiers, this is the advance-guard of the Irish-American army for the liberation of Ireland from the yoke of the oppressor. For your own country you enter that of the enemy. The eyes of your countrymen are upon you. Forward. March."

And march they did, O'Neill, as he departed at their head, instructing me to bring to his support on their arrival a party of 400 men then *en route* from St. Albans.

XVI.

CARELESS of consequences, I waited to see what would happen. As I stood on the brow of the hill where our company was situated, the scene was indeed worthy of my study. Ludicrous as were many of the elements which went to make it up, the charm of nature was superior to them all, and commanded my tribute of respect and admiration. Right below me was a pretty valley, down the very centre of which flowed a little creek marking the boundary of Canadian territory, and dividing by its narrow course the Canadian from American soil. A soft pleasant sward sloped gracefully down from where I stood to its bank, while on the other side there rose in graceful outlines the monarchs of a Canadian forest, overtopped by a rocky cliff standing out in bold and picturesque relief. The soft sweet breezes of the spring morning played upon our faces, while the brilliant sunlight sent its rays flashing upon our bayonets, and dancing on the waters underneath.

Nature was in her very best and sweetest mood, and yet little room for appreciation of her charms existed in the breasts of those who, sweeping down the valley's side beneath me, were seeking, in their own foolish way, to make " Ireland a nation once again." They were a funny crowd. All were armed, but few were uniformed. Here and there a Fenian coat, with its green and grey faced with gold, caught the eye, but only to stand out in contrast with the surrounding garments of more sombre hue and everyday appearance. The men marched with a certain amount of military precision, for all had received some degree of military training. At last they reached the little wooden bridge by which the water was crossed, and deploying as skirmishers in close order, they advanced with fixed bayonets, cheering wildly. Not a soul appeared in front. The dark Canadian trees hid from their view the ambushed Canadian volunteers ; and, fixed in their belief that nothing was known of their coming, they advanced in a spirit of effervescent enthusiasm. But not very far, however.

A few paces, and on their startled ears came the ringing ping, ping, of the ambushed rifles, as the Canadians poured a deadly volley straight into their ranks. Utterly taken aback, they stopped, broke rank, and fled as in 1866, an ungovernable mob, to return for a moment in order to pour a volley on their almost invisible enemy, and to finally retreat up the hill to where I stood, still under the fire of their adversaries, leaving their dead to be subsequently buried by the Canadians.

On the slope of the hill was a large structure known as Richard's Farm, to which the invaders retreated and continued their firing, ineffective as it was.

Seeing that all was over here, for a time at least, I hurried off to the point where the St. Albans contingent had by now arrived, and were arming. The process took some time, and while engaged in superintending it, I was afforded practical evidence of the termination of O'Neill's part in the fight. Standing in the middle of the public road where the men were forming into line—it was now half-past one, the "battle" which I have just described having taken place about 11.30—I was startled by the cry, "Clear the road, clear the road!" and almost knocked down by a furiously driven team of horses, to which was attached a covered carriage. As the conveyance flashed by me, I caught through the carriage window a hurried glimpse of the dejected face of O'Neill, who was seated between two men. I understood the situation in a moment, but said nothing. To have given the command to shoot the horses as they turned an adjacent corner would have been the work of an instant, but it was no part of my purpose to restore O'Neill to his command. I learned subsequently that O'Neill was in the custody of the United States marshal, General Foster, who, acting with that precision so peculiar to General Grant's administration, when contrasted with that of Andrew Johnson's, had, in consequence of the information furnished, arrived on the scene of the battle immediately after I left, and arrested O'Neill for a breach of the Neutrality Laws. O'Neill, who was in the company of his comrades, had at first refused submission, and threatened force, but on General Foster placing a revolver at his head, he gave in.

When the news of O'Neill's arrest reached us later on in the afternoon, a council of war was held, presided over by John Boyle O'Reilly, of whom I have already spoken, the council being held in a meadow, where we all stood in a circle. Contingents were hourly arriving, and a strong attempt was made to get Boyle O'Reilly to take command, and lead the attack at some other point, but in the end nothing was done.

Next morning, General Spear, the Secretary of War of the Fenian Brotherhood, arrived at St. Albans, and sought to do something practical in the way of continuing the invasion. Through his *aide-de-camp*, Colonel Brown, and subsequently in person, he appealed to me to supply him with 400 or 500 stands of arms and ammunition within twenty-four hours. Of course, it would never have done for me to have allowed further operations, and so I pleaded it was impossible under the condition of affairs then developed. Thousands of Canadian troops had arrived on the border, and the arms being located in places difficult to get at, they were out of reach for the moment. Luckily for me, the appearance of United States troops in the vicinity put any further attempt at war operations out of the question, for in order to avoid arrest for breach of the Neutrality Laws, the Fenians had to disappear with alacrity. I left this point with the rest of them, and hurrying to Malone, another of the places where rendezvous had been arranged, I found a similar state of things prevailing here, although the arrest of O'Neill, and the unexpected appearance of the United States troops, filled the in-

vaders with dismay, and utter demoralisation was
the result.

XVII.

On Friday, April 27th, under the excuse that I
was going to Burlington to see about O'Neill, I
went round by way of Rouses Point to Montreal.
I was elated with my success, and wanted to
report myself at head-quarters without delay. It
would not, however, have been safe for me to
have gone direct to Ottawa, and so I travelled
in a roundabout way. On the Friday night I
stopped with Judge Coursel, the Commissioner of
the Quebec police, and the following morning took
train to Ottawa. Before my journey concluded,
I found I had been altogether too premature
in my self-congratulations. In fact, that journey brought me even closer to discovery than
I had ever been before.

Nothing unusual happened till we got to Cornwall, where there was the usual half-hour's delay
for dinner. Taking full advantage of it, I was
enjoying a hearty meal, when both my meal and
peace of mind were disturbed by an unlooked-for
incident. Struck by an unusual commotion at the
door of the dining-room, I looked round to find
advancing towards me two men, one remarkable

for his tall military appearance, and the other for
his clerical attire. All eyes were turned upon
them, and as I ceased eating for the moment to
look up, I heard the clerical-looking person say,
as he pointed his finger towards me, "That is the
man." Advancing, the tall man, who subsequently
turned out to be the mayor of Cornwall, speaking
with a Scotch accent, said, "You are my prisoner,"
accompanying the words with a grasp of my
shoulder. I imagined there was some mistake,
and laughed as I turned to resume my dinner,
asking at the same time what was the matter.
Not a movement, however, disturbed the solidity
of my Scotch friend's face as he solemnly repeated
the words, "You are my prisoner," adding, "you
must come with me at once."

As I learned subsequently, the priestly looking
person was a wandering preacher, who had happened to be in the vicinity of Malone when I was
locating arms there, and I had been pointed out
to him then as the leading Fenian agent. His
memory was a very good one, and he immediately
recognised me when we met again.

Matters were beginning to look serious; but
still I could not comprehend what all this meant,
and being still hungry I said, "But won't you let
me finish my dinner?" "No," was the sharp
reply; "come." "For what reason?" quoth I,

indignantly. "Why am I arrested?" "You are a Fenian," came the reply, the words falling clearly and distinctly on the hushed room, where those present began to show signs of anger and indignation towards me. I hurried out with my captors, and was taken to a room adjoining the ticket-office, there to have demanded of me my luggage and my keys, with everything on my person. I had no luggage save a hand-bag, yet I had with me documents which would reveal everything, if made public. My position was dangerous—distinctly dangerous. The prospect before me was that of disclosure and imprisonment amongst a strange people, where I had no friend. Prompt action was called for, and so I asked the mayor for a few minutes' private conversation. Suspicious, and yet curious, he brought me into the ticket-office, where we were left alone. Here I told him the exact situation. It was true, I said, that I was a Fenian, but also a Government agent. I was even then on my way to Ottawa to see Judge M'Micken. To delay or expose me would mean serious difficulty for the Government. Let him send me on to Ottawa under guard, if he liked, and then he would prove my statements true. Did he want immediate proof, then here were my papers, and there a telegram to Judge M'Micken, advising him of my coming, which he himself would despatch.

My manner must have impressed him, for he decided to adopt my suggestion, and send me on by the same train in which I had been travelling (which had not yet gone, all this occupying but a few minutes), under the escort of a lieutenant who, with his Canadian regiment, was then returning from the scene of the invasion. The details of my arrest as a Fenian quickly spread amongst my fellow-passengers, and travelled before me on the route, and the reception I met with along my journey was most disagreeable. For safety's sake, the lieutenant transferred me to the care of a sergeant and couple of soldiers, and the carriage in which we travelled was the sole point of attraction in the train. Crowding round this carriage, the infuriated Canadians would hiss and hoot me, while their cries of " Hang him," " Lynch him," gave me a very uncomfortable idea of what would happen to me if left alone amongst them. So careful were my guardians of me, that they would not even allow me to have the window raised, so that I might smoke, fearing that in some way I might take advantage of the open window to escape. This was really a serious grievance with me, for they could not possibly have inflicted a greater deprivation than that in the matter of smoking. All through my life, even down to the present time, I have been a great smoker, sometimes consuming as many as sixteen cigars in the day, a statement which will probably puzzle some people who hold that tobacco ruins the nerves.

On reaching Prescott Junction, I found that the news of my capture—of course my name and rank never transpired—had created such a sensation that a special correspondent of the *Toronto Globe* had travelled to meet me, in order to find out who and what I was, and everything about me. He was doomed to be disappointed, however, for I could not be got to speak. When, eventually, we arrived at Ottawa, I found my telegram to Judge M'Micken had brought his representative to the station, and by him, myself and my guards were immediately conveyed to the police-office, where the Commissioner was awaiting us. Pretty certain of my safety now, I was quite prepared to smile, and really did laugh when brought into the presence of my friend the judge. Not so he, however. With proverbial soberness and solemnity he heard the details of my capture, received possession of my person, and gave a formal receipt for my custody. Armed with this, my guardians left, and then the old man's genial kindly nature asserted itself. By his instructions I remained in his office till nightfall, when, in a cab under cover of the darkness, I accompanied him to the club to take up my quarters there for the night.

In the club the Fenian prisoner of a few hours previously was made a most welcome guest, and had an exceedingly good time. My identity being known to some of the officers who crowded the club-house after their return from Franklin, I found myself quite the hero of the hour, and had most interesting chats over the experiences of the raid on both sides of the fight. Amongst the pleasant people whose acquaintance I then made was Dr. Grant, the physician to Prince Arthur, who was in Ottawa at that time.

With the following day came arrangements for my departure for home, and it was decided that, in order to avoid travelling over the same line again, I should be driven during the night to Ann Prior terminus—a distance of some forty miles from Ottawa—from which place I could take a branch line to my destination. Fortunate though I thought myself, my troubles were not at an end. This trip of mine to Ottawa was a chapter of misfortunes. As I was on the point of starting, I discovered that I had not sufficient money to bring me home. Accordingly, Judge M'Micken had to supply me with the needful funds. This, however, did not prove by any means an easy thing to do. A cheque was duly drawn, but of course I could not cash it, and the judge had to have recourse to a friend. The amount was a large one—three hundred and fifty dollars—and it was beyond the resources of the club at the moment. The services of the club porter therefore had to be utilised for the purpose of obtaining the money. Here, unknown to us, seed was being sown which was to bear evil fruit. The porter knew, of course, that I was the Fenian prisoner, although nothing more; and, gossip that he was, he let out the secret a little later. It became public property; and the Canadian press published the fact that an important Fenian had been in Ottawa immediately after the raid, and received a very large sum of money from the Government official with whom he was in communication, adding that the Fenians must have been nicely duped all through. This was bringing danger very, very near to me again; yet, marvellous to relate, suspicion never rested upon me in connection with the paragraph. I drove from Ottawa in the night, got safely home, and was never troubled further by my eventful visit. But, for a long time, I treasured very unchristian-like feelings towards that porter.

XVIII

WITH the fiasco at Pigeon Hill, and the equally inglorious termination of the musters at other points of the Canadian border, there died out altogether the idea of attacking and seizing any portion of Canada. O'Neill, after some confinement, was brought to trial, and sentenced to six months' imprisonment, and the Fenian organisation literally went to pieces for the time. I had no thought of its ever reviving again, and so turned my attention once more to my medical work, which I had had to completely neglect from the time of my leaving Joliet and attaching myself to O'Neill's staff.

I had scarcely resumed my studies, however, when a visit from O'Neill on his release showed me that there was still some fight left in himself and his comrades. He came to me as a matter of fact to enlist my co-operation in some work of a distinctly active character. In explanation of the position of affairs, he laid before me the originals of several letters to him from the Rev. W. B. O'Donohoe, a young priest of Manitoba, who was at the time acting as secretary for the notorious Riel. The correspondence gave all the details of a contemplated uprising of the half-

G

breeds in the North-West against the Dominion authorities, and stated, to my amazement and disgust, that he—this young priest—had received permission from his Archbishop—Tasché—to throw off his ecclesiastical garments and take a part therein.

In conclusion, O'Neill's assistance and co-operation in the attempt was sought, and as he put it, "anything to cripple the enemy" being his motto, he was only too eager for the fray. He had one great difficulty, however, and that was the want of arms. Knowing that a quantity remained in hiding since the second raid, he had sought to obtain possession of them, but had been referred to me as the person who had deposited them with their present custodians, and without whose permission they could not be given up. I cheerfully agreed to let him have 400 breech-loaders and ammunition, and accompanied him to the points where they were, for the purpose of their delivery, but not before I had surreptitiously obtained the use of the documents, and sent copies to both the Home and Canadian Governments with full information as to what was *sur le tapis*.

O'Neill, in company with a trusted confederate, J. J. Donnelly, fitted out his expedition, and on the 5th day of October 1871, after crossing the line at Fort Pembina, was arrested with his party,

and all his war material seized, in consequence
of the information supplied by me. Riel, thus
deprived of the expected assistance, surrendered
at Fort Garry to Lord Wolseley without firing a
shot. O'Neill and his party having been turned
over to the United States authorities, were, four
days afterwards, tried and acquitted. Strange as
it appears, these men, captured on Canadian soil,
were, by some egregious blunder, handed over
to the United States authorities, and by them
acquitted on the ludicrous technicality that the
offence was not committed on American, but
Canadian soil.

Subsequently O'Neill came back to me and
made my life a burthen. Discredited and dis-
heartened, he took to drink and went entirely to
the dogs, bringing to the verge of starvation an
affectionate but heart-broken wife, who, once a sister
of mercy, had nursed and grown to love him in a
hospital where he was confined, and, disregarding
all her vows, had in the end married him. Drifting slowly downward through disgrace and drink,
O'Neill, the once brilliant, if egotistical, Irishman
met a lone and miserable death.

XIX

On resuming my studies, I decided to enter the Detroit College of Medicine, and so, taking my family with me, I settled down there. There were many reasons for my change of residence, not the least important of which was that connected with the unpopularity which I found attached to me in my old home after my return from the Canadian affair. O'Neill had many opponents, and by these opponents I was attacked in company with O'Neill, and the others engaged in the affair, for having ruined the organisation by the premature "invasion" which had taken place. Therefore, I thought it better to remove to another quarter where this state of feeling did not exist, and where my Irish record would be of service to me in the future. As far as Detroit was concerned, I fixed upon it because of the desire of Judge M'Micken that I should become acquainted with, and obtain as much information as I could about, Mackay Lomasney—whose name will be familiar in connection with the London Bridge explosion—and others just settled down there.

Lomasney was, in the eyes of the authorities, an important man; and his subsequent career, terminating with the attempt to blow up London

Bridge, in which he lost his own life, fully justified their estimate. He had been engaged in the '65 and '67 movements in Ireland, had been charged with the murder of a policeman and acquitted, but sentenced to twelve years' penal servitude for his work as a rebel, and, with others whose names will appear later, had been amnestied in the year 1870. He had now settled down in Detroit as the proprietor of a book-store; and as he was known to be a most active revolutionist, much curiosity was felt as to what he was actually doing. I formed a very pleasant acquaintance with Mackay Lomasney, and found him a most entertaining man. The future dynamitard was at this time about twenty-eight years of age. Though of youthful appearance, his face was a most determined one, and the way in which it lent itself to disguise truly marvellous. When covered with the dark bushy hair, of which he had a profusion, it was one face; when clean-shaven, quite another, and impossible of recognition. Acting, as he constantly did, as the delegate from the American section to the Fenians at home, this faculty of disguise proved of enormous service, and may very well have had disastrous effects on police vigilance. I have seen Lomasney both shaved, on his return from Ireland, and unshaved, in his American life; and in all the men I have ever met, I never saw such a change produced by so easy a process. I may dismiss Mackay Lomasney from this point of my story by saying that, beyond his activity in connection with the establishment of the Irish Confederation, his movements gave little ground for apprehension, and, as far as the Confederation was concerned, its development proved of very little account.

But, if the Confederation was to accomplish little, the men who with Lomasney took part in its initiation were not without their claims to attention. Foremost amongst them were two bearing names destined to be familiar in latterday politics. These were O'Donovan Rossa and John Devoy. As both will be found constantly strutting across the stage of Irish-American affairs from this date, I will pause here to refer to them in some little detail.

Jeremiah O'Donovan—the " Rossa " was, he claims, added in early years as the outward and visible sign of the alleged fact of his being directly descended from the Princes of Rossa—was, at the time of his arrival, one of the most popular men amongst the Irish in the United States. Sentenced to imprisonment for life for taking part in the '65 movement, he had, according to general rumour, undergone the severest of sufferings and indignities in the British dungeons. A strong current of sympathy set in in his favour in consequence, and as both in public and private he lost no opportunity of dilating upon his grievance, the sentiment was in no sense allowed to waver or grow weak. The man whose name was to be so closely associated with dynamite and devilry in later years, did not at this time suggest by his appearance the possession of any undue ferocity. His face, though determined, was yet not without its kindly aspect, while his love for the bottle betrayed a jovial rather than a fiendish instinct. His fierceness, indeed, lay altogether in speech. Voluble and sweeping in his language, he was never so happy as when pouring out the vials of his wrath on the British Government.

Devoy, the notorious author of the "New Departure," was at once seen to be a man of weighty influence. Forbidding of aspect, with a perpetual scowl upon his face, he immediately conveyed the idea of being a quarrelsome man, an idea sustained and strengthened by both his manner of speech and gruffness of voice. Experience of Devoy's character only went to prove the correctness of this view. Quarrelsome and discontented, ambitious and unscrupulous, his friendships were few and far between; and had it not been for his undoubted ability, and the existence of those necessities which link

adventurers together, he could never have reached
the prominent place which he subsequently attained
in the Fenian organisation.

With their fellow - prisoners who had been
amnestied, General Thomas F. Bourke, Thomas
Clarke Luby, Edmond Power, and Henry S.
Meledy, together with James J. O'Kelly, late
M.P. for Roscommon, who is not a member of the
present House of Commons, Rossa and Devoy
brought the Irish Confederation into existence,
and formed its first "directory" or executive.
They indulged in the wild hope of being able
to gather in all the scattered Irish under one
banner, and to put an end once and for all to
the dissensions and divisions which had so disas-
trously affected Irish affairs in the past. They
were disappointed. Not by their unaided efforts
was this to be accomplished. Indeed, the Confederation was never popular. It was regarded
as a sort of close corporation "run," as we say in
the United States, in the interest of the exiles,
and, as a consequence, was jealously viewed by
the rank and file. Every effort that could be
made to bring about a fusion was tried by these
men, but without success. Even Stephens himself was brought over from France and put at the
head of affairs; but his name had lost its charm,
and he had to return to Paris a discredited man.

XX

WHILE my Fenian friends struggled on in this way, I looked after my own affairs. Completing my studies and business in Detroit, I moved myself and my family to Wilmington, where I settled down to make a home and secure an income. I was now a fully fledged M.D., and so I immediately commenced practising at Braidwood, a suburb of Wilmington. Success attended my start, my Irish connection and record bringing me an amount of patronage almost beyond my powers of attention. I had given up all idea of anything definite happening in the way of Fenian affairs, and turned my attention to local politics. Here, of course, my Irish friends were again of use. Failing to obtain a seat on the School Board, for which I had been nominated, I succeeded in getting an appointment on the Board of Health. The office was really a sinecure, with one hundred dollars a year attached. Not content with it, I gained the much more lucrative appointment of Supervisor of Braidwood, attached to which was a daily fee of $2\frac{1}{2}$ dollars, and travelling allowances when engaged on town business. Anybody acquainted with the American political system, even to a moderate

extent, will know how paying such offices can
be made.

Meantime I had joined the Medical Society of
my State, and assisted in founding the State
Pharmaceutical Society. My activity did not
even stop here, and, in addition, I took a very
active part in bringing about much-needed legislation on the question of the practice of medicine.
In these days there was no such thing as a State
law regulating the practice of medicine or phar-
macy, and I—let me frankly confess it—as much
for the sake of popularity as anything else, spared
no pains, even going to the extent of "lobby-
ing" in Springfield, the State capital, in the
interest of legislation on these matters, in which
I was very successful.

Little as I imagined it then, events were at this
time shaping themselves to an end which, frequently attempted, had never yet been wholly
accomplished by the aspiring leaders of the Irish
in America. This was the bringing together of
all Irishmen at home and abroad into one vast
and perfect organisation. The hour was coming,
and with it the men. Born in comparative poverty
and insignificance, but under an impressive name,
the association now being formed, the great Clan-
na-Gael of the future, was destined to be a powerful, rich, and far-reaching organisation, healthy of

limb and strong of hand, fated to leave its heavy mark upon the pages of this half-century's history. From small beginnings have come great results.

Away back towards the end of the sixties, there came into existence one of those temporal societies, an off-shoot of the permanent conspiracy known under the name " Knights of the Inner Circle," which was joined by many Irish conspirators, myself amongst the number. With its members there became associated, in the latter end of 1869, some three hundred members of the "Brian Boru" Circle of the Fenian Brotherhood in New York City, who, in consequence of a political quarrel over electioneering matters, seceded from their original body ; and by these men, acting in concert with others under the name of the " United Irishmen," what were really the first camps of the Clan-na-Gael were established.

The V.C. (the cypher was arranged on the plan of using the alphabetical letters immediately following those intended to be indicated) had for its object the same intention which governed the inception and development of all Irish conspiracy in America—the freedom of Ireland from English control by armed force. It was, however, to differ from its predecessors insomuch as, unlike them, it was to be of an essentially secret character. P. R. Walsh of Cleveland, Ohio, known as "the Father of the Clan," was the apostle of this new condition of things, and he, with others of shrewd and far-seeing minds, argued with great success, that if one lesson more important than another was to be learnt from the past history and miserable fiascos of the movement, it was that no possible success could be achieved with a revolutionary organisation working in the open day. The Irish people, reasoned these priests of the new faith, had not judgment enough to manage their schemes for freedom. They revealed their secrets to the heads of their Church; they were dictated to by these heads; they feared to obey their non-clerical leaders; and so were thwarted the best schemes of the most active workers. A revolutionary movement must be secret and un-scrupulous, and, to be successful, they could not enter on the contest for freedom with the yoke of the Church around their neck.

Language like this reads strangely indeed in the light of latter-day revelations, and the knowledge the world now has of Clan-na-Gael priests and their work. But at the time it was not without its appropriateness and significance. The priests at the period of which I write were, neither in Ireland nor America, the priests of these subsequent years. Then, as in those days of old, when religion was paramount and priestly control

salutary and effective, the ban of the Church was
not merely a phrase dangerous in sound, it was a
living dread reality, fearful in its consequences in
the eyes of those who in their lives worked out
that grand old characteristic of the Irish people,
faith in their Church and reverence toward its
rulers. It was reserved for the coming years to
bring to the view of a startled public a people
reckless and defiant of priestly control, because of
the teachings of their atheistic and communistic
leaders, and the self-surrender of all their higher
and priestly functions by those who were content to be led by, rather than to lead those whose
consciences were their charge and their responsibility.

XXI.

THE arguments were well put, and what was
more, they were well timed. They proved successful. Everything appeared in favour of the
new move; and the re-establishment of the
Fenian organisation in Great Britain on a more
compact secret basis, under the title of the *Irish
Republican Brotherhood*, was one of the many
satisfactory features of the moment. Matters,
however, moved slowly; and, although actually
established in 1869, it was not until the year
1873 that the movement became in any way

general. Then it was that, merging almost all other societies in itself, the Clan, now known as the V.C. or United Brotherhood, established subordinate bodies or " Camps," as they were called, almost simultaneously in all the leading centres of the United States. Secrecy was the text preached in every direction. Every member was bound by the most solemn of oaths to keep secret all knowledge of the order and its proceedings which might come to him, under penalty of death. A Masonic form of ritual was adopted ; grips, passwords, signs, and terrorising penalties were decided upon ; and all the pomp and circumstance of mystery, so dear to the Irish heart and so effective in such a conspiracy, were called to the aid of those who now inculcated this new doctrine.

Undoubtedly, there was no secret made amongst its members as to the treasonable character of the organisation. The official printed Constitution set forth the truth of the matter in no uncertain way. " The object," it stated, " is to aid the Irish people in the attainment of the complete and absolute independence of Ireland, by the overthrow of English domination : a total separation from that country, and the complete severance of all political connection with it ; the establishment of an independent republic on

Irish soil, chosen by the free votes of the whole
Irish people, without distinction of creed or class,
and the restoration to all Irishmen of every creed
and class of their natural privileges of citizenship
and equal rights.   It shall prepare unceasingly
for an armed insurrection in Ireland."

The Ritual and forms of initiation were framed
entirely upon Masonic precedent ; and, to the vast
majority of the members of the Clan, the statement will come no doubt as a great surprise that
the much vaunted secret forms of the Masonic
order need be secret to them no longer, inasmuch as that, when being admitted to a Clan-
na-Gael club, they were going through the same
forms and ceremonies as attached themselves to
that great source of mystery and wonderment in
the eyes of the non-elect, the Masonic Brotherhood.   I have often laughed to myself at the
surprise shown by some Masons on the occasion of their initiation to Clan-na-Gael clubs—for
there are Masons in the Clan—at being brought
once more into contact with the familiar procedure.   One great feature of similarity exists
between the two ceremonies.   In both the candidate is impressed with a deep sense of awe and
respect, to learn subsequently that nothing very
mysterious or wonderful is to come within his
knowledge.   Though the effect is the same, how-

ever, the causes are very different. In one case, that of the Mason, nothing very strange happens or is committed to his secrecy, for the simple reason that the practice of brotherly love and charity requires no unusual strain either on his powers of wonder or reserve ; while in the other the poor confiding Irishman is simply intended to play the part of a dupe, to move and subscribe to order, but to be trusted in no single regard, until by jobbery or manipulation he works his way to the higher ranks of the organisation.

The candidates for membership were balloted for in the usual club manner, three black balls excluding. The successful ones having answered different queries regarding their age, belief in God, &c. &c., were, after being blindfolded and shut out from view of their future associates, brought forward and addressed by the Vice-President of the meeting as follows :—

" My Friends.—Animated by love, duty, and patriotism, you have sought affiliation with us. We have deemed you worthy of our confidence and our friendship. You are now within these secret walls. The men who surround you have all taken the obligations of our Order, and are endeavouring to fulfil its duties. These duties must be cheerfully complied with, or not at all undertaken. We are Jsjtinfo (Irishmen) banded together for the purpose of freeing Jsfmboe (Ireland) and elevating the position of the Jsjti (Irish) race. The lamp of the bitter past plainly points our path, and we believe that the first step on the road to freedom is secrecy. Destitute of secrecy, defeat will again cloud our 'brightest hopes ; and, believing this, we shall hesitate at no sacrifice to maintain it. Be prepared, then, to cast aside with us every thought that may impede the growth of this holy feeling among Jsjtinfo (Irishmen) ; for, once a member of this Order, you must stand by its watchwords of Secrecy, Obedience, and Love. With this explanation, I ask you are you willing to proceed?"

The answer being satisfactory, the candidates were next placed opposite the President, and addressed by him as follows :—

"My Friends,—By your own voluntary act you are now before us. You have learned the nature of the cause in which we are engaged—a cause honourable to our manhood, and imposed upon us by every consideration of duty and patriotism. We would not have an unwilling member amongst us, and we give you, even now, the opportunity of withdrawing, if you so desire. Every man here has taken a solemn and binding oath to be faithful to the trust we repose in him. This oath, I assure you, is one which does not conflict with any duty which you owe to God, to your country, your neighbours, or yourself. It must be taken before you can be admitted to light and fellowship in our Order. With this assurance, and understanding, as you do, that the object of this organisation is the freedom of Jsfmboe (Ireland), will you submit yourself to our rules and regulations and take our obligation without mental reservation?"

At the conclusion of the address, the questions having been put, and correctly replied to, the candidate took the oath as follows :—

"I, ———, do solemnly and sincerely swear, in the presence of Almighty God, that I will labour, while life is left me, to

H

establish and defend a republican form of government in Jsfmboe (Ireland). That I will never reveal the secrets of this organisation to any person or persons not entitled to know them. That I will obey and comply with the Constitution and laws of the V.C., and promptly and faithfully execute all constitutional orders coming to me from the proper authority, to the best of my ability. That I will foster a spirit of unity, nationality, and brotherly love among the people of Jsfmboe (Ireland).

" I furthermore swear that I do not now belong to any other Jsjti sfwpmvujpobsz (Irish revolutionary) society antagonistic to this organisation, and that I will not become a member of such society while connected with the V.C., and, finally, I swear that I take this obligation without mental reservation, and that any violation hereof is infamous and merits the severest punishment. So help me God." (Kiss the book.)

And then, in conclusion, the President made the following remarks :—

" The name of this Order is the V.C. Its local sub-divisions are styled D.'s, and are known by members. This is D. No. —. The leading object of the V.C. is to co-operate with the J.S.C. (Irish Republican Brotherhood) in securing the independence of Jsfmboe (Ireland), and the special object is to secure the union of all Jsjti Obujpobmjtut (Irish Nationalists). As it is essential for the safe and efficient working of our organisation to preserve the strictest secrecy in reference to it, you will never mention the name of the V.C., or anything connected therewith, to any one whom you do not know to be a member thereof in good standing. And that we may be more effectually guarded from exposure, as well as to secure concentration of effort, you are prohibited by the supreme authority from contributing money to, or otherwise aiding, any other Jsjti sfwpmvujpobsz (Irish revolutionary) society.

" Should you desire to secure some worthy person for membership, you will first have him proposed here, and, if elected, you may then indirectly and carefully ascertain his sentiments on the subject of secret Jsjti Obujpobm (Irish National) organisations, and, should his views be favourable, you might then intimate that you believe there is a secret organisation in existence working for Jsjti (Irish) liberty; and, if he appears inclined to join it, you may admit that you are a member of it, or acquainted with a member of it, and that you think you can secure his admission therein; but no further information must you convey, nor use the name of any person connected with the Order. . . .

"Finally, my brother, be careful that you do not make an improper use of these instructions, and let not the cause of Jsímboe (Ireland) or the interests of the V.C. suffer through any want of prudence, perseverance, and courage on your part while travelling onwards on the path to freedom. (Two raps.)

"Brothers! It affords me great pleasure to introduce to you your new brother." (One rap.)

XXII.

Up to the year 1881, when the administration of the conspiracy underwent a change, with which I will deal at its proper time, the Clan-na-Gael was governed by an executive body (known in the cypher as F.C.), presided over by a Chairman elected by the body at the annual conventions, and a Revolutionary Directory known without any regard to the cypher by its initial letters R.D. This Revolutionary Directory was composed of seven men, three of whom were nominated by the

Executive, three by the Irish Republican Brotherhood (known as the J.S.C.) in Ireland, and a seventh selected by the six when appointed. The Revolutionary Directory was, as its name implies, a body dealing directly with revolutionary matters, and it was chiefly characterised by the autocratic power possessed by its members, about whose action no detailed information was supplied, and against whose proceedings there was, in consequence, no basis for appeal. The names of all these officers were known only to the delegates who elected them, and to the Presiding Officer of each camp, known as Senior Guardian.

To the Executive (or F.C.) was intrusted, amongst other things, the arrangements regarding the places and dates for holding the biennial and annual conventions of the order; and their decision in this respect was carefully guarded, and only at the very last moment communicated to the high officials, in order to prevent any spies or agents of the British Government from becoming acquainted with their proceedings. The head of each subordinate body was informed a week in advance of the date and place of the convention; and he was instructed to arrange for the immediate election of a delegate from his camp. So close was the secret kept, that the delegate, if other than the presiding officer, did not know till the very hour of his starting where he was bound for. Like convicts, the members were known by numbers, never by names. Camps (known as D.'s) were also numbered; and, in order the better to cover their doings from the outside world, each camp had a public name by which it was known. For instance, my own camp was known as the " Emmet Literary Association."

During the early years of its existence I was not a member of the Clan-na-Gael. Although, as I have stated, I was one of the " Knights of the Inner Circle," I did not take any prominent part in the early days, when the V.C. succeeded, or rather absorbed it. There were reasons for my not doing so. My prominence and action in the ill-fated Canadian raid had not been altogether forgotten, and I was still held responsible, in certain minds, for the premature undertaking of it. Another reason affecting my action was the difficulty introduced by a clause in the new constitution in regard to the question of nationality. This clause read as follows :—

" All persons of Irish birth or descent, or of partial Irish descent, shall be eligible to membership; but in cases of persons of partial Irish descent, the camps are directed to make special inquiries in regard to the history, character, and sentiments of the person proposed."

In view of the whole situation, I determined

that I should live down any ill-feeling which might exist regarding my previous exploits, and that I should take advantage of the interval thus brought about by arranging some plan for my election later, on the ground of my partial Irish descent. I had, of course, hitherto passed myself off as a Frenchman, strongly sympathising with Irish affairs, though never laying any claim to connection with the country. Now I had to change my tactics a little, and so I gradually got it put about that my mother—poor lady, she is living to-day, and will probably never know till she reads this of the liberty I took with her birthright—was of Irish descent. Of course, as the people out there had never seen or heard of my mother, and it was quite a common thing for French and Irish to intermarry, the deception was not likely to be discovered, as indeed it never was.

There was still yet another reason for my being cautious. The most insane and implacable enemy of O'Neill's—and through my friendship for O'Neill, of myself—Major William M'Williams, of old Fenian fame, was now high in the councils of the new organisation. In the O'Neill *régime*, presumably jealous of my position, he had denounced me as an adventurer, and the ill-feeling he had for me had culminated during the sittings of a Fenian congress in an open attack, reported in the New York papers as follows :—

" THE FENIAN CONGRESS AND A FENIAN ROW.

" The Fenian Congress was in session yesterday. A quorum of the Executive Committee appointed in Chicago was in session all day. They say they intend to commence work as soon as they obtain possession of the munitions of war. Major M'Williams and Major Le Caron, two of the delegates, had a little onset in front of the Whitney House last eve, and blood might have flowed had it not been for the interference of several delegates."

The altercation, I may add, on this occasion involved the use of revolvers, and created too pronounced a feeling between us to allow of my ever after expecting anything but the bitterest opposition from M'Williams. To my relief, however, M'Williams eventually got into a personal altercation with a fiercer antagonist than myself, by whom he was shot in Columbia, S.C., being killed on the spot. His exit cleared the way of the only difficulty which existed at the time of his death, and so I considered it prudent to accept the invitation, often extended to me, to join the Clan-na-Gael. I joined, and an appointment upon the Military Board of the organisation quickly followed. It must not, however, be thought that I had been "out of things" meantime. Not at all. Possessed, as I

was, of more than one confiding friend, I secured
information about everything that took place.

XXIII.

SLOWLY but surely the Clan-na-Gael was gaining
ground, despite all the forces arrayed against it.
Triumphing over Church opposition, conscientious
scruple on the score of joining secret societies,
and the single opposing Revolutionary faction
still faithful to the memory of Stephens, it had,
in 1876, a membership exceeding 11,000, which
included amongst its leading names those of
Alexander Sullivan, John Devoy, O'Donovan
Rossa, Thomas Clarke Luby, Thomas F. Burke,
Dr. Carroll, James Reynolds, Frank Agnew,
Colonel Clingen, Wm. J. Hynes, P. W. Dunne,
Michael Boland, Denis Feeley, J. J. Breslin,
Michael Kirwen, and General Millen.

These were the men who in the after years
were to be in the front rank of the Clan-na-Gael,
and by their position and influence to model and
direct the policy of the organisation. Of them
and their position at this time I shall now have
some little to say.

With Sullivan I have already dealt, and here I
need only state that, having established himself

in Chicago, he had taken to the study of law, in which branch of the profession he was now—in 1876—preparing to practise. He had been maintaining his questionable reputation, for he had shot a man in cold blood; and though twice tried, had been successful in escaping the consequences of his act, owing to the employing of that process so frequently charged against the Government in Ireland—packing the jury. Of Devoy and O'Donovan Rossa I have also spoken before. The former, drifting to New York, had since we parted with him been engaged on some two or three American papers, and he was now, if I remember aright, engaged on the *New York Herald* staff. Rossa, very much to the front for the moment, in consequence of his "skirmishing" theory, had meantime been living on the proceeds of the fund raised for himself and his fellow-exiles on their arrival in 1871, and a special subscription for himself, which Ford inaugurated in the *Irish World.* Luby had been a well-known patriot since 1865, when, in company with John O'Leary and Charles J. Kickham, he had been sentenced to a long term of penal servitude for the part he played in Ireland as one of the editors of the *Irish People.* General Thomas Fras. Burke had served with the Confederate Army, and had been amongst those who, in 1867, left America to lead in that most disheartening of fiascos, the Irish rising of 1865, as the result of his part in which he was sentenced to death, but subsequently amnestied.

Dr. William Carroll, one of the principal physicians in Philadelphia, whose name will appear prominently in the future, and who stood one of the sponsors for Mr. Parnell on the occasion of his arrival in America, was best known as the admirer, friend, and associate of John Mitchell, and was himself nothing if not a Revolutionist. James Reynolds of New Haven, Conn., whom I first met in connection with the secret organisation, was by profession a gas- and brass-fitter, and an avowed advocate of "extreme" measures. He was in fact a member of the Revolutionary Directory of this period. Frank Agnew had a Fenian record extending as far back as the Senate period of the Fenian Brotherhood. Strangely enough, I first came in contact with him when, on an inspecting tour, I had occasion to inspect a Fenian Company of which he was captain in Chicago. He was one of those who arrived too late to be of use in connection with the Fenian raid of '70. He was now a contractor of some importance in Chicago, and a great friend and ally of Sullivan's. Of Colonel Clingen I need not say much, save that he had been an old Fenian ally of mine in days gone by, and had sat with myself on the Military Board during O'Neill's *régime*.

Of the others I have mentioned, Hynes and Dunne perhaps deserve the most prominent place, by reason of the part they have recently played in the Cronin affair. Both these men, it will be remembered, came out as very strong opponents of Alexander Sullivan, whom they roundly accused of causing Dr. Cronin's death. Hynes I knew as far back as 1865, when, as a clerk to John O'Neill, he took a very active part in the work of the Fenian Brotherhood. Owing to a row between O'Neill and himself, he severed his connection with active Fenianism, and obtained a clerkship in one of the departments at Washington, finding his way, after a little time, to Arkansas. Although returned as a carpet-bag Congressman for the State, he failed to prosper, and at last he found himself without a dollar in Chicago. Here the first man to help him was Alexander Sullivan, against whom he is now arrayed. Through Sullivan's political influence, Hynes was engaged as professional juryman at a fee of two dollars a day, from which position he worked himself forward to that of a prominent politician and a well-known member of the bar at which he practises.

P. W. Dunne proved to be a duplicate of

O'Donovan Rossa, in appearance and in many other ways, with this one strong exception, that, whereas Rossa never sacrificed any of his means for the good of his countrymen, but rather lived upon them in fact, Dunne sacrificed an almost princely fortune.   In early years he had been a prominent distiller (a very lucrative business) in Peoria, Illinois; and he was one of the leading seceders from the Stephens wing of the Fenian Brotherhood, after the failure of 1865, in which he himself participated, in company with P. J. Meehan, editor of the *Irish American*.   He was now situated in Chicago, occupying the position of Superintendent of Streets, and had preceded Sullivan and Clingen upon the Executive of the Clan-na-Gael.

As for the remainder, Boland, once a lieutenant in the United States Army, was now a practising lawyer in Kentucky, having meantime taken part in the '66 raid on Canada.   He was also one of the most prominent of Clan-na-Gael officials, and an advocate of extreme measures.   Feeley, also an attorney-at-law, had been a member of the Royal Irish Constabulary in his early days, and was now, as of yore, one of the most prominent and bloodthirsty of rebels in the States.   Kirwen had been Brigadier-General and Fenian Secretary of War during the Canadian raid of 1870, and had preserved his Revolutionary record unbroken;

while Breslin, chiefly remarkable for the part he had played in helping James Stephens to escape from Richmond prison (Ireland) in 1866, now, as ever since then, a prominent and avowed Revolutionist, was occupying his public life in some municipal office of an important character, while, in secret, playing his part on the Revolutionary Directory of the Clan-na-Gael.

One name I have left to the last, and that is General Millen's. The discredited hero of the Jubilee Explosion Scheme of 1887 was at this time engaged on the editorial staff of the *New York Herald*. Unlike almost every one whom I have named, his military title was neither of Fenian nor of American extraction. He had, according to his own account, gained both his military knowledge and his rank when, out in Mexico on the part of the *New York Herald*, he had thrown in his lot with Juarez prior to the overthrow of the government of Maximilian and the establishment of the First Republic, of which Juarez was President. Be the claims to military knowledge which he advanced good or bad, they were accepted with a certain amount of good faith by the Clan leaders; and his usefulness in this regard being appreciated, he held a position of some importance at this time, being in fact Chairman of the Military Board.

XXIV.

My advent in the organisation, though gratifying
to a certain extent, did not satisfy me as fully as
I wished. I wanted to know everything that took
place on the inner side of the movement, and I found
that, as one of the rank and file, I could really learn
nothing. Accordingly, I set my wits to work to
see how I could accomplish my desire of gaining
such a position as would give me all I wanted.
Very little consideration was needed to show me
that, in a large centre like Chicago, where jealousy
and ambition governed every motive, it would be
impossible for a new-comer to get to the front, and
so I decided to work out my designs in a smaller
and more unimportant place, where internal dissensions would find little if any home. It will
be remembered that Braidwood was the place
where I had my drug-store, and where I had had
strong evidence of my popularity in my election
as Supervisor by a majority of 103 over my
opponents. In the end, therefore, I determined
to establish a camp in Braidwood, and with the
assistance of the official organiser, a most promis-
ing "camp" was got together, to the Senior
Guardianship or Presidency of which I was
unanimously elected. Sullivan unconsciously

assisted me in my design. It was through his influence, though at my suggestion, that the official
organiser was sent down in the first instance.

Having once obtained the position, I spared
neither pains nor money to make myself secure
in it. My status and extensive practice as a
doctor permitted of my playing the *rôle* of the
generous patriot, and there was no subscription
list on which my name did not figure in some
capacity as the patriotic, political, charitable, or
religious friend. The latter was not by any
means the most infrequent, for religion of a
certain type plays a very large part in Irish
politics. Where money and the other arts failed,
then I took to diplomacy. Year in, year out, I
continued president of my camp, though always
at election time asking to be allowed to retire in
favour of some better and more deserving brother.
Of course it was simply a case of "swearing I
would ne'er consent, consenting."

I was too useful to my brothers of "Camp 463,"
now 204, to allow of their permitting me to retire
to the ranks. If no other reason but the question
of money came in, then this of itself alone would
have been sufficient. When a delegate had to
be despatched to conventions or gatherings elsewhere, none were more ready to start than I,
while—more important still for the patriots—my

bills for expenses, instead of being of the large
and unjustifiable character usually associated with
such proceedings, could only be got from me under
protest, and with every manifestation of desire to
save them outlay. Of course, this travelling about
from centre to centre, this mixing with many men
from many points, and the opportunities thus
afforded for gaining information and opening
up new sources of supply, admirably suited my
purpose ; and by taking advantage of the varied
openings given me, I was enabled to extend my
usefulness as a Secret Service agent to a very
appreciable extent.

Matters, indeed, were satisfactorily situated for
me at every point. As Senior Guardian of the
Braidwood camp, I was in receipt of every document issued from head-quarters, and through me
many of these found their way to Mr. Anderson on
the English side of the water. My work in connection with these documents taxed all my powers
of resource; and had it not been for the popular and
trusted position which I held, I could have accomplished very little in regard to them. A stringent
regulation of the Executive required that all documents—when not returned to head-quarters, as
many had to be—should be burned in view of
the camp, in order that the most perfect secrecy
should be secured. It was, of course, impossible

for me to retain the originals of those which had
to be returned, and of them I could only keep
copies. With those requiring destruction in the
presence of my camp, I was enabled to act
differently. Always prepared for the emergency,
I was, by a sleight-of-hand performance, enabled
to substitute old and unimportant documents for
those which really should have been burnt, and
to retain in my possession, and subsequently
transmit to England, the originals of all the most
important. I was, of course, shaking hands with
danger and discovery at every turn, and yet so
marvellous was my success that I not only escaped
betrayal, but that which would undoubtedly have
led to it, namely, suspicion.

To this end, I was much assisted by the confidence reposed in me by my fellow-officials, the
Junior Guardians, who exhibited their trust to the
extent of giving me possession of their keys of the
strong-box, of which they held possession during
their period of office. This contained all the
papers of the camp; and with a view to its safety,
one key was given to the Senior Guardian, and
the other to the Junior Guardian, the locks being
different in construction, so that the box could
only be opened by the concurrence of both
officials. Had I not been able to obtain the
confidence of my Junior Guardians to the extent

of possessing their keys, I could never have brought my designs to such a successful issue. Strangely enough, when I appeared in the witness-box at the Commission — for I was even then Senior Guardian of my Clan-na-Gael camp — I had both keys of our strong-box in my possession, which I jokingly offered to Mr. Houston as a memento of our strange and unlooked-for meeting.

XXV.

Meantime, events had been developing themselves in a strange and unlooked-for way. O'Donovan Rossa — speaking to the Irish in America through the columns of the *Irish World* — had advocated the establishment of a Skirmishing Fund in the following style :—

"Five thousand dollars will have to be collected before the campaign can be started. England will not know how or where she is to be struck. A successful stroke or any stroke that will do her 500,000 dollars' worth of damage will bring us funds enough to carry on the work ; and by working on incessantly and persistently, the patient dirt and powder shock will bring out enough perhaps to carry on the war."

In the same issue of the *Irish World*, Patrick Ford, in the course of a commendatory article, said—

"What will this irregular warfare of our Irish Skirmishers effect? It will do this much. It will harass and annoy England. It will help to create her difficulty and hasten our opportunity. It will not only annoy England, but it will hush her too. This is what we look for from the Skirmishers. One hundred dollars expended on skirmishing may cause to England a loss of 100,000,000 dollars. That would be a damaging blow to the enemy; and what is to prevent the dealing one of three or four such blows every year?"

Here I shall drop Rossa and his Skirmishing Fund for the moment, to say a few words about Ford. The opportunity seems a favourable one for dealing with a man whose name has been so prominent of late years, and clearing up a few of the many misconceptions which appear to exist regarding him. Like O'Donovan Rossa, his colleague at this time in skirmishing matters, Ford's position in Irish revolutionary affairs has been quite misunderstood in British quarters outside the Parnellite party. As a matter of fact Ford is not, and never has been, a member of the Clan-na-Gael. True it is that he was a member of the old Fenian organisations which preceded it—as, for instance, the Irish Confederation, but in the membership of the last and most powerful of all the branches of the Irish-American conspiracy, the editor of the *Irish World* has had no place. The secret of his position and influence lies in his paper. This,

from the very moment of its start, has been a
pronounced success, reaching a high-water mark
of influence and circulation, which threw the puny
efforts of its competitors completely into the
shade.   The paper came into existence at the
proper moment for itself; it was well edited,
well printed, and splendidly equipped with news
from every quarter, and on every point.   It
caught the public fancy and "went" amazingly.
Ford, originally a printer and a man of no mean
attainment, gathered round him a staff of equally
clever writers, established correspondents at every
important centre, and working at very high pressure, was on the point of failing on several occasions, only to escape through the assistance of
friends, politicians, or capitalists, willing to oblige
for certain considerations.   Indeed, if I am not
very much in error, matters are not in the most
favourable way for the paper at this very time.

Patrick Ford, according to Michael Davitt, is
a most worthy disciple of the Christian principles,
and a man whose life would serve as a model for
very many of those who criticise this dynamite
advocate's character in no enthusiastic vein.
Speaking of the man simply "on the view" as
the American phrase has it, Davitt's observations are not so far-fetched as they would appear
to be at the first blush.   In appearance and

manner, the editor of the *Irish World* is quite
the opposite of the man you would figure to
yourself after reading his dynamite appeals and
exordiums in his own journal. Quiet and unob-
trusive alike in look and speech, he is as mild
a mannered man as ever scuttled a ship. Of
medium height, spare of build and spare of feature,
without any ferocity whatever marking the outer
man, he gives the observer the idea of being a
quiet, sedate, and rather retiring business person.
Although a vigorous and effective writer, he is
not remarkable for his platform utterances, and
while a good talker, is by no means an orator.

Associated with Patrick Ford in his connection
with Irish-American affairs have been his brother
Augustine and his nephew Austin. Augustine,
whose name comes into prominence with Rossa
in the Skirmishing Fund affair, was the publisher,
as distinct from the editor, of the *Irish World*;
while Austin, then a young fellow, was afterwards
to become a member of the Clan-na-Gael, and to
serve as the medium of communication between
the leaders of the Revolutionary organisation and
his uncle, the editor of what was undoubtedly,
though unofficially, their mouthpiece, the *Irish
World*. There were many reasons for an
alliance, unofficial though it might be, existing
between the *Irish World* and those charged with

the conduct of the vast secret conspiracy known to the initiated as the V.C. For what the *Irish World*, with its extended popularity, its great influence, and its enormous circulation, championed in public, the Clan-na-Gael worked for in private. Ford and his fellow-workers, in a different path, understood each other full well; and when, within a year after the establishment of the Skirmishing Fund, it became desirable that the Clan-na-Gael should take charge of it, there was no more ardent advocate of the change than he. And as in the early, so in the later years. When the new departure came to the front, Ford and his Clan-na-Gael friends were of the same mind as to its importance, and the necessity for supporting it. When dynamite came to be the order of the day, he was its loud-tongued apostle; and when, later still, "martyrs" like Brady and Curley suffered in Ireland the just consequences of their fiendish part in the Phœnix Park murders, the editor of the *Irish World* was first to fill the gap with a fund on behalf of their families, excluding from its benefits all connected with those who had had the good sense, though bad patriotism, to plead "guilty" to their part in the fell transaction.

XXVI.

To return, however, to Rossa and his Skirmishing Fund. As a prominent Fenian of "the old guard," and a member of the Clan-na-Gael, Rossa's influence, backed up by Ford's advocacy, succeeded in getting together no less than 23,350 dollars by the 14th March following the issue of the appeal—in something less than twelve months in fact. Although, however, this large sum had been accumulating during this period, and portions of it had been ready at different times for use if required, no skirmishing or pretence at skirmishing had taken place, and some little dissatisfaction commenced to manifest itself at the non-fruition of the many promises which had been held out of "hurting England." There then occurred the transfer of the fund to the Clan-na-Gael under very mysterious circumstances, which have never been thoroughly explained or understood. The nearest approach to an explanation was afforded by a communication from Rossa, which appeared in the *Irish World* of the 21st April 1877, which, I think, I cannot do better than quote here.

"When I started this Skirmishing Fund, the council-men of the two Irish revolutionary societies in America—the Fenian

Brotherhood and the Clan-na-Gael—took it into their heads that I was going to interfere with the regular revolutionary work, that I was going to play the deuce with everything, and they gave me no friendly help. I have been doing all I could to convince them that I am not the very desperate character I was in prison or out of prison ; and some six months ago, being telegraphed to visit a convention of one of those societies, I went there. I there proposed to receive into the trusteeship and Executive Council of the Skirmishing Fund one or two of their body, provided that the one or two meant skirmishing work such as was laid down in our programme. This proposition of mine was accepted, and all passed off harmoniously.

       •   •   •   •

"Here is how things stand now :—Mr. James J. Clancy, who acted as treasurer of the fund, got married a few weeks ago and ceased his connection with the *Irish World.* Then Austin Ford wrote me (on 14th March) the following note :—

"'I told you that, at a certain Irish convention, I had consented to admit to the trusteeship of the fund some members of their body. They gave me several names to select from ; and looking about for men who meant work, I took the names of John J. Breslin, who rescued the Australian prisoners, and who was the principal actor in the rescue of James Stephens in 1865 ; of Doctor William Carroll, of Philadelphia, who left his professional business (and being a particular friend of John Mitchell), came to New York when Mitchell was going to Ireland two years ago, went on board the steamer to see him off, went on the steamer with him to Ireland, having no other idea in his head but to take care of him. The other name I took was that of James Reynolds of Newhaven, Connecticut. He is the man in whose name the *Catalpa* was registered, and he mortgaged his property to raise $4000, when it was needed at a crisis in connection with the expedition. Now Mr. Clancy and Mr. Ford have resigned, I have in connection with these three men I have mentioned taken into the trusteeship John Devoy, Thomas Clarke Luby, and Thomas Francis Bourke.'

.   .   .   .

" Last night Thomas Clarke Luby went to Washington, carrying with him $17,500 in American bonds endorsed by me, to have them transferred for safe keeping to the names of Dr. Carroll, Thomas C. Luby, John Devoy, Tom Bourke, John Breslin, and James Reynolds. . . . John O'Mahony died. It was deemed well to send his remains to Ireland. There was no money to bear the expenses. I thought I might trespass on the skirmishing money. I consulted Mr. Ford and Mr. Clancy about a loan. They said it could be legitimately looked upon as within the pale of our work, and they paid me $2030 to defray the expenses. The Clan-na-Gael and the Fenian Brotherhood have promised to refund the money."

No secret was made of the connection which now existed between the "trustees" and the "fund," for a public address was issued "to the Irish people in the United States," and published in the *Irish World* of the 21st April, containing the following passages :—

" But since the 'skirmishing' project was first announced, circumstances have greatly altered. . . . Old Europe is threatened with a general convulsion. War on the most tremendous scale cannot much longer be staved off by all the artifices and subtleties of all the diplomatists in the world. Russia and Turkey are equally resolute to fight the inevitable fight. . . . The rest of the Great Powers of Europe will be drawn by an irresistible force into the arena. England, above all, whether she likes it or not, must draw her sword once more or meanly confess herself a third-class power. She is too proud of the part to yield her high place without a blow. She must first be beaten to her knees.

"England's difficulty then has all but come; in other words, 'Ireland's opportunity.' Is Ireland prepared to seize that opportunity? . . .

"In view of the altered circumstances of the time, 'big with fate to us and ours,' we propose to enlarge the basis of the 'Skirmishing Fund,' established by Rossa, and of the plans it was intended to further. We propose forthwith to create a 'Special National Fund' to aid the work of Ireland's deliverance.

"Action, some may think, has been postponed too long. Be this as it may, *we* are determined to lose as little further time as possible ere we furnish our countrymen with practical results of our work. But a blow must be followed up by blows. Unhesitatingly then" (they ask for) "the means to do what may give heart and inspiration to our brothers at home, and prepare the way for the last grand struggle.

. . . "We shall only add that it is plain that 'the Home Rule Agitation' has signally failed to satisfy the yearnings of the Irish people. The O'Mahony funeral demonstration, with its deep heroic significance, has exercised the vain misleading phantom. Every true Irishman in Ireland (and shall we not say in America too?) once more believes in the old creed of our gallant fathers — that the sole way to free or regenerate Ireland is by total separation from England; and that total separation can only be achieved by desperate sacrifices, daring enterprises, and the strong hand.

> "JOHN J. BRESLIN,
> "THOMAS CLARKE LUBY,
> "JOHN DEVOY,   New York.
> "THOMAS FRANCIS BOURKE,
> "JER. O'DONOVAN ROSSA,
> "WM. CARROLL, M.D., Philadelphia, Pa.
> "JAMES REYNOLDS, New Haven, Conn."

The names of the trustees will, of course, be familiar, as being amongst those regarding whom I gave some details some few pages back, and who were all remarkable for their past Fenian records and present prominence in the Clan-na-Gael ranks.

XXVII.

WHILE the Skirmishing Fund and its custodians were engaging public attention in this way, the secret work of the organisation was by no means being neglected. The ordinary work of shipping arms to Ireland, and communicating with the sister society as regards members, organisation, &c., was conducted with regularity and precision; while operations of an extraordinary character were indulged in as opportunity offered. Amongst these latter must be classed the negotiations, commenced about this time, for an alliance between the Revolutionary party in America and the Russian Government. Wild and absurd as the idea may at first appear, it is nevertheless an undoubted fact that these negotiations were not alone started in sober earnest, but they were in the end finally completed and developed to the stage of a regular diplomatic compact at head-quarters in Russia. As is well known, the rela-

tions between England and Russia were for some
three or four years previous to 1880 of a distinctly strained character, and war at many times
appeared imminent. Filled with the idea that
war would actually take place, the Clan-na-Gael
Executive caused overtures to be made to the
representative of the Russian Government, proposing that they in America should fit out privateers which, sailing with letters of marque from
Russia, should worry English vessels and assist
in every way possible in furthering the designs
of Russia, in return for which Russia should
pledge assistance to the Irish in their attempt
to wrest Ireland from English domination.

The matter assumed the proportions of a really
serious proposal, and Dr. William Carroll, of
Philadelphia, about whom I have already spoken,
and who was one of the trustees of the Skirmishing Fund, as well as Chairman of the Executive
Body of the Clan-na-Gael, was delegated by the
Executive to represent their interests in the
negotiation. Dr. Carroll, through the assistance
of Senator Jones of Florida, was placed in communication with the Russian minister at Washington, and to this gentleman the Clan-na-Gael
ambassador represented that some millionaires—
the names of two were mentioned—were prepared to subsidise the undertaking, and that

several points had been fixed upon for fitting out the privateers, San Francisco being notably one of them. So satisfactorily did the negotiations progress for the Clan-na-Gael people, that in a few months Dr. Carroll left America for the Russian capital, where, it was subsequently reported in an official way, the treaty between the Russian Government and the Revolutionary organisation was formally ratified.

It was a significant fact that shortly after this the Russian minister at Washington was recalled. The report in the official ranks of the Clan-na-Gael was that the proceeding was the result of an action taken by the British Government in consequence of what had occurred. Of course, regarding this view of the occurrence, as far as I can speak, there was neither definite information nor proof.

This was but one of the many wild schemes indulged in at this period. Another had to do with the manufacture of a submarine torpedo-boat, with which it was intended to inflict terrific damage on the British navy under water. After one failure, the boat was actually built at the shipyard on the Jersey side of the North River at a cost of some 37,000 dollars; but nothing ever came of it, for it was apparently completed only to be towed to New Haven, where it lay, and where, for aught I know, it may be rotting at the present day. Its principal use, as far as I could make out, was in supplying a certain number of patriots, charged with the control of its construction, some five dollars a day each as recognition for their invaluable services.

On the other plots and schemes I can only touch in the lightest possible way. They included the assassination of Queen Victoria, the kidnapping of the Prince of Wales or Prince Arthur, an attack on Portland Prison, with the rescue of Michael Davitt therefrom, and a hundred and one odd schemes in which Dhuleep Singh, General Carroll Thevis, Aylward, and other soldiers of fortune or discontent all figured.

XXVIII.

THE month of September '78 was remarkable for the arrival in America of Michael Davitt. He had been released from Portland Prison on ticket-of-leave several months previously, and having travelled through Ireland in the meantime, now came to the States with the ostensible object of lecturing. This first visit of his differed from the second one paid in 1880 by reason of the change which his opinions underwent in the interval.

When in September 1878 Davitt landed in America to be met by Devoy and others, and welcomed in an effusive address, he took pains, in replying, to state he was still faithful to the principles of his youth, for which he had suffered imprisonment, and that the dungeon had not changed his political convictions in the least. Apparently not, for during his visit Davitt put in an appearance at several Clan-na-Gael camps, and took part in their proceedings as a duly accredited brother and representative. Contact with Devoy, however, and with the theories on the subject of the " New Departure," to which Devoy at this time was giving prominence, must have changed Davitt's views somewhat, for references to past principles, life-long convictions, &c., soon made way for pleasant pictures and prophecies of the development known as the " New Departure," which was at last to bring the Irish political plotter within sight of his Mecca.

There is no need for me at this late day to deal at any great length with what has since been known as the " New Departure." It proved to be nothing more or less than the scheme which found its development and outcome in the Parnellite movement, viz., the bringing together the two forces of Irish discontent—the Constitutional and the Revolutionary sections—and, while allying

them for strategic and financial purposes, yet so
arranging the compact that each was allowed to
work in its own way for the accomplishment of
the object which all had in view—the repeal of
the Union between Great Britain and Ireland.

The exact terms of the treaty or alliance proposed by the American Fenians, after consultation
with Davitt, were set forth in a cable sent to Mr.
Parnell by Devoy and some of his fellow-trus-
tees of the Skirmishing Fund in the month of
October 1878, at a time indeed while Davitt was
still in the country. As the cable has a historic
interest, I will quote it in full here :—

"The Nationalists here will support you on the following
conditions :—

"First, abandonment of the federal demand, and substitu-
tion of a general declaration in favour of self-government.

"Second, vigorous agitation of the Land Question on the
basis of a peasant proprietary, while accepting concessions
tending to abolish arbitrary evictions.

"Third, exclusion of all sectarian issues from the platform.

"Fourth, Irish members to vote together on all imperial and
home questions, adopt an aggressive policy, and energetically
resist coercive legislation.

"Fifth, advocacy of all struggling nationalities in the British
Empire and elsewhere."

Following up this proposal, to which, by the
way, no direct public reply was ever given, there
appeared in the press letters from John Devoy
advocating the new move in arguments which I

think I can best summarise by using the following extracts from one of his epistles :—

"The question whether the advanced Irish National party —the party of separation—should continue the policy of isolati n from the public life of the country, which was inaugurated some twenty years ago by James Stephens and his associates, or return to older methods—methods as old at least as the days of the *United Irishman*—is agitating the minds of Irish Nationalists on both sides of the Atlantic just now; and certainly no similar incident has aroused such wide discussion in Ireland for many a day as the publication of the views of the exiled Nationalists resident in New York on the subject.

"The object aimed at by the Irish National party—the recovery of Ireland's national independence, and the severance of all political connection with England—is one that would require the utmost efforts and the greatest sacrifices on the part of the whole Irish people. . . . I am not one of those who despair of Ireland's freedom, and am as much in favour of continuing the struggle to-day as some of those who talk loudest against constitutional agitation. I am convinced that the whole Irish people can be enlisted in an effort to free their native land, and that they have within themselves the power to overcome all obstacles in their way. . . . I am also convinced that one section of the people alone can never win independence ; and no political party, no matter how devoted or determined, can ever win the support of the whole people if they never come before the public, and take no part in the everyday life of the country. I have often said it before, and I repeat it now again, that a mere conspiracy will never free Ireland. I am not arguing against conspiracy, but only pointing out the necessity of Irish Nationalists taking whatever public action for the advancement of the National cause they may find within their reach, such action as will place the aims and objects of the National party in a more favourable light before the world, and help to win the support of the Irish people."

K

XXIX.

WHILE the ball was thus rolling in this way, Davitt completed his tour in America, and returned to Ireland to resume his work there. He did not return alone, however, for in his wake there travelled his new colleague, Devoy, who, journeying as one of the secret agents of the Clan-na-Gael, went to Ireland to inspect and report on the condition of the Revolutionary organisation there to the V.C. Convention, to be held in Wilkesbarre, Pennsylvania, in July 1879. Associated with Devoy in this work of inspection was General Millen, acting in the capacity of military envoy. Devoy, while in Ireland, made good use of his time. While he organised the Irish Republican Brotherhood in their secret meetings, he openly advocated the proposed alliance with all his might and main. In Ireland, however, as the report which he afterwards made to the Clan-na-Gael showed, the Fenians were not so ripe as his colleagues in America for giving up, even temporarily, their secret methods for constitutional agitation; and the work which he was to accomplish was not destined to bear too early fruit.

As the report which Devoy presented of the

visit thus made gave an interesting account of how matters stood in Fenian circles there at this period, I give a few extracts. They are important as showing the condition of the Revolutionary forces, which gave Mr. Parnell so much trouble a year or two later, when, through me, he appealed to Devoy to come over and cripple the opposition he was receiving from this quarter:—

"Three of the best organised counties—Dublin, Louth, and Wexford—seceded from the S.C. (Supreme Council or Executive of the Irish Republican Brotherhood), and believing the statements, so often repeated, that the American organisation supported Mr. Stephens, transferred their allegiance to that gentleman. There still remained with the S.C. (Supreme Council), Ulster, Connaught, Munster, a portion of Leinster, Scotland, and South of England ; but the work in these districts was almost paralysed, and the attention of the men distracted by repeated visits and communications of a conflicting nature from contending factions, who all claimed to be 'working for Ireland.' The numbers stood at this time (1878) as follows :— About 19,000 men stood by the S.C., some 3000 acted independently in the North of England, and not more than 1500, chiefly in Leinster, followed Mr. Stephens. No real work could be done ; it was a struggle for existence, and ultimately the majority prevailed. When your former envoy arrived in Ireland, this was the state of things he found existing. As you have been informed, he succeeded, with the help of another member of the V.C. residing in Ireland, in first gaining over the Leinster men to the S.C., by telling them the real truth about the state of things in America.

. . . .

"A reorganisation of the S.C. satisfactory to all parties concerned was then effected, and an efficient secretary elected,

who has since then rendered invaluable service in repairing the
damage done during the short period of turmoil and contention.   Some years before the organisation had been a compact
body of over 40,000 men, acting under its elected council, and
making commendable efforts to arm its members in spite of the
most discouraging difficulties.   At the beginning of last year,
after the S.C. had triumphed over the difficulties above mentioned, it was reduced to about 24,000 men, the confidence of
many of its members greatly shaken, and much of the material
accumulated during past years badly damaged through neglect
or entirely lost.

" It was deemed better to endeavour to weld into a solid
mass the united fragments than to increase its size by the
addition of new members.   Some mistakes were made, but,
upon the whole, the action of the S.C. seemed to me judicious
and safe.   Some 17,000 dollars had been sent by the F.C.
(10,000 dollars came from the National Fund for arms) for the
purpose of introducing arms into the country ; but it was left in
the hands of the R. D. until my arrival, in the belief that the
machinery of the movement had undergone too great a strain
to be able to bear much pressure, and the hands of the S.C.
were too full with the work of restoration to allow them to
undertake any more.   The organisation was just beginning to
breathe a little freely, and to feel that it was again a solid living
body, when I arrived to confer with the S.C. as to the best
means to infuse new life and vigour into it.

   .   .   .   .   .   .

" I began with Tipperary, Limerick, and Clare, and continued my tour till I had a fair idea of the condition of the
organisation in all of the seven provinces. . . . Besides county and
circle meetings, I attended provincial conventions in Munster,
Ulster, Connaught, North of England, and South of England,
and local district meetings in Dublin, Cork, Limerick, Derry,
Ennis, Glasgow, Dundalk, and other towns.

" When Leinster and Munster shall have been thoroughly
reorganised, which will take some time, I hope to see 50,000

good members in Ireland alone, and I should not care to see many more. In Ulster, Connaught, Tipperary, and Clare the great bulk of the men are small farmers or farmers' sons, and, on the whole, there is a much better representation than in '65. I am glad to be able to report also the presence in the organisation, and in positions of trust, of a few of the smaller landed gentry, a few professional men, and a large sprinkling of comfortable business men."

Nothing calls for further attention in connection with this visit of Devoy and Millen to Ireland, beyond the fact that the expenses of it were defrayed out of a sum of 10,000 dollars taken from the Skirmishing Fund for the purpose. Nor need I speak in any detail of the proceedings of the Wilkesbarre Convention to which the delegates reported. There was no incident connected therewith which calls for any special mention, as particularly affecting events at this period.

XXX.

Though lacking official recognition and support, the scheme of the " New Departure " was creating a good deal of enthusiasm throughout the ranks of the Gaels; and the reports which continued to come from Ireland as to the condition of the Land Question kept the matter fully alive. The arrival, too, of Mr. Parnell in New York in

the month of January 1880 gave a fresh impetus
to the whole thing. And whatever doubt had
heretofore existed as to the possibility of working
the new move, and making it subservient to the
requirements of the Revolutionary organisation,
took immediate flight after a week's experience
of Mr. Parnell in America. In the view of the
conspirators scattered throughout the States, Mr.
Parnell had given himself over, body and soul, to
the chiefs of the Clan-na-Gael. At every point,
under every circumstance, without a single exception, well-known and trusted men of the secret
councils were by his side and at his elbow, push-
ing him forward into prominence here, bespeaking
a welcome for him there, and answering for his
thorough fealty to the grand old cause at all
manner of times. Nor did his own utterances
leave any room for question. Brimful of references of deep meaning, and constantly lit up with
the flashing of bayonets and rattling of musketry,
his speeches breathed the sounds of war and the
policy of the hill-side in every note, till men
listening to his accents thought that at last the
hour and the man had come. Poor fools! They
knew not that his enthusiasm was the enthusiasm
of the dollar, or its equivalent in English coin
when totted up to £40,000, and his only weapon
the House of Commons lie!

Mr. Parnell's efforts in America to collect funds for the famine-stricken Irish—this was the ostensible object of his visit—were cut short by the general election which took place in Ireland in the spring of 1880, and he left hurriedly, but not before he had laid the foundations of the Land League, and played into the hands of the secret conspirators by giving them a very leading share in its control. Exit therefore Mr Parnell to give way to Michael Davitt, and enter Mr. Davitt once more on the American stage in quite a new *rôle*. Flushed with the triumphs of his recent proceedings in Ireland in the establishment of the Land League organisation, and the position he had suddenly sprung into, he now came out as a Constitutionalist pure and simple. There were no more visits to Clan-na-Gael camps, for the time at least. All was open and above board. He had his fad; that fad was the Land League; and his fad was to win in the political race, hands down. No matter where he went, it was the same story. Travelling Braidwood-way in order to lecture in my district, he spent three days in my company, part of which time he was my guest, and fell ill on my hands, when I honestly and successfully ministered to his needs. In our intercourse at this period we had many talks over the situation, and with me as with everybody else, he could only speak of the new movement. At his request, I told him the whole story of the second Canadian raid; and so great was his enthusiasm in his new *rôle*, that he seized upon the fiasco I related as yet another proof for me of the utter impossibility of doing anything in the way of active operations. Amused and interested, I watched the dark determined face glowing with light and enthusiasm, and wondered within me how long this born conspirator would be content to walk in the trammels of a truly constitutional path. The opportunity, however, was too good to be neglected, and I improved it by getting some very useful information unawares from my patient and guest.

I was quite *au courant* with Land League matters, for as an official of the Clan-na-Gael I had been instructed to develop the movement in my district, which I accordingly did, following the usual practice of enrolling my colleagues of the Clan-na-Gael as members of the League Branch, and thus keeping the control in our own hands. At public meetings held in favour of the open movement—it will be noted I speak of the Land League as the "open," and the Clan-na-Gael as the "secret" movement—I frequently presided, and when the occasion arose, introduced Davitt and Devoy.

XXXI.

So matters progressed and developed, the only important incident of the interval being the discovery that James J. O'Kelly, late M.P. for Roscommon, after being despatched by the Revolutionary Directory of the Clan-na-Gael to England with moneys to attend to the shipping of arms to Ireland, had thrown in his lot with the advocates of the New Departure in Ireland, and been returned to Parliament. Davitt and Devoy had both drawn upon moneys subscribed for blowing up England, though Davitt conscientiously paid every farthing of his share back in 1882.

In the month of November 1880, John Devoy issued a very peculiar circular to the Senior Guardians of the V.C., or Clan-na-Gael camps, which was remarkable as showing how loyal after all this author of the New Departure was to the methods of revolutionary work, and how he regarded the Land League but as the stepping-stone to more decisive things. This is how he put the matter :—

P.O. Box 4, 479.

NEW YORK, *November* 1, 1880.

"DEAR SIR AND BROTHER,—I propose to give a course of lectures this winter on the subject of "The Irish National Cause and the Present Crisis," with a view to stirring up our people here and increasing the resources of the National movement. I will stipulate beforehand that the proceeds shall either go to the Revolutionary Fund of the V.C. or to the National Fund, so that we may be better prepared to meet any emergency that may be forced upon us by England. While believing that all our efforts should be directed to restraining the people in Ireland from any premature insurrectionary movement, I think the excitement at home. should be utilised for the purpose of procuring the funds necessary to enable the National party to complete the preparations for the struggle for independence. The *time* for that struggle must be selected by us and not by England ; but one must not forget that our hand may be forced in spite of all our endeavours ; and it therefore behoves us to commence stirring up our people in America now. I think the Land League has now money enough for present purposes, and that the state of things prevailing in Ireland demands that all money that can be got from our people here should be devoted to revolutionary purposes. I am convinced, in fact, that the doing of this is the best help we can at present give the Land League. The prosecutions have already given the agitation a more decidedly national tone. Let us help to broaden it into a truly national movement, and make it serviceable to the cause of independence.

"If you agree with this view of the situation, I should be glad to receive your assistance in organising lectures in your vicinity, *provided your doing so would not be detrimental to the interests of the V.C.*

"I intend to begin in the New England States, then to go through a portion of New York State and Penna, and thence west. Communicate to the P.O. Box mentioned.—Fraternally yours,

"JOHN DEVOY."

I was only too willing to arrange for such a lecture as Devoy wanted, for thereby I should be bringing Devoy and myself into contact, with every probability of getting useful information. Accordingly, Devoy lectured for me somewhere about January or February '81, and during his stay visited and addressed my camp. He made a visit of some three or four days to my district, and as I had hoped and anticipated, we had many and long confidential chats together. The position of affairs was fully discussed. Devoy was very pronounced in his views about money subscribed for Land League purposes. What had been only hinted at in his letter, he gave very plain utterance to in his speech. The money subscribed for the Land League, he contended, should not all go for bread, and in this connection he outlined to me the ideas of the Revolutionary Directory of the Clan-na-Gael (of which he was a member) at this time. These were, to put it shortly, to strike and damage the British Government where and when they could. "The organisation on this side," said he, meaning

America, "have agreed to furnish the means, and the organisation in Ireland have signified their willingness to carry out a system of warfare, characterised by all the rigours of Nihilism."

All, however, was not plain sailing to him, and with amazing frankness he explained to me what his fears were. There was, he admitted, no possibility of a rising, as the leaders in Ireland were all against such a movement in the weak condition in which the organisation was. But, on the other hand, all attempts made to restrain the fire-eating elements would be met with failure, unless something practical was done. The attitude of Rossa and his followers had also to be considered. If no active work was done, some of our best men would flock to Rossa's standard and so weaken the organisation (Rossa, I should explain, had by this time taken up an independent attitude, and was working in connection with the fragments that remained of the old Fenian Brotherhood). It was thoroughly understood that work had been done by Rossa's emissaries or rather some of them ; hence the danger. The name of Boyton, whom I did not know at the time, but who was, as I learnt, a brother of Boyton the swimmer, engaged as a League organiser in Ireland, then came up, and I was informed that Boyton was one of those occupied in developing the new policy. By this I mean active warfare *aux* Clan-na-Gael as distinct from the constitutional work openly advocated by the Land League. Devoy remarked regarding this active policy that it was being well looked after, but would take time to complete.

Devoy's confidences were in fact most exhaustive, and enabled me to send quite an interesting budget by the next mail to Mr. Anderson. I learnt, as a further item of news, that much trouble was being experienced in keeping the I.R.B. (the sister society) men in some parts of Ireland, notably in Mayo, where they had the best organisation and most arms, from making what Devoy described as "fools of themselves." He, it appeared, feared attacks on the military when the latter were attending evictions. This striking interview between the Clan-na-Gael leader and the Secret Service agent concluded with the important announcement on the part of the former that he had received a letter from Mr. Parnell, through a friend, in which Mr. Parnell stated he was exasperated and was willing to do anything. He (Mr. Parnell) had agreed to the calling of the 1882 Convention, and to its being a National Movement Convention; and, in conclusion, Devoy said Mr. Parnell's personal attitude towards the National (*i.e.*, Revolutionary) party was well and satisfactorily understood.

This was, indeed, a time of confidences with me. I had communications with Alexander Sullivan and Meledy within a very short period from this, and from them—Sullivan being one of the Executive, and Meledy a leading member of the Clan-na-Gael—I learnt, though at different times, that a new plan of campaign was coming into force, nothing more or less indeed than one of cold-blooded murder and destruction. It appeared that a man called Wheeler had invented a new hand-grenade, and had offered a supply to the organisation. They were of such a portable character as to be easily carried in a satchel, and were especially adapted for the purpose in view. Meledy told me he had offered to take part in the work of placing them in Ireland and England.

The significance of the matter was lost upon me at the time, but was fully appreciated by me later on, when I learnt of the informer Carey's evidence in connection with the Phœnix Park murders and the Invincible conspiracy, in the course of which he confessed that he and his confederates had arranged to kill Earl Cowper, the Lord-Lieutenant of Ireland, by a hand bomb just perfected in the organisation, which could be

easily thrown from a window in a house in Cork
Hill, Dublin, which they had selected for the
purpose.

XXXII.

My private affairs permitted of my taking a holi-
day in the early part of the year 1881, and so I
determined to make a trip to Europe. Happening to communicate my intention to my old friend,
Colonel Clingen, now the commander of the
Clan-na-Gael guards in Chicago, and a very
prominent member of the organisation, he gave
me to understand that the Executive would avail
themselves of my journey to send by me documents which could not be trusted to the mails.
Nothing could have suited me better, and I
willingly consented to be of any service I possibly
could. Devoy, it subsequently transpired, was
the correspondent whose communications I was
to convey, and by an arrangement of Clingen's
a meeting took place between Devoy and myself
at the Palmer House, Chicago, in the month of
March 1881. Devoy on this occasion handed
me sealed packets addressed to John O'Leary
and Patrick Egan in Paris. O'Leary was then
regarded as the representative agent and official
means of communication between the Clan-na-Gael

and the Irish Republican Brotherhood in Ireland; Egan was the treasurer and accredited representative of the Irish Land League.

Journeying by way of Liverpool, I reached England on the 12th of April 1881, and stopping in London in order to see Mr. Anderson and show him the packets, as well as to receive instructions, I eventually travelled to Paris. On arrival there I drove to the Hotel Brighton, where I had learned Egan was located, and where I determined to take up my abode. The first person I met with in the hotel was Egan himself. He was coming down the stairs in view of me, as I asked for him, in company with Mrs. A. M. Sullivan (wife of the late M.P.), both being bound for the opera, where, on their invitation, I subsequently joined them. I made myself known to Egan at once, only to find of course that he had received some hint of my coming, and was quite expecting me.

As I washed and prepared to take myself to the opera, to see some more of this strange man, I endeavoured to recall his appearance, and to see how far he fitted in with the idea I already held regarding him. A man of bright cheery presence, stout build, and jovial look and voice, the latter very marked in its Irish accent, with bright laughing eyes and warm handshake and

a closely cut head of tawny hair, he was the last
person in the world you would take for a deep
conspirator, and a constructor of murder. I was
puzzled and bewildered—I could not make it out ;
and so giving up all thought of trying to read the
man's character on the outward view, I determined I should leave my further studies in this
direction to a later date and go and enjoy the
opera, which I did.

The next morning saw me *en route* for the
residence of John O'Leary, to whom I wished to
deliver my second packet without delay. I discovered him without much difficulty in his abode
at the Hôtel de la Couronne, in the Quartier
Latin. I found the old man surrounded by his
books and manuscripts, and from his appearance
more fit for the patient secluded life of the student
than the troublous career of the rebel. Seated in
his room, and gazing affectionately on his different
treasures of old and rare editions, he seemed
to have little in common with my friends of
the Clan. Yet I found him fully posted, and
as keen to talk with me as possible. At first
somewhat suspicious and uncertain in his manner,
he gradually lost his appearance of distrust, and
in the end gossiped with me quite freely. As
he opened Devoy's packet in my presence, I was
enabled to discover that I had been the bearer

L *

of a very long document, with an enclosure, to which he paid great heed.

From the very start I found O'Leary opposed to the "active" policy. He was as strong and bitter an opponent of the murderous idea as one could wish to meet; and, unlike Irish patriots in general, he was not without the courage of his convictions. He showed me a copy of the Dublin *Irishman* (the unfortunate Pigott's paper), of some date in the month previous, containing a letter over his signature, denouncing all secret warfare. In fact, so far did this really honest patriot go, that he refused in his official capacity to take any responsibility for expenditure in connection with the "active" policy. While condemning such methods, however, he avowed himself in full accord with an open insurrectionary movement; and he spoke in the bitterest terms of the way in which several Irish patriots had played false, while acting as paid members of the organisation. Another point in connection with our talks was the opposition shown by O'Leary to the Parnellite alliance. He would have nothing to do with such a joining of forces as was proposed, and he was all against mixing up the honest rebel movement with one which was, in his opinion, worthy of great distrust.

I enjoyed my talks with O'Leary because in

him I found a fine, honest, fearless spirit. The
man was old and grey, with furrowed brow and
stooped figure, the result of his long confinement
in English prisons. There was little about him
then to remind one of the bright-eyed daring
prisoner who, fifteen years before, had, from the
dock of a Dublin court-house, hurled defiance at
judge, jury, and Government alike; but there still
remained with him the same fearlessness of tone
and honesty of conviction which marked him
out then, as now, a prince amongst his fellows
of the Irish conspiracy.

XXXIII.

IN strong contrast to O'Leary was another old
Irish rebel whose acquaintance I made in Paris
for the first time. He was a man whose name
was familiar to me as a household word, but with
whom I had never before been brought directly
into contact. I speak of James Stephens, the leader
with whose name it was at one time possible to con-
jure in Ireland, who had been the head and front
of the Fenian Brotherhood in Ireland in 1865,
whose word was law to its sworn thousands,
and who, after making his escape from Richmond Bridewell in Dublin, ended his inglorious

public career by an unromantic exit in petti-
coats.　Curious being that he was, he inspired
feelings of the sincerest affection on the part of
his immediate followers; and there were few
things that, in their regard for him, they would
not seek to accomplish on his behalf.

His escape from Richmond Prison, attended
with tremendous risk as it was for all concerned,
was a case in point; and as it is a matter about
which present-day folk remember little if anything, I feel tempted to give the story in the old
man's words, as he told it to me.

"The two brave men," said he, "brave men
and true, who were instrumental in releasing me
were J. J. Breslin and Daniel Byrne.　Breslin
was a man of great expediency, or he never could
have procured the impression of the key which
opened my cell, and which was hung on a nail
in the Governor's safe.　He had to distract the
Governor's attention; steal the key, putting
another in its place; get the impression, and then
return the key to its proper place again.　The
most singular circumstance connected with my
escape was that while Kickham, who was deaf,
occupied the cell on my right, M'Leod, a thief,
was in the cell on my left.　A gong was placed
in his cell communicating with the Governor's
office, in order to allow of his giving the alarm if

necessary; and he could not have helped hearing me get out, when Breslin and Byrne, at one o'clock in the morning, stood beside my cell. He did hear me; but that thief, base as he was, was not base enough to sell me to the British Government. But then my trouble began. We had only a few minutes to do our work in. It was pitch dark, and the storm howled furiously. The ladder provided for my scaling the wall proved too short. Breslin, who was chief hospital warden, and Byrne, who was night-watchman and 'lock up,' were armed with two revolvers each. They had also provided for me. Our intention was to fight, if discovered, until killed.

"The short ladder nearly proved fatal. I could not reach the top of the wall, which was twenty feet high, so Byrne got a table out of the dining-room and placed the ladder upon it. Even then it was too short. I had to come down again. Breslin was fairly wild. Another table was procured, and again I tried. After a dreadful struggle, I succeeded in getting outside of the wall. It was no joke to jump twenty feet into the darkness. I had to do it, however, or be caught. Breslin gave me directions where to go if I did not break my neck in falling; and he and Byrne returned to their duty. I let go my hold, and down I went, fortunately falling on soft ground.

"My directions were to follow a gravel walk (for I was in a garden) until I came to another wall twenty feet high, where I was to throw a stone over as a signal to eleven men, all armed, who were waiting outside to receive me.

'I had some difficulty in finding the walk, and could get no stone of any size in the dark. At last I reached the garden wall, and threw over a handful of gravel. A rope with a weight attached was thrown over the wall. I climbed up by its aid, and soon found myself in the arms of my body-guard. We embraced with joy, and I soon made them disperse. I went to a house in sight of the jail, and remained there fourteen days. I afterwards went to a fashionable boarding-house in the finest part of Dublin and stayed two months. I left Dublin in the brigantine *Concord*, in company with Flood and Kelly, on the 12th of March, and landed in Ardrossan on the afternoon of the 15th."

Poor Stephens now lives in his humble garret in Paris, an exile broken in fortune, health, and hope, smoking his short black pipe and brooding over these days that are no more.

XXXIV

ALL this time Egan and I had been constantly together. My desire was, of course, to make a study of the man, and to get to know as much about him as I possibly could. Everything played into my hands. Egan was ignorant both of the geography and the language of the French capital, and he very largely availed himself of the help which I was enabled to render him, as the result of my supposed French nationality and knowledge of the city. My position, altogether, was a very pleasant one at this period. Egan lived in a most extravagant fashion, and as he would pay for everything and would not allow me to share in any outlay, I had the best of all things without any strain on my pocket whatever. He frequented the most expensive cafés, had the choicest of dishes, would only be content with the best boxes at places of entertainment, and, in a word, spent his money right royally. The information should be pleasant reading for the poor dupes in America and Ireland who subscribed the funds over which he was then presiding.

We cemented a strong friendship, and I was with him almost at all times. I made a point of being in his rooms when his letters arrived, and he was certainly very frank and open in acquainting me with their contents. As a result, I obtained full and accurate information as to the position and progress of affairs in Ireland during my stay. There was not the faintest shadow of a suggestion of secrecy between us as to our attitude towards Revolutionary matters. I remember well on one occasion Egan summing up his own position in these words—which I noted at the time—"I am a Land Leaguer, and something else when the opportunity presents itself." He boasted to me of his having been the backbone of the Fenian organisation in Dublin for many years, and admitted the fact, with which I was acquainted, that he was a member of the Supreme Council or executive body there.

In our talks on Revolutionary organisations, I found Egan an enthusiastic advocate of the "active" policy spoken of by Devoy, and he heartily entered into a discussion with me as to the ways and means of carrying it out. In this connection reference was made to Mr. Parnell, and he assured me most emphatically that "Parnell was all right as a Revolutionist." In support of this statement he cited the fact that some twelve months previously Mr. Parnell sought admission into the ranks of the Irish

Revolutionary Brotherhood, but was refused. "Parnell," remarked Egan with a wise look, "thought a good deal of the organisation, but it was not then in a flourishing condition, and we thought he would think a great deal more of it by being on the outside rather than in it."

Our conversations naturally tended in the direction of finance; and when the topic cropped up, Egan dealt with it in no nervous spirit, regarding me as quite a worthy recipient of his confidence. About this time a demand was being made for a public audit of the accounts of the League. He explained that an audit committee of three members of the League had already gone over his books, and this was all the audit that could possibly take place. His reasons for such a strong statement were very frankly given. A public audit would, he said, be the very thing Dublin Castle—meaning the Irish Government—would like to have, but this was out of the question. It was impossible for him to make public many of the items of his expenditure! I laughed to myself as he said this, wondering whether the expenses of our many extravagant trips about Paris came under this head.

But he was dealing with far more dangerous matters. He stated explicitly, in a very significant way, that the money had been used for other

purposes than those of constitutional agitation.
Amongst these sources of outlay were the expenses of the Dutch officers from Amsterdam to
assist the Boers in their revolt against British
control in South Africa; and coming nearer home,
the varied expenditure in connection with parties
attached to the Irish Republican Brotherhood in
Ireland. Altogether our talks on this branch of
the subject enlightened me on many points, and
supplied me with sufficient material to form a
fixed belief in my mind that his idea, at least,
was identical with that held in the States—that
the open agitation was but a branch of the movement to obtain the separation of Ireland from
England.

I use the phrase "his idea," but to be really
accurate I should say "their idea," for Egan
always spoke on behalf of his colleagues—with one
exception, which I can recall—and represented
that a complete harmony of view prevailed. And
in everything that happened subsequently during
my stay in England, I found this representation
of his sustained by fact, save the single exception of which I speak—namely, in the case of Mr.
A. M. Sullivan. I had not long to wait for an
opportunity of putting the statement to the test as
far as several of the M.P.'s were concerned; for
very shortly after this conversation, Egan and I

travelled to London, and by him I was introduced into the House of Commons, and to several Irish M.P.'s, with the significant description "one of our friends from America." I well remember that amongst those I first met in this way was Mr. Parnell himself, from whom I received a very warm greeting. On this occasion I was accommodated with a seat under the gallery of the House. This was but one of several visits I paid to the House at this time, in the course of which I constantly came in contact with Egan. When alone I generally sent in my card to Mr. Parnell, and he obtained the necessary admission for me, much to his disgust, I am sure, when a later day came and I put in an appearance in the witness-box of Probate Court No. 1, London.

At every point I, of course, made careful notes of what occurred, and, either verbally or in writing, reported them to my chief, so that the Government were not really so deplorably ignorant as the Parnellites then proudly hoped and believed. In fact, not one occurrence of importance with which Egan became acquainted — and he really knew everything, and kept nothing back from me — was delayed by a single post from headquarters at the Home Office in London. To resume, however. After

*

this first visit to London, Egan and I returned
to Paris by different routes, and on arriving
there the same close intercourse prevailed between us.   I had not been very long back,
when Egan informed me that Mr. Parnell had
written him expressing a very strong desire to
see me before my return to America. Nothing
loth, I promised to call upon the Irish leader
when next in London, and I duly carried out my
promise.

XXXV.

MAKING my way down to the House on the
occasion of my next appearance in London, I
obtained admission to the Lobby—admission was
then an easier matter than now—and encountered
Mr. J. J. O'Kelly in my search for Mr. Parnell.
The late envoy of the Clan-na-Gael had a long
chat with me over the situation, before the Irish
leader put in an appearance. While we talked
in this way, O'Kelly complained bitterly of
the opposition which the open or constitutional
movement known as the Land League was still
receiving from the Irish Republican Brotherhood
or secret organisation in Ireland, and he stoutly
advocated coercion on the part of the directors of

the American branch of the conspiracy in order
to bring the Irish malcontents into line.

His remarks, however, were cut short by the
appearance of Mr. Parnell, who, leading the way,
conducted us to a corridor outside the Library of
the House, where an interview of over an hour
took place, O'Kelly remaining for a little until
the conversation was well under way. O'Kelly,
while he remained, did almost all the talking.
His remarks were a repetition of what he had
already said to me in private. When he left, Mr.
Parnell adopted the same line of complaint, speaking in low tones, as we walked up and down the
corridor, to prevent any one being continually
within ear-shot. I was told detectives were
watching us, and that spies held a place in every
corner. As I afterwards learnt, the statement
was not without foundation, for every movement
of myself and my companion was noted, with
details as regards time, and duly reported to
Government officials within twenty-four hours.

The whole matter, said Mr. Parnell, following
up O'Kelly's remarks, rested in our hands in
America. We had the money, he said, and if
we stopped the supplies the home organisation
would act as desired. He expressed his belief
that Devoy could do more than any one else to
bring about a clear understanding and alliance;

and he commissioned me to use my influence with
Devoy, and to arrange for his presence in Paris
at as early a date as possible. So anxious was he
to bring Devoy over that he undertook to pay all
his expenses. Still speaking in this connection,
he asked me to at once proceed from New York,
after seeing Devoy, to other prominent members
of the organisation, mentioning particularly the
names of Alexander Sullivan and William J.
Hynes, the presence of either of whom, upon this
side of the water, he desired for the purpose of
bringing about a thorough understanding and
complete harmony of working. Special reference
was also made to Dr. William Carroll of Philadelphia, and his attitude towards the open movement.   Dr. Carroll, I may here explain, had
been elected Chairman of the Executive Body at
the Wilkesbarre Convention of 1879, but had
resigned in 1880 in consequence of his opposition
to the way in which the New Departure was
being worked, and the treatment he received.
This was the same Dr. Carroll who had spent
the previous year in Europe, having been specially
charged with the carriage of negotiations between
the V.C. and the Russian Government.

After arranging these matters with me, Mr.
Parnell entered into details regarding the position
of the Irish Question at this time.   His remarks

on this point were a veritable bombshell to me.
He started off by stating that he had long since
ceased to believe that anything but the force of
arms would accomplish the final redemption of
Ireland. He saw no reason why, when we were
fully prepared, an open insurrectionary movement
could not be brought about. He went carefully
into the question of resources and necessaries.
He stated what the League could furnish in the
way of men and money, and informed me as to
the assistance which he looked for from the
American organisation. He spoke of having in
the League Treasury at the end of that year an
available sum of £100,000. He discussed with
me the details of the position occupied by the
home and American Revolutionary organisations,
and defended the American policy for the time
being. I parted with him with the assurance that
I would do all he wished.

The interview had certainly proved a startling
one for me; and as I proceeded to my seat under
the gallery of the House, I pondered over the
manner and method of my late companion, to
discover, if I could, any incident in the course of
our hour's talk which would materially affect all that
he had said. But there was none. The manner
of the League chief had been grave and impassive,
as was his wont; he had been business-like all

through; there was no uncertainty, no indistinct-
ness in his utterance. He had certainly made
a plunge, but it was a plunge taken with all
deliberation and premeditation. I went over
all the points in my own mind again, carefully
impressed them on my memory, and took my seat
in the house beside General Roberts, with whom
I had an interesting talk in an undertone, and to
whom I pointed out some of the celebrities on
both sides. If I remember aright, it was the
occasion of a vote of thanks to General Roberts
for his march on Candahar; and when the vote
had been recorded, a large number of members crowded round to speak to him, whereupon
I left.

Reaching the street, I called a hansom at once,
and late hour though it was, I drove direct to
Mr. Anderson's private house in order to acquaint
him with what had happened, while the facts
were fresh in my memory. Carefully I went
into every detail, and as carefully Mr. Anderson
followed, taking a note as I went along of the
principal points. The early dawn had crept
upon us ere my report was finished, and concluding at last, I took my departure, to lose no
time in getting that sleep for which I commenced
to pine, and which I considered I had very fairly
earned.

XXXVI

I saw Mr. Parnell once more. This was when I went to say good-bye to him. I found him in the tea-room of the House of Commons, as cordial as ever. Indeed, he was particularly agreeable on this occasion, presenting me with a photograph of himself, on which he wrote, " Yours very truly, Charles S. Parnell." This portrait, which is here reproduced, I kept as an interesting souvenir for a long time, but had to surrender it at last to the Special Commission, amongst the records of which it is now duly numbered. Soon after I left London for Ireland, not, however, before I had seen a good deal of Egan, and spent several pleasant evenings in his company, at the house of Mr. A. M. Sullivan, M.P., who now, poor man! is no more. I well remember Egan's impressing upon me the necessity for my covering my revolutionary sentiments whenever Mr. Sullivan was near. It would never do, I was told, to talk of revolutionary matters, for he was ultramontane. This advice I followed, noting the fact in my own mind to Mr. Sullivan's credit.

Talented, witty, and brilliant, Mr. Sullivan made a magnificent *raconteur*. Even now I can

M

recall many of his happy efforts which would well bear reproduction. I shall not, however, yield to the temptation of bringing them in here, but will content myself with recalling one pleasant story told about the irrepressible Mr. Biggar. Mr. Biggar, as I was informed by way of preface, was known as the great objector and "counter-out," sometimes, sad to relate, moving that the House be counted when it was not to the interests of the party to take any notice of the want of a quorum. Very pious in disposition, he rarely failed to attend early mass, in spite of late sittings and consequent fatigue. One morning Mr. Biggar, fatigued after a very heavy night's sitting, but still devotionally inclined, attended mass at St. George's in Southwark. So tired out was he that he fell fast asleep in his chair as the service proceeded, and so he remained until all had been concluded and every one had gone. Upon being vigorously aroused by the verger, Mr. Biggar started up, rubbed his eyes, looked at the roof, and fancying himself at the moment in the House of Commons, with the master instinct strong within him, loudly exclaimed, "Mr. Speaker, I move that the House be counted."

Thanks to Egan, I travelled to Dublin under happy circumstances. I was the bearer of letters of introduction to Dr. Kenny, M.P., O'Rorke,

Yours very truly
Chas. S. Parnell

Egan's brother-in-law, and to those in charge at
the Land League head-quarters. I anticipated
an interesting time, and I was not disappointed.
Dr. Kenny, though his memory is now very
deficient—shall I say?—proved the most entertaining of men, and I had both lunch and dinner
at his hospitable board in Gardiner Street. It
was in his company I paid my visit to Kilmainham Prison, and through his kind introduction
that I made the acquaintance of John Dillon,
P. J. Sheridan, M. J. Boyton, and the others I
met on the occasion. My visit and its incidents
afforded a very good insight into how matters
were conducted, and proved to me how very
easy it was to carry on communication with the
outside world—at least when you were an Irish
political prisoner. To my surprise there was no
attempt made by the warder to hear the conversation I had with Boyton. On the contrary,
this interesting official most obligingly took himself off.

This meeting with Boyton was full of interest
to me. He was the man, it will be remembered,
who had been named by Devoy as carrying out
the arrangements for the "active" policy of
Ireland, and who was best known as the brother
of Captain Boyton the swimmer. From him in
the secrecy of conversation, undisturbed by the

presence of a warder or fellow-prisoner, I learnt
that the Land League had placed the Fenian or
National cause in a far stronger position than
ever in Ireland. Could the Clan-na-Gael only
see the national spirit which had been developed
all over Ireland, they would never oppose it, he
believed. In counties where the Revolutionary
organisation had been dead for years, continued
he, there was now material for work, and men
ready to go as far as any one. All these men
wanted was organisation and leaders. He
besought my assistance in proving his claim to
be a naturalised American citizen, which, if
established, would mean his release. I left him
with no doubt in my mind as to his being a
thorough-paced Revolutionist. When I got outside the prison, I received from Dr. Kenny a
letter which Boyton had intrusted to him after
leaving, containing a couple of his photos.
Boyton, need I state, was a paid Land League
organiser like Sheridan, the director of the
Invincibles. My meeting with Sheridan was,
by the way, almost a momentary affair, and that
with Dillon in the presence of a warder.

After a very interesting time in Dublin, I
left by North Wall boat, being "seen off," as
the phrase is, by Egan's business partner and
brother-in-law, O'Rorke, and Andrew Kettle,

both Leaguers remaining on the bridge of the
boat talking to me till we left. The detailed
report of all I had seen and heard was duly
submitted to Mr. Anderson. I was commended
for my success, said good-bye to everybody,
and once more took ship for home, in order to
get back in time for the Convention of the Clan-
na-Gael, which was to take place very soon. Of
course there was another matter which prompted
my speedy return, and that was the work I had
undertaken to do on behalf of Mr. Parnell. I
had to see Devoy and the others, to report the
Irish leader's views to them, and having acquitted
myself of all I had to do as a Revolutionary
envoy, to find out as much as possible of the
result, in order that I might utilise the information in my capacity as an agent of the Secret
Service.

XXXVII.

I REACHED New York somewhere in the month
of June 1881. Devoy was not there when I
arrived, and so I had to telegraph to him
at New Haven, Conn., in order to arrange an
interview. My telegram was followed by a
written report of all that had happened; and as
Devoy was detained at New Haven, a lengthy

correspondence took place between us. Though at first reluctant to go to Europe, he eventually undertook to do so. His consent, however, was conditional on his colleagues agreeing to the undertaking, and with them he promised to confer immediately on his return. Later on he telegraphed me to lay his correspondence before Sullivan and Hynes, when I discussed the matter with them. The following is one of the letters I had from Devoy in connection with this matter. It is, unfortunately, the only one I retained in my possession, the others having been forwarded with my despatches at this period, as they were of a far more important character.

> "41 ORANGE STREET, NEWHAVEN,
> "OFFICE OF MR. REYNOLDS,
> "*June* 24, 1881.

"DEAR FRIEND,—I am sorry I was obliged to leave here for New York last Saturday, consequently I did not get your letters till my return last night. They would have been sent on to me, but I was expected to return. I am much obliged for the information you have given me, and the interest you have taken in a matter that affects us all so closely. I have not heard from H. (Hynes), but yesterday I received a note from E. (Egan) urging me strongly to go over, but I did not understand for what purpose till I got your explanation. I should like to go very much if I could spare the time, and if I thought my visit would produce the effect anticipated, but I am afraid it would not. I have no authority to speak for anybody, and no man would undertake to speak for the V.C. without its consent, and which must take time to get; and

none of us, even if we had that consent, could give any
guarantee for the individuals on the other side, who are
hostile, and who, I feel certain, do not represent the opinion
of the home organisation. There can be no change there
until there is a change of persons, and that is sure to come in
time. All I could do would be to tell E. (Egan) and P.
(Parnell), on my own responsibility, what I believe would be
satisfactory to our friends here, and make propositions that I
might have felt morally certain would be approved of; but I
would not, on any consideration, have them pay my expenses;
that would place me in a false position at once. I have asked
advice, and if certain friends here think it the right thing to do,
I shall start next Wednesday; but, at present, I do not think
I shall be so advised. They seem to misunderstand our dissatisfaction here. It is not their action in Ireland, but the
action they allow their friends to take in their name here.
There is little difference of opinion about the essential point,
but we cannot tolerate the kind of thing begun in Buffalo.
Please drop me a line to P.O. box 4,479, New York City, and
even if I should go it will reach me. I will write again.—
Yours in haste,   "JOHN DEVOY."

Before proceeding to Sullivan and Hynes, I
took a trip to Philadelphia, in order to see Dr.
Carroll and convey Mr. Parnell's views to him.
With him I found very little sympathy for the
proposal. He was as antagonistic to the open
movement as possible. As for Davitt, he had
lost all faith in him. "When Davitt ceases to be
a Revolutionist," he remarked, " I have no further
use for him." As for any practical alliance between the two forces, his idea was that no two
or three people should take upon themselves to

decide, but that the whole question should be brought up before the coming Convention. Altogether, Dr. Carroll appeared anything but an enthusiast on Mr. Parnell's behalf, although in the end he went the length of saying that he was glad to find by Mr. Parnell's attitude that there was a returning sense of reason on his part. From Philadelphia I journeyed to Chicago, where I saw Alexander Sullivan and William J. Hynes. I dealt with them separately at first, but in the end a conference took place between the three of us. The news I brought them appeared to be a source of gratification. They apparently fully realised the importance of the situation, and determined in the end that one of them at least should go.

I had now completed my part of the work, and so, content with my labours, I returned home, wrote a full account of my proceedings to Mr. Anderson, and turned my attention to my business. I communicated fully with Egan in two lengthy letters, but I did not write Mr. Parnell, for Egan had purposely asked that I should not communicate direct with his chief. As far as any further public action on my part was concerned, I dropped out of the affair at this point. I knew that I should learn everything in time, and I was quite content to wait.

As I had anticipated, I did hear the result, and
on no less an authority than that of Sullivan himself. He informed me some time later that the
sanction of the executive body of the Clan-na-
Gael or V.C. had been given to the bringing
about of an "understanding." Sullivan, however,
did not anticipate that it would be all plain sailing.
Even then he expected trouble from the members
of the home organisation, but he pointed out that
their opinion was not that of the organisation in
its collective capacity. On one point he was
very strong, and that was the getting rid of poor
old O'Leary. The old man's independence of
mind and speech was not by any means relished,
and so it was determined that he should go.
There could be no radical change brought about,
Sullivan confessed, while O'Leary was there, and,
I might depend upon it, a change of the representative was certain to come very soon. As
he talked, Sullivan grew quite enthusiastic over
the new move, and he showed me by his manner
that he had given the subject a great deal of
thought.

"I feel morally certain," he continued, "that
the propositions I will make will be approved of.
I for one am opposed to bringing up this matter
openly at the coming Convention. I shall most
certainly object to Parnell or any of his friends

compromising themselves by allowing such a course. The whole matter must be left to the Revolutionary Directory and the F.C." (Executive Body). [As it will be seen later, this is exactly what happened. There was no public discussion of the proposal in open convention, but matters were satisfactorily arranged in the quiet caucuses of the responsible committees.] Sullivan, continuing, said, " They (that is, the Parnellites) seem to misunderstand our dissatisfaction here. Our quarrel is not with their action in Ireland, but with the action they allow their friends here to take in their name. I know there is but little difference about essential points, but we cannot tolerate the kind of thing begun in Buffalo."

This reference to Buffalo dealt with some proceedings in connection with the first American Land League Convention of a few weeks previously, which had attracted a good deal of attention and comment at the time. I had no personal knowledge of what took place, owing to the Convention having been held while I was in Europe, but I heard fully of the affair on my return. The whole thing was nothing more or less than an attempt on the part of the clerical element to gain the controlling power in the League Councils, to the exclusion of the Clan-na-Gael influence. Certain speeches had been made and action taken with this view, and although the result had not weakened them, the Clan-na-Gael leaders felt very bitter on the point.

XXXVIII.

THE month of August at length arrived, and with it the Great Dynamite Convention of 1881. It was pretty well known that "active" work was to be the order of the day, when the future plans and schemes of the organisation came to be discussed. Nothing was talked of throughout the camps but the utter lack of practical effort which had characterised the past few years; and now, when funds were pretty large, and the organisation itself in a very flourishing condition in every way, it was determined that some outward and visible sign should be given England of its power of doing mischief. The stories which were daily reaching America of the alleged brutalities being practised by the British Government, only served to inflame the blood of the rank and file of the conspirators, and to make them the more eager to force on some exhibition of their strength. The leaders, however, were in no sense behindhand in the way of bloodthirsty sentiment; indeed, as will be seen by what I have already stated about Devoy and others, arrangements had ere this been completed for giving expression to the popular desire.

The Convention, which assembled in the club room of the Palmer House, Chicago, lasted from the 3rd to the 10th of August 1881 ; and although the word dynamite finds no single place in the official records of the assembly, it was in the air and in the speeches from start to finish. The whole question of active operations came up and was debated at great length in connection with the statement of accounts furnished by the trustees of the Skirmishing Fund. Many of the delegates present attacked both the Revolutionary Directory and the Executive Body for having practically done nothing, while an enormous amount of money had been spent from this fund ; and wild demands were made for particulars. The fight raged so fiercely that disclosures were made compromising people on the Irish side of the water ; and, in order to prevent a complete *exposé*, a resolution was suddenly passed forbidding the mention of names and other compromising particulars. Explanations were, however, tendered as to the schemes which had been discussed and in part arranged. These included the treaty with Russia, the supply of officers to the Boers, the torpedo-boat, the hand-grenade, the purchase and shipment of arms, the purchase of 200 six-pound cannons at $25 each, and the attempt to rescue Michael Davitt on two occasions.

In the end a resolution in the following terms was adopted which, read by the light of the many and excited debates, was a clear instruction to the Executive Body to be up and doing at once in the way of "active" warfare :—

"That it is the sense of this Convention that, while we do not dictate to the F.C., whatever action they may inaugurate, however decisive, will meet the full approval of the delegates present and the V.C. at large."

This, however, was not the only important resolution they recorded. While the fight over an active policy was being engaged in, I secretly attended by request before the Committee of Foreign Relations, and explained to them the views of Mr. Parnell and Patrick Egan. As the result of what took place in connection with this matter, the following resolution was proposed and adopted in open convention :—

' ' That it is the sense of this Convention that both branches of the S.F. (*i.e.*, the Irish and the American members of the Revolutionary Directory), in so far as they can give their time and energies to it, should devote themselves to the work of revolution ; and if such bodies cannot give their approval to public movements that are intended to promote the political and social regeneration of Jsfmboe (Ireland) when they are supported by a large proportion of the Jsjti (Irish) people, they will at least refrain from antagonising them, and that the members of the I.S.C. (the Irish Republican Brotherhood) and the V.C. (Clan-na-Gael) should not arbitrarily be prevented from exercising liberty of action in regard to such movements."

XXXIX.

In this way did both of Mr. Parnell's ideas receive recognition and support. In the first place, the Revolutionary Directory was instructed to prepare for the rising of which he spoke, while, in the second, a pretty strong hint was given to the home organisation that members in their individual capacity should join the League and support its programme. It is only right that I should state at this point that I was not the only one charged with representing Mr. Parnell's views. My attendance before the Foreign Relations Committee brought me into contact with John O'Connor, *alias* Dr. Clarke, *alias* Dr. Kenealy, the travelling agent of the Clan-na-Gael in Europe, who informed me that he specially attended in his representative capacity to support the "understanding." This was not my first meeting with O'Connor by any means. When in Paris I had been introduced to him by O'Leary, and had frequently met him in the company of Egan, with whom he was on the most confidential terms, and working in perfect harmony. O'Connor's statement was followed by one on the part of Devoy, who informed me that " the matter was now all right."

This Convention saw the initiation of the Sullivan *régime*, Alexander Sullivan, ere its close, being elected to the position of president of the organisation, with head-quarters at Chicago. His election was attended by many changes in the constitution. Up to this the executive body, or " F.C." as it was termed, had consisted of a chairman, secretary, and treasurer, with eleven district members or " E.N.'s," elected to control the society in their several districts. The Convention now reconstituted the " F.C." by excluding these eleven " E.N.'s," and limiting the number to six, including the secretary, who was *ex-officio*, but without a vote. This was quite a revolution in the management of affairs, and Sullivan, in his new position, acquired a power and prominence never enjoyed by any previous president. It was after gaining possession of this important and powerful post that he visited Europe, in accordance with the arrangement I had been the means of first proposing to him. Of course it was not publicly announced that Sullivan was in Europe. By some he was understood to be ill, by others in Florida. It would never have done for him to have publicly admitted or allowed the fact to be known that he was so far east as Paris.

I had very many interesting conversations at this Convention, but none more so than those with Dr. Gallaher, now in Portland Prison for complicity in the dynamite outrages, and Mackay Lomasney, who had just returned from Ireland, where, like Devoy in 1879, he had been acting as the inspecting envoy of the Clan-na-Gael. Gallaher, at the time I speak of, was making experiments in the manufacture of explosives, and advocating their use. He was quite enthusiastic in their praise, and so carried away by his subject that he expressed his willingness to personally undertake the carriage of dynamite to England and to superintend its use there. Lomasney was an equally ardent dynamitard, not foreseeing then the fate which awaited him under London Bridge.

I think I cannot better conclude this chapter than by quoting the following statement of accounts, furnished at this Convention, of the Skirmishing Fund, which, in all its details, even to the amount stolen by the messenger of the *Irish World*, should prove of interest.

RECEIPTS, &c.

Total receipts by *Irish World* up to May 31, 1881	$88,306 32	
Received by trustees from other sources	1,603 50	
Interest	1,072 50	
Profits on Exchange	471 25	
		$91,453 57

EXPENSES, &c.

Purchase of bonds	$31,488 87	
Lent per F.C. to S.C. for tools	10,000 0	
Lent to F.C.	5,875 0	
Irish volunteers	1,000 0	
J. J. O'Mahony's burial	2,030 0	
O'D. Rossa's defalcations	1,321 90	
Old submarine vessel	4,042 97	
New submarine vessel	23,345 70	
Miscellaneous expense	321 4	
Lent Dr. Carroll	860 0	
Luby and Burke	100 0	
Cheques dishonoured	78 68	
Reception, Condon and Meledy	249 79	
Allowed A. Ford on old money, Rossa's not cashed	41 90	
Irish World overcharged	5 4	
Subsidising foreign newspapers (J. J. O'Kelly)	2,000 0	
Land League trial (Davitt)	1,532 0	
Special to O'Kelly	177 63	
Author, New Departure	1,003 90	
Stolen by messenger of *Irish World*	27 50	
Reception of Parnell	165 0	
		$85,666 92

ASSETS.

Balance in bank	$5,745 82	
Balance on hands	40 83	
		$5,786 65

XL.

I HAVE found this subject of Irish secret conventions so interesting to the many people who
have talked with me about Clan-na-Gael affairs
since my appearance in the witness-box that I
almost think I might venture on some slight description of the *modus operandi* of these gatherings
without wearying the reader. Like all proceedings from which the general public are shut out,
a Clan-na-Gael assembly becomes interesting in
proportion to the amount of secrecy by which it is
attended. Not indeed that a Clan-na-Gael Convention is anything very exciting or terrible after
all. It possesses none of the weird features of
that scene in which our three old friends of Mac-
beth figure. It is on the contrary very Irish—
very Irish indeed. But what it is and what it is
not can best be demonstrated by some few details
by way of description; and so, transforming my
gentle reader for the nonce into a V.C. delegate,
I will take him with me for a flying visit to the
Clan Convention of 1881 in the club-room of the
Palmer House, Chicago.

As we pass along down the corridor to the iron
doors of the club-room, we find our passage barred
by two stalwart Irishmen. They are members of

the local camp, stationed as sentinels to prevent
the entry of the unauthorised. We have already
presented our credentials and been intrusted with
the necessary passwords, and on giving the outside
password to these guardians of the door, we are
duly admitted. On the other side, however, we
are brought face to face with another couple of
trusted Gaels, and to them we have to give the
inside password. 'Tis done, and, freed now from
further question, we enter the charmed assembly.
What a sight! What a babel of voices and a
world of smoke! You can scarce see for the
clouds which curl and roll round you as the
breath of fresh air is admitted by the opening
door, while, as for hearing, your ears are deafened
by the din and clatter of many tongues and stamp-
ing feet. Yes, we are at last in the Irish Parliament, as it is grandly termed, in full session.
These are the hundred and sixty odd delegates of
the great V.C., sworn "to make Ireland a nation
once again," who are now assembled in the year of
grace 1881 to clamour for dynamite as the only
means of achieving their patriotic ends.

Let us sit down in the corner and study the
scene with attention. It partakes, on the first
view, more of the character of a "free and easy"
entertainment than a grave portentous gathering
of conspirators ; but you must not judge by first

appearances or outward characteristics. It is the way these men have of doing their business, and the dread character of their work is in no way affected by the almost ludicrous phases of the preliminary performance. Always you must remember that you are dealing with Irishmen, who in their wildest and most ferocious of fights still retain that substratum of childishness of character and playfulness of mood, with its attendant elements of exaggeration and romance, which make it as difficult for an ordinary House of Commons member to rightly understand his Irish colleague when he launches forth in description or invective, as it is for the civilised foreigner to know where the actual grievance now comes in.

Well, we are seated, and we must proceed to make the most of our time. And so I hurry on with my description. That is the chairman seated over there on the platform, with his two secretaries in attendance. The permanent presiding officer, as he is termed, is on this occasion no other than our friend Wm. J. Hynes, the gentleman who received his start in Chicago politics as a professional juryman through the instrumentality of Alexander Sullivan, and who since that time has put together flesh as well as riches, and is now one of the strongest-looking men here, possessed of that which, if he had no other qualification, would yet constitute a strong claim for the office of chairman—a voice capable of rising above the din caused by fifty excited patriots all yelling with their greatest might. Seated round in semi-circular fashion are the different delegates who, in the language they love so well, may be described as the flower of Irish-American patriotism. They are a funny crowd, as lolling with arms akimbo, and thumbs resting in their waistcoat arm-holes, they hang their feet on the chairs in front, which for comfort's sake are tilted to an angle of some 40 or 45 degrees, and puff their cigars—on such an occasion there is nothing so vulgar as a pipe indulged in—high up into the air, changing their position now and again in order to have a pull at those interesting-looking black bottles, or to disrobe themselves of coat or waistcoat, the better to cool their heated frames.

But hark! there is a row on now. Listen to the oaths and foul epithets which fill the air. These two patriots to our left have apparently disagreed about something and want to fight it out. See how they jump to their feet, kick the chairs about, throw a curse across the floor at the chairman as he seeks to stop their rowdy proceedings, and enter into grips with each other. Watch how friends hurry up on either side, and note the general confusion which now reigns.

The business of the Convention of course is
brought to a standstill, but not for long. See,
all is quiet again now. These incidents are of
hourly occurrence, and the fun of it all is that
these two combatants will be drinking whisky
in the most amicable way out of the same black
bottle in less than a quarter of an hour's time.
Do you notice these few men hurrying in with
handkerchiefs to their lips? Thirsty souls! They
have been taking advantage of the interval to
pay a visit to the bar.

XLI.

AT last we turn to business again. Luckily the
topic is an exciting one—nothing less indeed
than the Skirmishing Fund discussion—and so
matters will be interesting. O'Meagher Condon
is on his feet, and he is launching forth in vehe-
ment style against the whole of the governing
powers. Condon is one of those men who were
mixed up in the Manchester Martyr affair, and
since his arrival here a couple of years since, on
being amnestied, he has been quite a hero. He
has now a position in a Government department
at Washington, and is much esteemed in the
ranks of the Gaels. How his face works with

excitement and passion as he attacks Devoy and his fellows on the Revolutionary Directory for their want of practical work. He finishes at last, and up jumps Devoy, more sour-looking than ever, with the perpetual scowl growing heavier and heavier. As he proceeds, the author of the New Departure has recourse to the usual method of controversy. He asserts that Condon is a coward, and was guilty of the grossest neglect at Manchester. If Condon had but distributed the twenty odd pounds which were found on him on his arrest, many of the men would have escaped, instead of being captured with empty pockets. Gruffer and gruffer becomes Devoy's voice, as losing partial control of himself he trembles with excitement and flings charge after charge across the floor.

We are in for another personal quarrel, and so have to wait patiently while Condon, for the hundredth time, recites the threadbare narrative of his glorious deeds in Manchester. Matters are very electrical when the Rev. George C. Betts of St. Louis craves a hearing, and with his well-known smile seeks the suffrages of his fellow-patriots for the moment. Truly, a strange figure in a strange place. Tall, erect, in the black garb of the Church, with priest-like face and priest-like form, he woos the assembly to a

strange quietness as his clerical style of utterance
falls upon the audience.   He is as hot a dynamitard as any, but he wants no personalities.
If they are to accomplish anything, they really
must be more practical.   And so he proceeds,
winning applause and spreading enthusiasm, till
Devoy and Condon, and their personalities, are
swept into forgetfulness, and all are engaged in
applauding revolutionary sentiment spiced with
religious quotation, and served up in the most
orthodox of fashions.

The reverend dynamitard concludes, and
resumes his seat amidst most enthusiastic evidences of his popularity.   He gives way to an
equally inharmonious figure in this motley
gathering.   The man who now rises is one of
medium height, whose every movement bespeaks
the professional man, as awhile back the picture
presented by the Rev. Dr. Betts bespoke the
cleric.   A young man too is this, with his neat
attire, trim beard, and gold-headed cane.   No
less a person is he than Dr. Gallaher, who, in this
year of 1892, in the convict suit of grey with
its regulation arrows, works out his weary life
in Portland prison.   As you watch, and as he
speaks in that quiet gentlemanly fashion of his,
you can well believe that he is a man of whom
it might be afterwards boasted that he was

introduced to Mr. Gladstone himself. Save in his sentiments there is nothing of the dynamitard about him, but in the matter of his speech there is no room for doubt. Quiet and self-controlled though he be, his talk is the talk of war, and the enthusiasm which lights up his countenance is that strong steady flame which will steadily burn till England's dungeon doors close upon him and cut short his career of recklessness.

Following him on the floor is the familiar form of Denis Feeley, the fellow "Triangler" of Sullivan in later days, and with him the object of attack on the part of Cronin's friends. Cool, calm, and deliberate, he carries his audience with him as he advocates " a secret blow at the enemy"; while his big form shakes with indignation as he works himself up to an excited pitch over "the wrongs of their beloved country." At last Feeley concludes, and there rises another well-known figure, that of T. V. Powderly, for years the chief of the largest working-men's organisation in America, known as "The Knights of Labour." Little doubt can there be as to his views. Listen to what he says :—

"The killing of English robbers and tyrants in Ireland, and the destruction by any and all means of their capital and resources, which enables them to carry on their robberies and tyrannies, is not a needless act. Hence I am in favour of the torch for their cities and the knife for their tyrants till they agree to let Ireland severely alone. London, Liverpool, Manchester, and Bristol in ashes may bring them to view it in another light."

And so the talk goes on, and seven hundred years of grievances find expression from the lips of excited patriots, while quarrelsome delegates destroy all decorum. There is little purpose in our waiting further. One hour will be but the repetition of the other. As we rise to leave, however, one figure catches the eye and impresses itself upon us. It is that of the arch-plotter Sullivan, who, through all this din and turmoil, sits and makes no sign. He knows that later on he will be the candidate for the highest place amongst them, and so he takes no side. There is no possibility of your missing him as you pass him by. There he sits, quiet, watchful, and alert. You cannot mistake the man. There is a sense of power and intelligence in that clean cut, clean shaven face of his, lit up by its bright daring eyes. Had you but heard him speak, the lesson of his presence would have been complete. His clear trumpet voice, rising and falling with the play of a practised orator, his choice finished diction, his well-reasoned, well-arranged argument, and the graceful gesture and movement of his whole body would prove to you that there at least was a man gifted to command and competent to control.

And so we terminate our flying visit to the Eighty-one Convention of the Clan-na-Gael, wherein there were assembled forty lawyers, eight doctors, two judges, clergymen of both leading religions, merchants, manufacturers, and working men, all mixed up in glorious confusion, almost all reduced to the level of the whisky bottle, and none removed from the struggles of personal avarice and ambition.

XLII.

NOTHING of a very stirring character happened for the next couple of months, and so, much to my satisfaction, I was permitted to attend for a little without interruption to my private affairs. They sadly lacked some notice on my part, for business was growing, my drug-stores were increasing in number, and so was my family. Patients were very numerous too, but expenses were not without their increase, for I had to employ a regularly qualified M.D. to take my place in my absence. If I could have settled down and simply minded my own business from this henceforth, I would have been in a very satisfactory

position to-day. But 'twas not to be. I was constantly on the move, and living at high pressure
right through. To keep myself thoroughly posted
I had to be here, there, and everywhere, and, in
the end, my ordinary business had to take a very
secondary place. Even at this time my leisure
from political affairs was to be of very short
duration, for, in my capacity as Senior Guardian,
I received the following in the month of November 1881 :—

" *Private.*
" For S. G. alone.

" HEAD-QUARTERS, K.,
" *November* 21, 1881.

"S.G. of D.

" DEAR SIR AND BROTHER,—It is the desire of the F.C. that
as many members of the V.C. as can possibly attend the Irish
National Convention at Chicago, November 30, 1881, will do
so without entailing expense on the organisation.

" You will therefore make every effort to get the members
of the V.C. elected as delegates from any Irish society that
may have an existence in your neighbourhood, whether it be
as representative of the Land League Club, the A.O.H., or any
other organisation.

" The F.C. particularly desires your presence as a delegate,
if it is possible for you to attend as such.

" Fraternally yours,
" K.G.N. OF THE V.C."

I thoroughly knew what this meant. Under
the new *régime* of Sullivan there was to be no
more of the " Buffalo business," and to prevent it
things were to be done in a thoroughly practical

manner. The members of the secret revolutionary organisation were to capture the representation at the coming Land League Convention, to act unitedly in the development of a policy in harmony with the Clan-na-Gael, and to officer the future executive in such a way as to prevent further misunderstanding. In order to do all this, the Clan-na-Gael men were to obtain election as League, or Ancient Order of Hibernian, delegates, the latter organisation being a purely benevolent body, whose branches had largely affiliated with the League or open movement from the start. This was accordingly done; and thus it came about that, when I met my fellow-delegates to the open Land League Convention of 1881, I found almost every second man a brother from the camps of the Clan-na-Gael.

The whole scheme worked in the most perfect manner. On arrival in Chicago each Clan-na-Gael man reported himself to the chief officer of the district, to whom credentials were presented. Official intimation was then given as to what would happen, and each conspirator learned that, prior to the sessions of the convention, caucuses of the Brotherhood would be held in the hall of Camp 16, Twenty-second Street, Chicago. The usual precautions were taken, and admission only gained by passwords exchanged on each occasion.

As the chairman at the first gathering—the Rev.
George C. Betts—humorously put it, "our object
was to make things easy for the Land Leaguers,
and to save them as much trouble as possible."
At each meeting the plan of procedure at the
coming session was decided upon, and the election
of temporary and permanent officers arranged.
Nominations for various committees were fixed,
and no opportunity neglected for adapting the
constitution and officials to our requirements.
The resolutions subsequently adopted in open
convention were drafted by our committees.

It therefore came about that John F. Finerty
of Chicago, the well-known dynamite advocate
and prominent member of the Clan, " called the
convention to order," and made the opening
speech. William J. Hynes of the Revolutionary
Directory, and the chairman of the late Clan-na-
Gael Convention, was appointed temporary chairman, and Joseph E. Ronayne, who had acted in
a similar capacity at the Dynamite Convention,
was appointed secretary, while T. V. Powderly
of the Clan Executive, whose fiery speech at the
same Convention was given a few pages back,
was nominated assistant-secretary. The nomination of these men led to a trial of strength
between the two forces of the Convention, but
the real tug of war was reserved for the second

day, when resolutions previously adopted at the Gael's caucus were proposed, nominating the Rev. George C. Betts of St. Louis as permanent chairman, and Patrick Ford, John Devoy, Mrs. Parnell, and a number of priests as vice-presidents. Of course the priests were put forward for politic reasons. The vice-presidents were not objected to, but the appointment of the Rev. George C. Betts, a Protestant clergyman, was strongly opposed by the priestly party. A very excited debate took place, but in the end the opposition to Betts was withdrawn at the instigation of the Irish visitors—Messrs. T. P. O'Connor, M.P., T. M. Healy, M.P., and Father Sheehy—and so at the close this Vice-President of the Clan-na-Gael was elected, and the secret organisation triumphed all along the line.

The Irish political controversy was darkened the following year by the sad event in the Phœnix Park, Dublin, when Lord Frederick Cavendish and Mr. Burke met their deaths at the hands of the Irish Invincibles. As regards the Invincible conspiracy, I have little or nothing to say. It was in no sense an American affair, and no matter how little or how much certain sympathisers in the States may have known of the murderous conspiracy, nothing was said on the subject in public or in secret to connect the Clan-na-Gael in any way with the proceedings of Carey and his friends. There was, of course, a certain amount of sympathy with the affair, as was shown by the attitude taken up by John Devoy in his paper the *Irish Nation*, which was, by the way, the official organ of the Clan-na-Gael at this time, and subsidised from its fund. Devoy gave great prominence to the refusal of Egan to offer a reward for the discovery of the murderers, printing the following telegram in his issue of 13th May 1882 :—

"PATRICK EGAN ON BLOOD-MONEY.

"PARIS, *May* 10, 1882.

"Mr. Egan, the Treasurer of the Land League, has telegraphed the following to the *Freeman's Journal* of Dublin :—

"'EDITOR, *Freeman*, Dublin.—In the *Freeman* of yesterday Mr. James F. O'Brien suggests a reward of £2000 out of the Land League Fund for the discovery of the perpetrators of the terrible tragedy of Saturday. Remembering, as I do, the number of innocent victims who in the sad history of our country have been handed over to the gallows by wretched informers, in order to earn the coveted blood-money, and foreseeing the awful danger that in the present excited state of public feeling crime may be added to crime by the possible sacrifice of guiltless men, I am determined that if one penny of the Land League Fund were devoted for such a purpose I would at once resign the treasurership.

"'PATRICK EGAN.'"

And commenting upon it in the following vein :—

"Patrick Egan has spoken out like a man against the

adoption by Irishmen of the base English policy of suborning informers. He declares that should a penny of the Land League funds be devoted to such an object, he will resign the treasurership. Mr. Parnell should at once repudiate the attempt made from this side to connect him with action so culpable and un-Irish. By consenting to become the trustee of the Irish-American blood-money he would forfeit the sympathies of his warmest admirers."

It was in this year, too, that O'Donovan Rossa was finally expelled from the Clan-na-Gael. He had been in very bad odour for a long time previously, owing to his unsatisfactory connection with the Skirmishing Fund ; and at last, after a couple of attempts to get rid of him, he was summarily kicked out, and from henceforth repudiated by the recognised officials of the secret organisation.

XLIII.

EIGHTEEN hundred and eighty-three proved a very busy time with me. There was another Land League Convention : Egan, Sheridan, Frank Byrne, and other Invincibles "on the run" arrived in the country, and altogether my time was pretty well occupied in obtaining information and passing it on to my chief. The year opened amidst rumours in the public press of the secret movement having captured the open

o

organisation of the League.   Mr. Parnell himself
had taken action previously in connection with
the Kilmainham Treaty, and in other ways which
were not understood or appreciated, and, as a
consequence, a partial breach had occurred.   So
strained were matters becoming that in February
it was announced that both Mr. Parnell and
Egan would come to America in April for the
purpose of discussing the whole situation and
fixing upon some new mode of operations for the
future which, while equally effective as regards
joint working, would not impair Mr. Parnell's
usefulness.   Many weeks, however, had not passed
ere the fight between the clerical and revolutionary elements in the States began to wax
exceedingly hot, and, changing his plans, Mr.
Parnell determined not to interfere, and so failed
to put in his promised appearance.

Egan, however, thanks to the revelations of
Carey, had to make a speedy and somewhat undignified exit from Dublin, and not waiting till
the month of April, he put himself *en evidence* in
American life in the month of March.   I met
him a week or two after his arrival, when he was
the guest of Alexander Sullivan, the President
of the Clan-na-Gael, at Chicago.   We renewed
our cordial friendship, and the same close inti-
macy prevailed between us as had been the case

in Paris. Egan told me that the programme now to be proposed would give full satisfaction in America; while, as for Sullivan, he (Sullivan) remarked to me significantly about this time that, though he had never doubted Egan, he was now more than satisfied.

The public Convention of the Land League, henceforth to be known as the National League of America, took place at Philadelphia on the 26th April and following days. The same plan of campaign as had been developed in 1881 was put in force by the Clan-na-Gael. A secret circular was issued instructing the camps to send delegates, and these delegates when assembled in Philadelphia pursued the same line of policy in their caucus gatherings. The whole thing worked like an exquisite piece of mechanism, and produced the most satisfactory results for the Clan leaders. Of course I was a delegate, and of course I attended all the secret caucuses. Well for Egan that it was so. He considered it impolitic to appear at any of the secret gatherings, and so, much to my satisfaction, he asked me to acquaint him daily with what transpired, which I did, and received in return many interesting pieces of private information. The Convention was remarkable for the presence of Egan and Brennan, the runaway treasurer and secretary of the Irish Land League, both of whom took part in the proceedings, and of Frank Byrne and his wife, who were accommodated with seats on the platform.

In accordance with the arrangements made at one of the caucus meetings, Alexander Sullivan was appointed president of the new organisation. He played his part well on the occasion, and succeeded in entirely overcoming the scruples of those opposed to him in consequence of his being chief of the Clan-na-Gael. Not once but twice did this prince of intriguers decline the honour respectfully but firmly ; and not till after repeated appeals from Mrs. Parnell, the mother of the Irish Home Rule leader, did he consent to take the office. Another leading Gael was appointed secretary, and out of the Executive Committee of seven, five were members of the Clan-na-Gael.

Although Mr. Parnell did not make his promised appearance, he sent a lengthy and significant telegram, in which he asked that the platform should be so framed as to enable himself and his friends to continue to receive help from America, and to work in such harmony as would allow of their achieving those great objects for which, through many centuries, the Irish race had struggled.

This was a pretty plain hint from the leading

spirit on the Irish side to keep matters moderate in appearance, and it was not lost on those charged with the conduct of affairs, as the following extracts from my official report to my camp on my return will show :—

"The various reports were read and routine business transacted. These developed that the Land League had not increased in members, but, on the contrary, had decreased during the past year ; that a majority of the patriots of America had become tired of giving their earnings for 'Simon Pure agitation ;' of the 900 branches existing a year ago, 105 had disbanded, and 298 had failed to report. The total receipts for the past year from all sources were 79,138 dollars, 40 cents, and the disbursements 74,123 dollars, 40 cents, leaving on hand a balance of 4915 dollars.

"There was an evident desire upon the part of clerical delegates and lady Land Leaguers (who evinced a fear of amalgamating with dynamiters and secret society Revolutionists) to retain the organisation intact, dropping the word land, adopting the platform of the Dublin Convention of last October, electing their officers for the ensuing year, calling themselves the National League, and adjourning *sine die*. This policy received an able but unscrupulous supporter in Miles O'Brien of New York, a renegade member of the V.C., who exhibited the last circular of instructions from the F.C. to a number of priests to show them how they were to be manipulated by the terrible Clan-na-Gaels. Had this source been successful it would have prevented union, it would have continued the various factions, and the formidable front presented to-day of all the societies of the country pledged upon one platform to work united with one object in view would never have been achieved.

"Brother Brown of St. Louis moved a substitute for all resolutions to declare the Land League dissolved after the adjournments of this Convention, and the delegates to attend the National Convention the next day. This eventually was practically carried by a large majority.

"The Convention, to which I presented credentials from this body on Thursday morning, presented the grand array of nearly 1200 delegates upon the floor, the stage being decorated with portraits, paintings, statues, flags, and flowers, and graced by some fifty ladies—conspicuous amongst them being Mrs. Parnell and Mrs. Frank Byrne—the galleries packed to overflowing, some five thousand interested spectators being present, a sight not soon to be forgotten.

"Again the V.C. showed the work of its second conference of Wednesday night, the proceedings being opened by Brother Sullivan, and Brother Dorney being unanimously elected temporary presiding officer, the temporary secretaries being Brothers Roach of Troy, Brown of St. Louis, Hines of Buffalo, and Gleason of Cleveland. The appointment of the Committee on Credentials, after the opening speeches, constituted the first work on hand, and here again the perfect organisation of the V.C. developed itself; and the first breeze created by the Rossa-Dunne faction, who moved an amendment that each society have a member upon the Committee on Credentials, was promptly voted down. Rossa presented his credentials as a member of the National Party of New York, but was admitted only upon a press ticket.

"The knowledge of a blood and thunder set of resolutions being in the pocket of Major Horgan of New York, ready to be fired, regardless of consequences, into the Convention, required the passage of a resolution that, until permanent organisation was effected, all resolutions offered should be referred to the Committee on Resolutions without being read. A permanent organisation was effected in the afternoon by the unanimous election of Brother Foran of Cleveland as presiding officer. The various committees being appointed, the Convention adjourned till Friday morning, the result of the day's work summarised showing that there was nothing to warrant the fear that the Rossa faction would develop any strength or discord;

that the V.C. were in the majority everywhere; that by every action it was desired to follow out the instructions of Mr. Parnell as cabled to the Convention on that day; and at least, so far as the public policy was concerned, to drop all nitro-glycerine methods of procedure, and to perfect the union of the united societies of the country and Canada upon one platform, for the purpose of sustaining Parnell and his policy by acting and existing permanently as an auxiliary body, or rather further, to the Irish National League.

"One straw to show which way the wind blew was the nomination in committee of P. A. Collins of Boston for permanent chairman. His candidature was unitedly set down with a will for his action in offering a reward of 5000 dollars for the discovery of the killers of Burke and Cavendish last year.

"Friday morning found the Convention in session with the various committees on Plan or Organisation, Platform, Resolutions, and Permanent Organisation ready to report. After some spirited speech-making by Fathers Boylan and Agnew, and others, Dr. O'Reilly of Michigan submitted the report of the Committee on Resolutions, in which was included the platform of the National League of America. After reading, an attempt was made by Finerty to adopt them *seriatim*, for the purpose of getting inserted some more favourable to the turbulent Rossa-Dunne faction. They were, however, adopted as a whole. . . .

"The Committee on Organisation presented their report, which was unanimously adopted.

"It was then in order to elect officers for the ensuing year. Alexander Sullivan nominated Dr. O'Reilly of Michigan as treasurer. He was elected without opposition, Father Walsh having declined, stating privately that he had to choose between his parish and the treasurership; and that being the case, he would have to decline.

"The nomination for president resulted in the almost unanimous choice of Brother Alexander Sullivan, who, after twice diplomatically declining, finally was prevailed upon to accept. The Executive Council of one from each State was elected, a large majority of whom were members of the V.C.

"Brother Hines of Buffalo was unanimously elected permanent secretary. Various sums of money were subscribed for the new league, principally by the ladies. Resolutions were passed turning over the books, balances on hand, and property of the old Land League to the new League.

"Speeches expressive of God-speed and goodwill followed by everybody, and the Convention adjourned to meet again next year at the call of the Executive.

"The Executive Council subsequently met and elected the Council of Seven, five of which are members of the V.C.

"To briefly summarise the results of the Convention, we find the unification of all Irish societies pledged under one leadership to follow the lines laid down by Parnell and the party at home, not to lead but to follow them whence they may go with all the energy, practical and financial support possible—a proof to the world that the ten millions of Irish nationality upon the continent can be represented in convention by their 1200 delegates, and work harmoniously and unitedly, and giving to those, and their number is legion, who believe in force alone, the supreme satisfaction of knowing that the machinery of the cause is now under the control and direction of their comrades, who believe, as they do, that dynamite, or any other species of warfare that can be devised is perfectly legitimate, so long as it can be made effective, and accomplish results permanent and tangible.

.　　.　　.　　.　　.　　.　　.

"Michael Boyton arrived upon the second day of the Convention with two members of the Supreme Council, who, as it will be readily understood, did not figure publicly upon this occasion."

XLIV

It was shortly after this—I think somewhere about the 29th of May—that I was fortunate enough to learn from Sullivan some particulars as to what was going on in connection with the Dynamite Campaign. A demonstration had been arranged at Milwaukie, Wisconsin, in honour of Patrick Egan, and at Sullivan's pressing invitation I accompanied him in order to participate in it. We travelled together and conversed almost all the way, Sullivan, as was his wont, supplying me with very interesting details. He told me that the management of the secret warfare was entirely in the hands of the Revolutionary Directory in America. Men, it appeared, could not be obtained at home to do the work, for from some lack of courage or discipline they could not be relied upon.

The rule adopted was that no volunteer should be accepted. Special choice would be made of men without families, and a special course of instruction in the use of explosives would be necessary after a man was chosen. So great was the care taken in the selection of agents, that their whole career and character would be inquired into beforehand without their knowledge. No new members would be chosen for the work, because forty of the Royal Irish Constabulary had been sent on full pay to America to join the organisation with a view to selling it. Sullivan imparted the further interesting information that Dr. Gallaher, when on his mission, purposely abstained from coming in contact with Irish members, and obtained introductions to, and acquaintance with, English members. He was often in the House, I was told, and had been even introduced to Mr. Gladstone himself.

Contrary to expectation and the requirements of the existing constitution, no Clan-na-Gael Convention took place in this year—1883. In the ordinary course of events such an assembly should have met in August 1883. For reasons best known to themselves, however, Sullivan and his colleagues on the executive of the secret organisation postponed the gathering, and in the end, by a system of manipulation which Sullivan developed to a perfect science, in connection with his management of Irish affairs, the approval of the organisation was gained to certain changes which included the putting off of the Convention to the following year, 1884. To allow of these changes being approved of, it was necessary to hold a series of district Conventions, and delegates were there elected to represent the districts at the general Convention which would follow. Sullivan's adherents were generally in the majo-

rity at such district assemblies, and so it was a
matter of ease for him to have supporters elected
at almost every gathering, which, in other words,
meant that the delegates then elected were
nothing more or less than ardent Sullivanites, who
in the future Convention would question nothing,
whereas ordinary delegates would undoubtedly
prove curious, if not embarrassing, in their search
for information as to the conduct of the affairs of
the Clan-na-Gael.

All was not clear sailing, however, and murmurs
were heard in several quarters regarding this
attempt to burk discussion and inquiry as to the
work of the past two years. Several of the camps
eventually ceased their allegiance and were
immediately expelled, and the organisation split
up into two sections, the one being Sullivanite
and the other anti-Sullivanite. Devoy and his
whole camp were amongst those expelled from
the Sullivan wing. The seceders formed a new
organisation under the old name, and the
Sullivanites became known as the U.S. Sullivan
was still the strong man, and had the greatest
number of supporters; and, following my usual
rule, I acted with the majority and became a
U.S. man. At the start a change was made as
regards the number and title of the governing
body. Three members formed the executive,

and they were now known as the Triangle—
a name taken from the Δ sign which was used
by way of cypher signature on all documents
coming from head-quarters. The fight between
the two sections was now raging bitterly, and the
oath of the U.S. was so drawn as to exclude
members of any other Revolutionary body, thereby
denying the right of any person to be a member
of both organisations.

Meantime, under the plea of imminent danger
of discovery, the books of the organisation were
all burnt, and no record whatever was left in
existence which would allow of investigation.
This had driven very many men to desperation,
and loud and sweeping were the charges which
the seceders made against the Triangle for misappropriation of funds and other like matters.
None were more prominent in leading the attack
on Sullivan and his colleagues than Dr. Cronin,
whose murder has recently been the subject of
such lengthy investigation. Indeed, from this
point onwards, almost down to the end of 1888,
the history of the Clan-na-Gael is the history of
the dispute between Cronin and Sullivan. And
now, having purposely excluded all special mention
of Dr. Cronin from my story heretofore, in order
that I might the more fully and clearly deal with
the matter in a compact form, I shall proceed to

sketch the life and career in Irish-American politics of this last victim of political assassination. In explaining the situations in Irish affairs as they affected or were affected by Dr. Cronin, I shall have to travel rapidly over points already dealt with; but I think it better to do this than to improperly represent the ill-fated Cronin by omitting from my reference to his career the points which told in favour of himself or his adversaries.

XLV.

PHILIP H. CRONIN was born in Ireland, but when very young emigrated to Canada. From thence when a young man he went to St. Louis, Missouri, where he studied medicine at the St. Louis College of Physicians and Surgeons. Before this he had been clerk in a chemist's store, and had thus acquired a very considerable practical knowledge of medicine. He graduated with high honours, and became eventually Professor of Materia Medica and Therapeutics in the college. He also attended a medical college from which he secured the degree of M.A. Cronin was a man of fine presence, good looking, almost six feet in height, and very well formed. He was a clever man in every way, and a good forcible speaker, though in style aggressive and combative to a degree. Very ambitious, like his future enemy Alexander Sullivan, he was never happy in a back seat, always thrusting himself forward and fighting for the place of leader. In fact, so pronounced were his ideas in favour of his supremacy, that where he could not rule he was quite prepared to ruin.

He moved to Chicago in the latter part of 1881, and immediately entered upon the practice of medicine, taking up his residence at 351 Clark Street, at the corner of Oak Street. At this time he was about thirty-two years of age, so that he was only some forty years old at the time of his murder. From the moment of his arrival in Chicago, he went in enthusiastically for Irish politics, and took a leading part in both Revolutionary and Land League matters. He identified himself with the Clan-na-Gael, and was prominent at all gatherings of the Irish of every kind. He was strong in social instincts, and was quite a figure at social gatherings, where he used to great advantage the fine tenor voice of which he was possessed, singing national songs especially with great spirit and enthusiasm. As a consequence he rapidly came to the front in Chicago, and in six months was better known than an ordinary resident would have been in ten years. Towards the

Land League movement he was especially sympathetic, and he took a very large part indeed in building it up. He was in a short time elected President of the 18th Ward League, then known as the "Banner League" of Chicago. Equally active in the secret movement, he was a guiding spirit of Camp No. 96 of the Clan in Chicago, publicly known as the "Columbia Literary Association," and so great was his influence that, on the appointment of the notorious Frank Agneau to the position of district member, Cronin succeeded him as Senior Guardian of the camp. This was the camp which held its weekly meetings in the well-known Turner Hall on the north side of the city.

It was at this time that the policy of dynamite had been decided upon, and that the campaign against English Government buildings and persons was being inaugurated. Cronin (who was anything but a saint in character) was an ardent advocate of the policy ; and, owing to his scientific attainments, he was appointed as chief instructor in the use and handling of explosives, acting all this time, be it marked, as the President of the Banner League (or Chicago branch of the Land League) as well. In fact, he held the position of President of the Land League branch down to the year 1888. Cronin, unfortunately

for himself, succeeded at a very early stage in
falling foul of Alexander Sullivan. Living as
he did till 1887 at the corner of Clark and
Oak Streets, within a few doors of Sullivan
himself, he gained such an amount of prominence that he was rapidly throwing Sullivan
into the shade. He threatened to become more
powerful than Sullivan, and this Sullivan,
equally ambitious and more unscrupulous, could
not brook. In a short time Sullivan and his
adherents came to detest the Doctor, and as
I found—for I lived within a stone's throw of
each, knew them both intimately, and saw them
continuously—the relations between them were
becoming more strained and bitter every day.

In June 1881, as I have related, Sullivan
obtained a victory over all his rivals by being
chosen President of the Clan-na-Gael, or Revolutionary organisation, at the Dynamite Convention
held that year at the Palmer House, Chicago.
It was after this that Cronin gave the first
pronounced sign of his enmity in public. The
opportunity for its display was brought about
by the attack made by O'Meagher Condon upon
John Devoy, the principal of the three members
of the Revolutionary Directory, Devoy with his
colleagues being charged with responsibility for
the failure of the many schemes of active war-

fare proposed by Condon. Devoy, evidently jealous of Sullivan's election, indulged in a good deal of incrimination, not confining his attacks to Condon alone, and he was afterwards supported by Cronin, who was possessed of the same grievance. The two joined forces, but without any effect, for Sullivan's position was assured. From the dispute, however, which occurred at this Convention, dates the commencement of undisguised hostility between Sullivan and Cronin.

Early in 1883, when the call was issued for the Philadelphia Convention (at which was formed the first branch of the American National League as distinct from the Land League), a meeting of Cronin's branch of the League took place in Chicago for the election of delegates to the Convention. Sullivan and his friends, determining to crush Cronin if they could, packed this meeting, and had elected as delegates Alexander Sullivan himself, his brother, and other personal adherents, much to the disgust of Cronin and his supporters.

Sullivan was equally successful later on when, under the new constitution, the Executive called district Conventions in lieu of the general convention they had managed to postpone. The Convention in Cronin's district was held in Millionaire Smythe's Hall in Chicago — Smythe being Senior Guardian of Camp 458;

Cronin, as Senior Guardian of his own camp, attended in the capacity of delegate therefrom. Mackay Lomasney, my old friend from Detroit, also attended from his district in a like capacity. Although an attempt was made to impeach Sullivan's action, it was not successful. His friends were in the majority, and his conduct was upheld. All attempts on the part of Cronin to bring about a different state of things—and they were not a few—were voted down, and Alexander Sullivan, in company with Mackay Lomasney, the London Bridge dynamitard, was elected delegate to the Triangle Convention of 1884.

Cronin, filled with fury, returned to his camp and made a series of most sweeping charges against the Triangle. In return charges were preferred against him of being a traitor, liar, &c. &c., Sullivan of course being the instigator. A Trial Committee, of which I was one, was appointed, and by it Cronin was promptly found guilty and formally expelled. I voted, as I always did, on the side of the winning party. Cronin on his expulsion immediately joined the ranks of the seceders, which by this time included such well-known men as Devoy, Dillon, M'Cahey, and others, and he immediately obtained a seat on the executive of the new body. And here, for the moment, I must leave him.

XLVI.

THE next matter of public importance in which I was interested was the Boston Convention of the Irish National League of America, which took place in the Fanieul Hall, Boston, on the 13th and following days of August. Of course I went in my dual capacity as League delegate and Revolutionary official. The same plan of campaign was practised with the same successful results. The Rev. Dr. Betts was again to the front as president of the secret caucuses, while Egan, grown more bold by this, was a regular attendant. When the nomination of officials of the League came up, Sullivan was named for re-election as president. He, however, declined, and made way for Patrick Egan. Egan, after some refusal on the ground that the British Government probably knew of his connection with the secret movement, and that his taking office might compromise Mr. Parnell, eventually agreed, and so he took the chair vacated by Sullivan. This Convention was attended by Mr. Thomas Sexton, M.P., and Mr. William Redmond, M.P., on the part of the Parnellite party, and by P. J. Tynan, the famous "No. 1" of the Phœnix Park murders—shall I say on behalf of the Invincibles? Sullivan undoubtedly was the pet boy of the period, for he was the object of the most adulatory references on the part of Mr. Sexton. He was, we were told, a man who did honour to the race from which he had sprung; a man of whom any race might well be proud — and so on. Egan, however, came in for his fair share of attention too. He was, according to another speaker, " that clean handed, that patriotic, that heroic exile," although, of course, no reference was made to the reasons for his exile as supplied by the Phœnix Park crimes.

If, however, no reason was given in public for his exile, Egan was not slow to refer to the matter in private. I had journeyed in his company to Boston, and had had a very exciting chat with him, in which the question of his flight had largely figured. His description of how he was enabled to get away from Dublin was most graphic. He started off by boasting how he had got information from the Castle; and to show how readily it could be obtained he said that, within twenty minutes of the order being issued for the warrant for his arrest, he knew of the fact. He was at his office at the time, and at once proceeded to his house and packed his satchel. He had two children sick then, and Dr. Kenny was attending them. He destroyed a number of documents which he

"NUMBER ONE"

P. J. TYNAN

had in the house, some of them pertaining to his
connection with the Irish Republican Brotherhood, and also some letters of James Carey. In
fact he destroyed all papers tending to incrimi-
nate him in case he was arrested. Fortunately
for him there happened to be in Dublin at
the time a Scotch friend in the Belfast flour
trade, who assisted him in getting away. He
gave this friend his rug and valise, and instructed him to purchase a ticket for Belfast
at the Northern Terminus. He himself arrived
at the railway station one moment before the
train started, took his valise and rug from his
Scotch friend, slipped into the train, and that
night was in Belfast. On his arrival at Belfast
he found that he could not get out by boat, and
he went to an hotel, where he slept. In the
morning he purchased a return ticket to Leeds,
travelled with that as far as Manchester, and
then got off the train. There he purchased
another ticket from Manchester to Hull, took
the steamer from Hull to Rotterdam, and thus
got out of the country.

From the account of his own escape, he passed
on to tell me how his fellow-official Brennan, the
Secretary of the Irish Land League, had got
away. Brennan, it appeared, gained the first
hint of his being implicated by reading the an-

nouncement of Carey's evidence on a news sheet
displayed on the pavement in the Strand. He
was accompanied by Mr. Thomas Sexton, M.P.,
at the time, and on reading the announcement
they at once turned down a side street where
arrangements were made for Brennan's flight.
Brennan started off for his lodgings in order to
pack a valise, while Mr. Sexton, going to Charing Cross, purchased a ticket for Paris. On this
ticket he travelled to London Bridge, and there
by arrangement he met Brennan, who immediately proceeded on the train to the French
capital. Egan was very generous in his confidences on this occasion, and amongst other
things he told me that he was satisfied the new
Executive Body would continue the "active
work," and it would be done by men who would
not go further than their orders, as Dr. Gallaher
had done. This was news to me, and I inquired
how. "Why," replied Egan, "he (Dr. G.) got
in with some of Rossa's men, and MacDermott
(a reputed informer) got it from them, and gave
him away." Previously to this I had met Egan in
camp gatherings, and knew that he was now an
actual member of the American Revolutionary
organisation. It was, by-the-bye, at a camp
meeting in Philadelphia in this year that Egan,
addressing some sixty members, said, " I have

been reading up the records of the Italian ban-
ditti, and from them I have come to believe in
this rule : Let us meet our enemies with smiling
faces, and with a warm grasp of the hand, having
daggers up our sleeves ready to stab them to the
heart." Strange words these, and yet I thought
when I heard of their being uttered of the smiling
face and warm hand clasp which had puzzled me
not a little on that first night when I met the
speaker on the staircase of a Parisian hotel.

The Convention of the secret organisation
followed immediately after that of the National
League, but as I was not a delegate I had no
intimate connection with it. It was at this Convention, as I learnt subsequently from Sullivan,
that arrangements were made—few, if any, Anti-
Sullivanites were present—for the destruction of
the records of which I have already spoken, and
which gave rise to so much bitterness on the
part of the Cronin faction.

The principal fact worthy of notice in connection with the secret Convention of 1884
was the acknowledgment by the "Triangle" of
118,000 dollars as the sum received and expended
for dynamite purposes from the date of the holding of the Convention of 1881. No vouchers or
detailed statements were forthcoming, and their
absence was sought to be explained on the ground

that it was inexpedient to supply information in
view of the risk and exposure of brave men
engaged in the enterprises. No detailed statement of the expenditure of this vast sum has ever
been made to this day.

As one result of this unsatisfactory condition of
things, a circular was drawn up by Cronin and
his friends, making definite and formal charges
against the " Triangle " of stealing the funds of the
organisation. Cronin was very aggressive in giving
currency to these charges in the most offensive
language, and the feeling against him on the part of
Sullivan's adherents became extremely embittered.
As it grew in intensity it spread to more than
Cronin, and soon the followers of both men were
ranged in hostile camps, fighting a wordy war of
the deadliest type. All attempts to heal the
breach proved fruitless, although much outside
influence of an important character was brought
to bear upon the different parties concerned.

XLVII.

WHILE the contest raged between the opposing
factions, I was up and doing, travelling about, and
gaining as much information as I possibly could.
I made many trips to various points of the country,
and so was enabled to gauge pretty accurately

the condition of public feeling and the probabilities of the future. My pretexts for all this travelling were admirably adapted to divert suspicion from my real object. When a journey for my health's sake was not possible, I got appointed (through Irish political influence) to a seat on the Mississippi Valley Sanitary Commission ; and when no more work was to be done under this cover, I connected myself with one of the largest pharmaceutical houses in the States, and travelled as their representative in whatever direction suited me. So successful was I in combining business development with my secret work, that I had great difficulty in resigning this latter connection, the proprietors strongly urging my continuance in it, and only parting with me after many fruitless attempts to change my decision. When at home I was of course an ardent politician, and a volunteer on every committee in the Democratic interest. So prominent was I in local politics, that on one occasion I ran for election for the House of Representatives, only being defeated by a majority of 128 votes on a poll of several thousands. It was the cry of " The Fenian General " that lost me the seat with the English voters.

I was frequently in communication with Egan through all this period, for he made many trips to Chicago, both for business purposes—he had now embarked in the grain trade—and with the object of consulting with Alexander Sullivan, whose worthy *fidus Achates* he proved. It was as the result of one of my interviews with him that I received the following passport to the faithful, which proved of such service in the way of corroboration when I appeared before the Special Commission :—

Irish National League

of

AMERICA

OFFICES OF PRESIDENT AND SECRETARY

Lincoln, Neb. November 24 1885

It affords me great pleasure to introduce to all Friends of the Irish National League with whom he may come in contact during his visit in the south my esteemed friend Dr. H. Le Caron of Chicago—

Dr. Le Caron although French by name and descent has ever proved himself one of the most devoted friends of the Irish National Cause and since the formation of the Land and National Leagues has been most indefatigable in promoting the ends of those Organizations—

Patrick Egall
President,

Alexander Sullivan meantime occupied himself very busily in purely American politics, and for the purpose of making his position in this regard the more favourable, he caused it to be understood that he had withdrawn from the Clan-na-Gael. This, of course, was only a blind, for as a matter of fact, for twelve months at least after he had so announced his withdrawal, his name continued to appear on circulars and documents. This, however, is immaterial. What is important to note is that Sullivan warmly advocated the election of J. F. Blaine to the Presidency, and that he in secret circles made much of the fact that Blaine's foreign policy would do all that the Clan-na-Gael desired. Mr. Blaine paid a high tribute in the public prints to the services rendered him by Sullivan.

The year 1886 saw the introduction of the Home Rule Bill by Mr. Gladstone, and consequent inactivity on the part of the American conspirators. I therefore had rather an easy time of it. Enthusiasm ran pretty high, because it was thought that with Home Rule granted the way to complete separation would be cleared in a wondrous degree, and that at last we were in sight of the point for which all had struggled and many had bled, "the making of Ireland a nation once again." Mr. Parnell now appeared to have a distinct claim upon Irish American indulgence, and particular pains were taken to prevent anything happening which might unfairly affect his position in any way. So complaisant were "the men beyond the sea" in America, that the open Convention called for January 1886 was postponed in order that Mr. Parnell might be present. The gathering eventually took place in the month of August 1886, but there was no Mr. Parnell, his place being taken by no less than four of the leading Parnellites from the English side—Messrs. Michael Davitt, John E. Redmond, M.P., John Deasy, M.P., and William O'Brien, M.P. As usual, the whole proceedings were governed by the Sullivanite wing of the secret organisation. I was myself a delegate, attended the secret caucuses presided over by Patrick Egan, and assisted in developing affairs in the interests of the conspirators.

The fact that Devoy, Cronin, and others were now in opposition was an element of danger in connection with the satisfactory working of the intrigue to "nobble" the open movement; but by a system of proxy voting success was achieved, and the adherents of the Croninites driven from the field. The way in which this was accomplished was remarkable, and very suggestive of

the position which Egan, the ex-Land League
official, and friend and adviser of Mr. Parnell,
held in the Revolutionary organisation. By a
circular issued by the " Triangle" on the eve of
the Convention, it was ordered that each Senior
Guardian should secure proxies for all branches
of the National League in his vicinity unable to
send delegates to the open Convention, and immediately forward such proxies to Patrick Egan.
Here was a clear confession of the close connection between the two movements—open and
secret—existing in the person of the present
United States minister to Chili, the then President of the Irish National League of America.

XLVIII.

I HAVE already touched at several points on the
Dynamite Campaign, and I will now pause in my
narrative for the purpose of dealing in some detail
with the incidents attending the development of
the plot to " blow up England." Although there
had been several attempts made by O'Donovan
Rossa's adherents to damage public buildings,
notably the Mansion House, London, the barracks
at Chester, the police-station and the Town Hall
at Liverpool in 1881 and 1882, the Dynamite

Campaign as organised by the Clan-na-Gael did not really commence till the latter end of 1882, or rather the beginning of 1883. Indeed the attempts on the part of Rossa's people were simply gunpowder explosions, and had no connection with dynamite at all. They were of a very miserable character, and quite in keeping with O'Donovan Rossa's reputation in the States. With him experience proved that it was always, as the homely phrase has it, a case of "great cry and little wool."

To Dr. Gallaher, our friend of the professional appearance and gold-headed cane, was intrusted the task of inaugurating the work undertaken by the Revolutionary Directory of the Clan-na-Gael. At the time he set out all was enthusiasm in the ranks of the Clan, and great things were promised. In one secret circular the F.C. (or governing body) had informed the members "that it had no delicacy or sentimentality about how it would strike the enemy, or when or where. . . . They meant war, they meant that war to be unsparing and unceasing. They meant it to be effective. Their policy would be to make assaults in all directions, so that the suffering, bitterness, and desolation which followed active measures should be felt in every place."

Under the pretence of taking a voyage to Europe for his health's sake, Gallaher set out in the steamship *Alaska* on the 15th October 1882, reaching Liverpool in good time, and from thence travelling to Glasgow, in order, as he explained, to see some relatives. Glasgow, by the way, has always had a prominent representative of the British branch of the Fenians in residence there. From Glasgow he came on to the London Wall Hotel, and here he remained for a month spying out the land and making the preliminary arrangements for the work which was to follow. His work finished, he took a trip to Dublin, where at the Gresham Hotel he lived as befitted a man of his position. From thence he proceeded to Donegal to visit more "relatives." From Donegal he eventually made his way to Queenstown, where in the *Bosnia* he took passage for home on the 10th December, having, as he subsequently reported, made all necessary arrangements for commencing his branch of the "active work."

He was with Sullivan in Chicago in the following month, and here he and I met and had many chats together. We were fellow-doctors, and we "chummed" together in a fashion very agreeable to me. He soon wearied me, however, for I found he could talk of nothing but dynamite, its

production, its effectiveness, and the great weapon
it was soon to prove against the British Government. He spent the next couple of months in
communication with the powers that were, and
placed them in full possession of all he had done
and all he hoped to do. They took an equally
sanguine view of the possibilities of success, and no
time was lost in enlisting the first dynamite band
which visited Europe. By the middle of March
there were eight men embarked on the dangerous
enterprise, Gallaher being the leader and pay-
master; and at this date the first of them set out
for England in the Cunarder *Parthia*. Every
precaution was taken to avert suspicion, and so
much care was exercised that some travelled as
steerage passengers, while the rest, like Gallaher,
journeyed in gentlemanly fashion. The band
was made up of Gallaher and his brother Bernard,
Dowd, Wilson, O'Connor, Curtin, Whitehead,
and Norman, all being Clan-na-Gael men, though
none save the doctor held any important position
in the organisation.

The first arrivals of this precious assembly of
dynamitards reached Liverpool on the 27th of
March, and, of course, separated at once. Gallaher
went to the Charing Cross Hotel, which he made
his head-quarters. His men were quickly put to
work, and in a very short time a nitro-glycerine

factory was established in Birmingham, under the
superintendence of Whitehead. From here large
quantities of liquid were conveyed to some few
points in London in rubber bags and rubber
shooting-stockings. All the elaborate arrangements, however, were destined to come to naught,
for before any "active" work could be done,
thanks to the vigilance of the police in London
and Birmingham, Gallaher and his associates
were arrested, and the whole of the nitro-glycerine
seized. The month of May 1883 saw the trial
and conviction of the leader and three of his
associates, Whitehead, Curtin, and Wilson, the
case for the Crown being completed by the testimony of Norman, *alias* Lynch, who played the
rôle which never lacks an exponent in the case
of an Irish conspiracy—that of informer. All
of the unfortunate prisoners were sentenced to
penal servitude for life. An interesting feature
in connection with Gallaher's arrest was the
discovery on his person of no less a sum than
£1400.

What the actual designs of this dynamite band
were, are not, and probably never will be known.
Quite sufficient for the public must be the fact
that so enormous was the quantity of nitro-
glycerine discovered that according to experts,
it was quite equal to the blowing up of every

Q

house and street in London, from one end to the other. Pleasant discovery this for the ordinary British citizen who laughs at dynamite and pooh-poohs the existence of any condition of things calling for a more elaborate Secret Service. The arrest and discomfiture of the Gallaher band had one very useful result. It effectively put an end to all idea of manufacturing dynamite on English soil. Unfortunately, however, it did not put an end to the Dynamite Campaign. It simply affected the weapon, not those who were prepared to employ it.

The next group of dynamitards who visited England included Cunningham, Burton, Mackay Lomasney, Luke Dillon, and a man known as Ryan of Philadelphia. These men did not all come at the same time, but they worked together in harmony so far as it was possible. During their visit to London explosions occurred in October 1883 on the Underground Railway; in February 1884, at Victoria Station; in May 1884, at Scotland Yard; in December 1884, at London Bridge; and in January 1885, at the House of Commons and the Tower. The dynamite employed in these cases was all brought from America, secreted about the persons of the conspirators, and of women who were sent over with it, as well as by an employé of one of the steamers of the National Steamship Line, who belonged to the organisation. The explosive was generally made up in slabs of Atlas powder, obtained from, amongst other sources, the Atlas Company and the Repauno Chemical Company of Philadelphia.

Of the second group, only two men were brought to trial, Cunningham and Burton ; and these men, for the attempts on the House of Commons and the Tower, were sentenced to penal servitude for life. The remainder, with the exception of Lomasney, escaped to America. Lomasney, in company with a man supposed to be named Fleming, met his fate under London Bridge in his attempt to blow up that structure. Luckily for the Londoners, the bridge escaped without any injury, but Mackay and his companion apparently came to their end by the discharge of the explosive, for they were never seen more.

There were two other men whose part in the Dynamite Campaign of this period deserves mention. These were "Jack" Daly, as he was called, and his confederate, J. F. Egan, who were tried and sentenced at Warwick in 1884, the former to imprisonment for life, and the latter to penal servitude for twenty years. Daly was perhaps the most daring and desperate criminal

of all, and his intended crime merits special
reference. This was the blowing up of the
House of Commons while in session, by the
throwing of bombs on to the table in front of
the Speaker. So ardent was Daly in planning
this foul enterprise that he twice gained admission to the Strangers' Gallery of the House.
When arrested, some of these bombs were found
upon him, and examination showed that one of
them, if used, would have been quite sufficient
to send every stick and stone, to say nothing of
the members of the House of Commons themselves, heavenwards or thereabouts. Luckily,
this desperate man was arrested in time, for
assuredly his character was quite sufficient to
warrant the belief that he would have carried
out his intention.*

Of all the schemes indulged in by the dynamite
men, none seems to have been more far-fetched
than that of the theft of a certain stone from
within the walls of Westminster Abbey. This

---

* As this same Daly has more than once been the subject of lengthy
debates in Parliament, and his release demanded by the Irish members
on the ground of his being the victim of a wrong conviction, I think it
well to state that his sentence and the subsequent refusal of the Home
Secretary to accede to these demands, were based on letters written
by him to the notorious J. J. Breslin of the Revolutionary Committee of
the Clan-na-Gael, and now in existence among the records of the Home
Office.

was the famous "Stone of Scone," which serves
as the seat of the Coronation-chair in the Abbey.
To an outsider the possession of such a stone
as this seems of no importance whatever. Yet,
ludicrous as it may appear, the idea of securing
it gave rise to great enthusiasm and led to a
very generous subscription with this object.
According to the originators of the scheme, this
"Stone of Destiny" was really the property of
Ireland for a thousand years before Christ, and
upon it were crowned the Irish kings, for hundreds
of years, on the sacred Hill of Tara. Its restoration to the land of its original and only lawful
owners, it was contended, would inspire confidence
in the course then being pursued, and the people
would be strengthened by the well-known tradi-
tion "that so long as this stone remained in
Ireland, so long would she remain a united
nation," while its loss to the English would work
wonders. Elaborate preparations were made for
carrying out the scheme. Men were sent from
America to work in conjunction with certain
Fenians in London, and it was decided that some
of the conspirators should secrete themselves in
the Abbey, and at night seize the police, remove
the stone, and pass it out through a window to
others who would be in waiting outside to take it
to a place of safety. For months these men waited

and waited, but the opportunity never came, for
one of the group gave the whole thing away to
the police, and the detectives who surrounded the
sacred edifice made the seizure impossible. In
the end the three principals had to leave the
country for fear of arrest, and the whole affair
ended in smoke—as usual!

The close of the year 1885 brought the announcement of Mr. Gladstone's conversion to
Home Rule, and the termination of the Dynamite Campaign for the time being. How the
political situation was viewed at this period, can
best be represented by the following extracts
from a secret circular of the Clan-na-Gael, or
United Brotherhood, issued two days before
Christmas :—

"The operations so far conducted have compelled the
enemy to recognise the Constitutional party, and we are now
in a fair way to reap the benefits and results of the heroic
work of the members of the U.S. (United Brotherhood). . . .
We expect to resume active operations after the present
exigencies of the Constitutional party are passed. We have
purposely and advisedly abstained from doing anything likely
to embarrass them during the crisis of the elections. It is to
be hoped that during these operations, members will abstain
from making inquiries or discussing the subject in any manner,
for we cannot say when we undertake to answer members, but
that at the same time we are answering the inquiries of our
enemy, furnishing important information, and giving important
clues to detect and suppress our work. The mystery of an
unknown power striking in the dark, always able to avoid

detection, is far more terrible than the damage inflicted. We caution you, therefore, above all things, to be silent; but if compelled to speak, disavow all knowledge, or better still, mislead all inquirers. In the meantime, we wish to impress on you the necessity of mutual forbearance and faith."

So, for the time, in deference to " the exigencies of the Constitutional party," the Dynamite Campaign was brought to a close, leaving as its record little or no damage to the enemy, but no less than twenty-five of the unfortunate instruments in prison, sixteen undergoing life sentences, two, sentences of twenty years' penal servitude, and seven, sentences of seven years each. Of course, some of these prisoners are not men from the American side. In many cases those coming from America picked up colleagues in England, and, unfortunately for these latter, the knowledge which the local police possessed proved disastrous to them.

XLIX.

THE secret convention of the Revolutionary organisation—or rather, of the principal section which had remained faithful to Sullivan—met in due course, in August 1886, but as I was not a delegate, I had no personal knowledge of what took place. The spirit of the time, however, was very fairly reflected in some circulars, issued prior to its assembly, from which I take the following extracts :—

"The indications all point to the conclusion that the measure of Home Rule offered will be emasculated and pared down in such a way as to make it unacceptable to those for whom it is intended. We are now preparing for those contingencies, and the estimates for the cost of making a rigorous campaign with 'delusion' (dynamite) will absorb more funds than are at present available from the prescribed percentage. The Executive, therefore, in order to meet the great outlay necessary at this crisis, take this occasion to request that, in addition to the usual percentage, each camp at once, by a vote of the camp, send on such additional funds as they may deem proper. . . . It is suggested that in voting this fund it be credited in forwarding it entirely to 'delusion' (dynamite). In the meantime, in the next few months, important operations are likely to take place ; you are cautioned to use every device to mislead those engaged in tracing our operations."

And again :—

"We have some members who are opposed to the active operations of the last few years, and who, therefore, favour a more enlarged representation. It would seem to us that the operations objected to are fully vindicated by the concessions wrung thereby from England. However, we offer no suggestions as to what line of policy you may see fit to pursue. It will be the business of your Convention to frame that policy, and the business of the Executive Body to execute them without regard to individual opinions. . . .

"The silent secret warfare has been productive of results. It would be well, therefore, to instruct your delegates as to your wishes on those points fully and clearly. Having

instructed your delegates which of these policies you wish to
pursue, the details will not be difficult. It would be well,
therefore, to put your instructions to your delegates in one of
the following general terms, with such alterations as you deem
proper :—

" Viz., ' Our delegate is instructed to favour an active secret
policy, similar to recent operations ;' or, in the alternative of
favouring a return to open insurrectionary operations, as follows :—

" Viz., ' Our delegate is instructed to favour the planting of
ploughs (distribution of arms) and an open insurrectionary
movement.'

" 'There can then be no insinuations of misrepresentation,
and whatever policy is adopted will have the overwhelming
support of the organisation at its back. It will be well, also,
to embody such changes as are desirable in the constitution in
your instructions. It is to be hoped that, in the short time
intervening between this and the Convention, you will fully,
wisely, and carefully consider the policy of the future, and the
character, intelligence, and experience of your delegates. . . .

" 'The active operations of the U.S. (United Brotherhood)
have brought about the probable granting of Home Rule. It
is desirable that delegates to the National Convention shall be
fully informed of your desire to follow up these operations on
the same lines, or whether you desire to fall back on the old
work of putting ploughs in. The latter course does not seem
to us fruitful of results or practical. The former policy has
been vindicated by great destruction with little loss to us. It
is for the Convention to decide, however, what the future
policy shall be."

From the official report of the secret Convention which reached me subsequently, I learnt that
the votes in favour of dynamite had been in the
majority, for the policy of the late Executive had

been endorsed, and the new Executive given a free hand for the future. What, however, was perhaps the most important proceeding of all at this Convention of the Revolutionists, was the passing of the following resolution :—

" Resolved :—That we maintain the same relations in the future to open societies, working for the same purpose as ourselves, that we have in the past."

If further proof were wanted beyond that already given of the "understanding" which existed between the open and secret organisations, it could not be supplied in a more emphatic manner than this.

Although the Executive were given full power to act as they thought best, it was apparently considered undesirable to do anything during the latter part of 1886, and so nothing of importance came to pass up to the month of April 1887, when I made another trip to Europe, without, however, any letters or credentials on this occasion. My visit was, nevertheless, not of an uneventful character. I visited the House of Commons more than once, and in the social intercourse which took place between myself and some of the Irish M.P.'s, learnt many facts of an interesting character. It was during this visit that I set myself to find out some particulars regarding

Dr. James G. Fox, M.P. I was rather curious about this gentleman, who now failed to recognise me in the House of Commons lobby, although we had met on more than one occasion at Land League Conventions in the States, where we had been brother delegates. His associations, his position as State Executive for the League in New York, and his well-known National proclivities as evinced during his fifteen years' residence at Troy and elsewhere in the States, all made me anxious to know something of the man in his new position of M.P., and of how his thoughts now inclined.

I learnt casually that he was in the habit of frequenting Gatti's Restaurant in the Adelaide Gallery, Strand, and there I determined to renew my acquaintance with him. The opportunity for doing so was not long wanting, for on an early day I found myself seated at the same table with him, where he was deeply engaged in perusing the *Irish World*. Making this fact an excuse for opening a conversation with him, I asked, in an interested way, if I could obtain copies of the paper he was reading at any place in London. I spoke with a marked American accent, and my appearance did not belie the suggestion I wished to convey as regards my nationality. He replied that he thought not, explaining that he received it regularly from the other side, asking me in conclusion if I was interested in the publication. I replied in the affirmative, and then followed his query as to whether I was not from the United States. To this I made answer by producing my card, whereupon he looked intently at me as he remarked, "Why, I ought to know you; I have met you in conventions. My name is Fox." The information was rather unnecessary as far as I was concerned, but, maintaining a quiet face, I thought for a moment, and in the end confessed to a recollection of him. We were soon on familiar terms, and discussed American matters with great freedom.

There was one fact that I wanted particularly to discover, and that was whether or not Fox was a member of the Clan-na-Gael. I had had no opportunity of learning this at the open conventions at which we had previously met, but yet my view very strongly inclined to the belief that he was. In the course of our conversation, therefore, I took occasion to give him the "hailing sign," but he did not return it, merely remarking significantly that he was not a member of any secret society, a remark which, taken in connection with my sign, tickled me not a little. I never ascertained the truth of the matter, but I remembered the circumstance

IN THE SECRET SERVICE.

when, in June 1888, at the Clan Convention in
Chicago, a burly delegate near me mounted his
chair, announced himself from Troy—where Fox
had lived—and in a loud voice demanded recognition by the chair.   On this being accorded him,
he said, holding up the *Times* pamphlet, "Behind
the Scenes in America," that he held in his
hand a little book which had been sent to him
by a Member of Parliament who was a member
of his camp.   This book was being sold by the
thousand at the price of one penny, and the information it contained could only have been
supplied by a traitor high up in the ranks of
the organisation.   He moved for a committee
to inquire into the matter.   This committee
was appointed, but their inquiry ended in smoke,
the "traitor," as I was termed, having another
narrow escape.

While in England on this trip, the authorities
learned of the presence of General Millen in
Paris, and to Paris I was despatched, in order
to find out if possible what Millen was doing.
I found "le brave Général" of the Clan-na-Gael
very comfortably settled in the *Hôtel des Anglais*
in the Cour de la Reine, accompanied by his wife
and two interesting daughters.   I called upon
him, representing that I had heard of his being
in Paris through the *Herald* office, and was

anxious as an old friend to say "how do you do." I did not, however, gain very much by my visit, for the simple reason that at this time Müllen had not, as far as I believe, any close connection with the dynamite business known as the Jubilee Plot, with which his name was subsequently associated. At this point his business in Europe had to do with the bringing about of a reconciliation between the British and the American branches of the Revolutionary organisation.

The fact was, that for two or three years previously the relations between the two sections of the conspirators had been of a very strained character. Sullivan, finding that the home organisation was not in favour of dynamite, when the campaign was started, had argued that they should not have any more money to spend on organisation and arms, which, for all that was known to the contrary, were simply rusting away in Ireland; and, accordingly, supplies were stopped, and the home Fenians were not notified of the last couple of conventions, with the result that no envoys from Great Britain and Ireland attended. This led to a very bitter feeling in Ireland, and the contention was strongly urged that the conduct of the American Executive was distinctly *ultra vires*. Now, when dissensions raged in America, Sullivan, long-headed as usual, sought to strengthen his section by the allegiance of the home organisation; and accordingly, Millen was despatched to Europe to bring about a more satisfactory condition of affairs. His mission, in this regard at least, was unsuccessful.

As for Millen's connection with the Jubilee explosion, I know very little. The whole undertaking was shrouded in mystery, but it is pretty certain that it was not a Clan-na-Gael affair alone. The best description that could be given of it would be that it was in its inception a Rossa undertaking financed by the Clan-na-Gael. For political reasons the secret organisation could not openly ally themselves with dynamite for the moment, because tactical considerations dictated the giving of a free and untrammelled hand to Mr. Parnell to hoodwink Mr. Gladstone and his supporters. As, however, the circulars I quoted a few pages back showed, dynamite was not by any means thrust aside; so, in order to keep a fair front to the open movement, and yet a satisfactory stand in the eyes of the fiery rank and file, Rossa was temporarily taken into the good graces of the Executive, and some of his adherents despatched with funds from the secret organisation to kick up a row in England. Millen, at the time I saw him, was not in the plot, which at that moment

indeed had not been hatched; but on his return
to America he fell in with the scheme and returned
to Europe to work it out. His bungling, however, led to his being superseded by John J.
Moroney, a tried and trusted friend of Alexander
Sullivan, who was despatched to London with
a large amount of money and distinct orders
to show some value for it. What happened is
a matter of too recent history to need recapitula-
tion here. The introduction of Moroney and
his colleagues to the House of Commons by
Mr. Joseph Nolan, M.P., and the facts associated with the working of the conspiracy, are
of too late a date to be forgotten so soon.[*]

I returned to the States in October, only to
remain a couple of months there, and to come
back again to Europe at the end of the year.
This time my visit was of a purely private character, and the sluggishness of affairs allowed of
my having a complete rest from all sorts of in-
vestigations and interviews. I came to Europe
in connection with a business speculation which
promised highly satisfactory returns, and I was
successful in laying the foundation for a very
encouraging enterprise. Unfortunately for me,
however, I was not to reap the fruits of my
work. As a consequence of my appearance

See Appendix (i.).

in the witness-box, I was prevented from returning to the States at the time when the profits were accruing, and so had to undergo the loss of this as well as many other sources of income.

L.

THE following year—1888—was my last in America, and ere its close I left for the purpose of attending the dying bedside of my father. I left for England in December with the full purpose of returning in a month, but as matters turned out I really left my home for the last time. I had written twice to Mr. Anderson, offering my services in connection with the Special Commission, but nothing had come of my proposal, and I had no idea that anything would happen in connection with the matter. My idea was, as I have explained, that the Government were really prosecuting the Parnellite party, and I could not understand how all the information which I knew them to be possessed of was not appearing. The charges and allegations had made a great stir in America, and the disclosure of the whole working of the Clan-na-Gael in the "Behind the Scenes" articles had created such a sensation as seemed to me to make a full disclosure imperative, so that the American public might have accurate and com-

R

plete data for arriving at a proper conclusion regarding the foul conspiracy existing in their midst.

I must not, however, travel too fast; and so
shall have to go back a little, in order to complete
the story of the Cronin-Sullivan dispute, which, in
a way, came to a conclusion in the year of which
I write. As I have already stated, the history of
the Cronin affair while it lasted was the history
of the Clan-na-Gael for the time being, and thus
in completing my statement of it I shall be bringing the record of revolutionary matters down to the
date at which they and I parted. To return, therefore, to the Cronin matter, which I left at the point
in 1886 where appeals from outside quarters failed
to heal the breach. As a last resort, a conference was arranged in September 1887 between
committees from each organisation, the Sullivan
section and the Cronin section; and a final effort
was made to settle the differences. Cronin was
one of the committee from his section, but he did
not help the settlement. The conference continued up to April 1888, when a basis of union
was arrived at. The rock upon which the dispu-
tants invariably split was the demand made by
the Cronin section for the appointment of a committee to try their charges of misappropriation
against the Executive, and the expulsion of the
Executive from the organisation if found guilty.

In the end, this was conceded; and a united Convention was called in June 1888, which, meeting first in Maddison Street Theatre, was eventually moved to Green Baum, in consequence of the allegation that British detectives had gained admission to the former place of meeting.

Here was pandemonium let loose for eight days, during which the Convention sat morning, noon, and night. I was a member of this assembly, and I never heard such a row in my life. The Sullivanites had it all their own way at first; but the seceders, with Cronin at their head, threatened to "bolt" if they did not get fair play; and they appealed to the patriotism of their countrymen to give them a chance. They were, accordingly, given a representation on all committees, but were always in a minority. Cronin perhaps took as prominent a part in the Convention as any man, and his conduct naturally incurred the enmity, and eventually the vengeance, of his opponents. He and Devoy submitted formal charges of fraud, &c., against Sullivan's executive.* Strong language was used, but Sullivan's friends defended him warmly. Finally a Trial

---

* John Devoy, in the course of a speech delivered at Cheltenham Beach prior to the death of Mr. Parnell, made the following statement as regards the Cronin affair :—

"The men to whom I refer and whom I charge to be in alliance with the men who instigated the murder of Dr. Cronin, are Michael Davitt and John O'Connor, one of the members from Tipperary. (Cheers and cries of

Committee was appointed to try the parties charged. Cronin, strange to say, was a member of this Trial Committee, though he was one of the persons making the charges. There was a terrible scene when his appointment was made known, but the Convention had to put up with him in the end.

All the Trial Committee were sworn by the oath in the ritual to truly and justly try the charges submitted to them. The committee consisted of seven members, and as subsequent events showed, four of them were Sullivan's friends. They met in November 1888. Previous to this, however, Cronin had been playing a very objectionable part. He spoke against the accused whenever occasion offered, wrote to the papers

Hear, hear). I say here that there is a combination between the coterie which brought about the murder of Dr. Cronin and the Davitt clique in Ireland, to oust Mr. Parnell from the leadership and place Michael Davitt in his place. In Michael Davitt's sworn testimony before the Parnell Commission, he said, ' I sought out John Devoy, because I heard he was going to make trouble in the Convention, so that I might learn his plans and frustrate them.' I am glad of that admission from Michael Davitt himself, and for the payment of a thousand dollars given to him for one speech in Ogden's Grove, and the full proceeds of a lecture tour given throughout the United States under the auspices of the Triangle. The Cronin murder was as much a part of the infamous work of this alliance to down Parnell, and to down every man in this country who believes in giving his movements a fair, full, and reasonable trial, as the puffs of Michael Davitt at a thousand a puff."

In corroboration of Devoy's statement, I find in the financial report of the Clan-na-Gael the sum of one thousand dollars charged ; and while Mr. Davitt had for some years disassociated himself from the party of violence, he does not appear to have been averse to receiving a portion of their spoils. Mr. Davitt may plead, as other well-known Irish patriots have done, that he did not know the source from whence this money was derived ; but no man was in a better position to have found out than he, had he so desired.

in accusation of them, and in no way showed
himself the unbiassed person he had sworn
himself to be. Sullivan naturally felt very bitter
over all this, and he fell out with a number of
friends who sided with Cronin in the claim for
full investigation. When the trial came on, it
was found that all the vouchers, papers, and
indeed every evidence of expenditure, had been
destroyed, in accordance with the resolution
which had been adopted at the Boston Convention. This increased the uproar, and after two
weeks of inquiry the majority, consisting of
Sullivan's friends, expressed themselves satisfied
with the statements made by the accused ; while
the minority could only admit the proper expenditure of 33,000 dollars, which left a deficiency of
85,000 dollars, or £17,000. The result of the
trial was that Michael Boland was convicted of
misappropriation ; Sullivan was acquitted, but
censured for the loose way in which the Executive
had done its business, and D. C. Feeley was like-
wise acquitted but censured. The details of this
finding were given me, by the way, by Sullivan.

At the time I left for Europe, the Trial Committee had adjourned, and Cronin was back in
Chicago. The Executive had refused to sustain
the action of the Trial Committee by a majority
of one, and there the affair stood. But Cronin

would not let well enough alone.   He had been
talking very plainly, and denouncing Sullivan right
and left.   I figured in this trial by furnishing Sullivan with affidavits for his defence.   Cronin afterwards charged Sullivan with getting me admitted
into the organisation, and with putting me into a
position of trust.   This did not help matters, and
altogether Cronin proved himself to be a very
dangerous man in the eyes of Sullivan.   Doubtless he possessed much information, the publication
of which would damn Sullivan for ever.   What
followed is a matter of recent inquiry.   Cronin
was foully murdered, and Sullivan, with others,
was charged with participation in the crime.
Sullivan was released, but three men, well-known
members of the Clan, were convicted, and sentenced to penal servitude for life.*   The inquiry
was fruitful in many ways, and brought to light a
vast amount of corroboration of the most important portions of my testimony.   There were,
however, no two more sensational incidents
than those produced by the report issued by
Cronin after the Trial Committee had dissolved,
and the positive proof now supplied for the first
time of the statement frequently made, that Sullivan had in May 1882 received in his position as
chief of the Clan-na-Gael a sum of £20,000 from

* See Appendix (ii.).

Patrick Egan, then Treasurer of the Land League in Paris.

The report issued by Cronin stated amongst other things—

"That the Trial Committee appointed at Chicago was unable to elicit all the facts connected with the charges placed before it, because of the refusal of several of the witnesses to answer many of the questions asked, and because of the inability of others to remember events and figures that might be supposed to be indelibly impressed on their memories. From the evidence presented, I am obliged to report—

"That the family of one who lost his life in the service of this order was scandalously and shamefully neglected, and continued to be neglected for two years after their destitute condition was known, and that Alexander Sullivan, Michael Boland, and D. C. Feeley are responsible and censurable for that neglect.

.   .   .

"That the defendants, Sullivan, Boland, and Feeley, issued a deceptive report to the Boston Convention, leading the order to believe that its affairs had been examined by independent committees, and that the order was $13.000 in debt ; that, in fact, Alexander Sullivan and Michael Boland were on the Committee of Foreign Affairs, and the Treasurer states that there was a balance in the treasury, and not a debt.

"That, prior to the Boston Convention, one hundred and eleven thousand ($111,000) dollars was expended without any direct or indirect benefit to the order, and most of it in a manner that could not in any way have benefited the order, and that the same three defendants are censurable and responsible for this enormous and wasteful expenditure.

.   .   .   .   .

That the $80,491 reported to the district Convention as having been spent in active work was not spent for any such work, no such work having been done or contemplated during the eleven months within which this large amount was drawn from the treasury. The active work done between the Boston and district Conventions was paid for out of the surplus held by the agent of the "Triangle" at the time of the Boston Convention, and not out of the $87,491 drawn from the treasury months after such active work had ceased."

I give these extracts in order to show the reader how matters stood between Sullivan and Cronin on the eve of the latter's murder. Into the details of the £20,000 transaction I need not

enter, beyond stating the fact that banking officials were called to prove by their books that on May 15, 1882, Sullivan cashed, through Monroe and Co. of Paris, two cheques amounting to the sum I name. This, I may state, was about the date when Sullivan, in response to Mr. Parnell's request, crossed to Paris in order to settle the difficulty with the Revolutionary body on the British side. As the following extracts will show, the matter had been one around which a great deal of controversy had raged for many years :—

"The O'Donovan Rossa resents Mr. Patrick Egan's imputation against his character for truth and veracity. The O'Donovan, when in this city a few days ago, intimated to a *Chicago Tribune* reporter that Mr. Patrick Egan, while Parnell, Dillon, Davitt, and other members of the Executive of the Land League were in jail in Ireland, was visited in Paris by Revolutionary Irish patriots from this country, who induced him to give 100,000 dollars of the money contributed to Land League purposes to them for revolutionary purposes, *i.e.*, making war on the British Empire with dynamite and such things. Mr. Egan having seen or heard of O'Donovan's statement, denied that there was a particle of truth in it, and sent the *Tribune* a telegram to that effect from Denver. Now comes O'Donovan with a rejoinder. We have received from him the following telegram :—

"'*Editor of the* "*Tribune.*"

"'Mr. Patrick Egan denies my statement. I say my statements are more worthy of belief than Patrick Egan's. I stated in Chicago that money sent from America to support the no-rent movement in Ireland was followed over by some parties who got 100,000 dollars of it ; that it was not used for any such work in Ireland, and that Patrick Egan knows all about it. I repeat my assertion. Will Patrick Egan meet me in the presence of John Finerty and Denis O'Connor of Chicago, or in the presence of Patrick Ford and Major Horgan of New York, both answering all questions under oath ?

"'O'DONOVAN ROSSA,
"'*Editor* "*United Irishman.*"

"'NEW YORK, *July* 15, 1883.'"

LII.

LONG before these final developments, however, I had sailed for England, and severed for all time my connection with Irish politics in the United States. I had come, as explained, to my father's dying bedside. Unfortunately for me, I was not in time to find him conscious, and did not reach the house where he lay till the day on which he died. When the sad offices connected with his death had been fulfilled, I turned my thoughts again to home, and set about preparing for another voyage to the States. Everything had been completed for my departure, when I suddenly learned from Mr. Anderson that the *Times* had approached him with a view of obtaining a witness regarding the American side of the conspiracy. Before this point was reached, I had chatted over my proposal of going into the witness-box with Mr. Anderson, but he had very frankly told me that he had no intention of giving up such a useful informant of his own initiative; and as he had no connection with the *Times* case, he did not think it likely that any approach would be made to him on the subject.

Matters, however, turned out differently to what he expected, and on the eve of my departure for America I learned that my services might, after all, be utilised, and my desire to drive the truth home given full play. To be effective, however, my coming appearance should be kept a profound secret, and so I appealed to Mr.

Anderson to make such arrangements as would allow of this being the case. As a result, I was informed a little later that the *Times* people had arranged that Mr. Houston should be the person with whom I should deal, and that to him alone should I be known pending my appearance in the witness-box. This was the first mention I had ever heard of Mr. Houston, and it was with no little curiosity I made my way to No. 3 Cork Street in search of the gentleman to whom I bore a single line of introduction. I remember well how, when I was first ushered into his now familiar room by his faithful " Rogers," I gazed suspiciously at the tall youthful figure which met my view. As Mr. Houston took my letter of introduction from me and carelessly opened it, answering my suspicious glance with a slight smile hovering about his face, I could not help the remark, " Sir, you are a much younger man than I was led to believe I would meet." The smile broadened into a laugh as the reply came back, " I am sorry, but I cannot help being young, you know. However, I am Mr. Houston." And so we two people met for the first time.

I informed Mr. Houston that it was always an understood thing on my part that my letters to Mr. Anderson were private property, and that whenever I liked to ask for them they would be at my disposal.   Accordingly I had, on learning that my evidence would be accepted, requested that Mr. Anderson should allow me to go over all my documents and select such as appeared necessary for the corroboration of my statements, as well as for the assisting of my memory.   To this he had assented, excluding any of the papers which he had made official by passing them on at the time of their receipt.   It was then arranged between Mr. Houston and myself that I should get the documents from Mr. Anderson, and go to work at once in the preparation of my evidence.   Much to my disappointment, I learnt there was not time for me to make a last hurried trip home, and that if I was to carry out my intention of testifying I should have to be content with the many losses which would result from my stopping in England. One thing, however, I stipulated for, and that was the bringing over of all my family to England before I appeared in the box.   I was willing to let all my private affairs go to ruin by my non-return ; but I was not prepared to leave my wife and family to bear the brunt of the popular ill-will which would result from what was to follow.

One of the first things I did, therefore, was to cable for my wife and children ; and having eased my mind on this score, I went to work with a will in the preparation of my evidence.   For ten long

working days, Mr. Houston and I waded through
the hundreds of letters and Clan-na-Gael documents I had now at my disposal, he taking notes
as he went along, and I dictating many items
brought to my recollection by the letters I was
perusing. We worked in this way from ten to six
o'clock each day, undisturbed by visitors of any
kind; and when I left him, Mr. Houston, with
the assistance of his clerks, worked far into the
night, copying the circulars, and transcribing the
notes which remained at the end of our day's work.

On Tuesday morning, the 5th of February 1889,
the curtain was rung up, and throwing aside the
mask for ever, I stepped into the witness-box and
came out in my true colours, as an Englishman,
proud of his country, and in no sense ashamed of
his record in her service. On what followed I need
not dwell. While I was under examination, my
old employer, Mr. William Baber of Colchester,
was brought into court by the well-known detective Meiklejohn, in order that he might identify
me. Nothing, of course, came of the incident;
but as I once more saw Mr. Baber, I thought to
myself how little he knew of the part I had
played at his father's death-bed. It was in 1884
that I was hurriedly called one day to see a
patient who was said to be dying. I found him
an old man of eighty, surrounded by his family

and friends. In a few minutes he was dead; and
finding that all round about me were strangers
to the grim monster, I performed the last offices
for the body. As I was so employed, the poor
people related to me their history, and then I
learned to my surprise that the man whose eyes
I was now closing in death was none other than
the father of my former employer at Colchester,
who had emigrated to America some few years
previously.

Great as was the sensation produced by my
strange and weird but true story, it was as
nothing compared to that brought about by the
perfect corroboration afforded by the assassination
of poor Cronin, of whom I have said so much.
Little did I think, when day after day I stood
in the witness-box to tell my tale, and morning
after morning read the scoffing references of
those who believed it not, that in a little while
the blood of a murdered Gael would cry out in
judgment against those of whom I spoke, and
that in the outcome truth would prevail, and
the black foul conspiracy be dragged into the
open light. Yet so it was; and to-day there
are none who question the existence of the
murderous alliance to which I testified, and of
men within its ranks prepared to obey its leaders,
even unto the shedding of blood.

LIII.

I HAVE told my story, and little more remains to
be done. Yet I cannot lay down my pen without
rendering some little tribute to one whose care
and caution on my behalf I can never repay.
I refer to Mr. Anderson. For twenty-one years
I served under this gentleman in the Secret
Service, and no greater honour can I pay him
than to say that during all this time I was never
discovered. Only those who have played my
part can fully appreciate what this means. Not
always careful, not always guarded enough in
the rattle and bustle of my life, there were times
when, had it not been for my chief's watchfulness,
discovery might have overtaken me. But he
never wavered or grew lax in his care. He
proved indeed to me, not the ordinary official
superior, but a kind trusty friend and adviser,
ever watchful in my interests, ever sympathising
with my dangers and difficulties. To him, and
to him alone, was I known as a Secret Service
agent during the whole of the twenty-one years
of which I speak. Therein lay the secret of
my safety. If others less worthy of the trust
than he had been charged with the knowledge
of my identity, then I fear I should not be here

to-day on English soil quietly penning these
lines.

If my identity remained undiscovered, it was
not for want of attempts on the part of colleagues of Mr. Anderson to find it out.   It
was but natural, of course, that those associated
with my chief should seek to penetrate his reserve regarding such a voluminous correspondent
as myself, and to gain, at first hand, possession
of the many important pieces of information
which he alone appeared to be able to supply.
All attempts, however, in this direction, and
they were many, proved fruitless.   So determined was a certain public official at one time
to discover my identity, that having in some
way got hold of my Christian name, Thomas
— I always wrote in the name of Beach to
Mr. Anderson—and assuming it to be my sur-
name, he despatched a detective to Chicago to
discover the man called Thomas in the organisation there.   Of course there was no chance
of getting at me in this way, but, nevertheless, I was warned in time, and left no possible
loophole for discovery.   Imagine, dear reader,
the weakness of such a policy as this, which
would commit the safety of an important informant to the irresponsible knowledge of an
ordinary detective !

When this attempt failed, communications were sought to be opened up with me by the same official through Sir John Rose and Judge M'Micken, with whom I had acted at the time of the Fenian raid of 1870. So strong, indeed, was the pressure brought upon Judge M'Micken, that the old gentleman travelled specially to Chicago to see me on the point. However, I would have none of it. I was quite contented, and too well assured of my safety as I was; and so, much to my own satisfaction, I was left undisturbed in Mr. Anderson's charge.

There was only one thing about which he had frequently to remonstrate with me, and that was my expenditure. Many a lecture did I receive from him on the subject of money spending. It was not, of course, his fault, but rather that of the system. Indeed, so kind and friendly was he that he at times advanced me money for which he himself had to wait for repayment for some time, if indeed he ever got all of it back, which I very much doubt. Of course I could not help spending the money. I tried to be as sparing as possible, and, whenever I could, debited my expenses to those other undertakings which I allied with my Secret Service work. But it was not always possible to pursue such an economic course,

s

and in very many instances where Mr. Anderson could not pay, I had to pay myself. I
occupied a certain position; I had to live up
to that position. The expenditure of money
amongst the Irish patriotic class was an absolute necessity for my purpose, and consequently
I could never put any money by, but rather
lived up to, if not, indeed, at times beyond
every penny of my income.

On this question of Secret Service money I
could say much. The miserable pittance doled
out for the purpose of fighting such an enemy
as the Clan-na-Gael becomes perfectly ludicrous
in the light of such facts as I have quoted in
connection with the monetary side of the Dynamite Campaign. Gallaher, as I have said, had
no less than £1400 on his person when arrested
in 1883; while, coming down to a later date,
Moroney, when despatched from New York in
1887, in connection with the second stage of the
Jubilee explosion plot, carried with him some
£1200. How on earth can the English police
and their assistants in the Secret Service hope to
grapple with such heavily financed plots as this,
on the miserable sums granted by Parliament for
the purpose? There are, I believe, some thirty
men charged with the special duty of circum-
venting political crime in London. All praise

and honour to them for the work they have done, and the sincerest of congratulations to Chief-Inspector Littlechild, who so ably conducted the arrests of all the principals of the latter-day dynamite plots. But these policemen have succeeded more by chance than anything else ; events have played into their hands, and, clever men that they are, they have been sufficiently capable to take advantage of the little that came to their knowledge, and from small clues to work out great things.

Some day, however, a big thing will happen, about which there will be no leakage beforehand, and then the affrighted and indignant British citizen will turn on his faithful band of thirty and rant and rave at them for their want of capacity and performance. The fault will be the want of a perfect system of Secret Service, properly financed. If plots are to be discovered in time —and already there are some whisperings of coming danger—they can only be discovered through information coming from those associated with them. As I have shown, the men engaged in them are very highly paid. If it is to be made worth their while to speak, then the price offered by the British Government must be higher than that of the other paymasters. There is no use in thinking that mere tools like Callan and Harkins—the men now in prison in connection

with the Jubilee Explosion Plot—would be of any
service. These men know nothing. It is the
Millens and the Moroneys of the conspiracy who
should be in Government pay, and they have no
mean price. Imagine offering either of these
men a retainer of £20 a month with a very odd
cheque for expenses thrown in! The idea is
ridiculous. I have heard it urged that the
thought of Secret Service is repugnant to the
British heart, wherein are instilled the purest
principles of freedom. The argument has
sounded strange in my ears when I remembered
that London, as somebody has said, is the cess-
pool of Europe, the shelter of the worst ruffians
of every country and clime. America is called
the Land of the Free, but she could give England
points in the working of the Secret Service, for
there there is no stinting of men or money.

LIV.

This, then, is my story ; and in it must be found
the justification, if such be needed, for the part
I have played. I have no apology to make for
my twenty and odd years' work in the Secret
Service. I took up that work from a conscientious motive, and in a conscientious spirit I

pursued it to the end. I have in no sense been an informer, as the phrase is understood. I allied myself with Fenianism in order to defeat it ; I never turned from feelings of greed or gain on the men with whom I at first worked in sympathy. I never had any sympathy with Irish Revolutionists. Quite the opposite. Nor have I been an *agent provocateur.* Although I always voted for politic reasons on the side of the majority, even to the joining in the vote which meant dynamite, on no single occasion was I instrumental in bringing an individual to the commission of crime. True, I had to take many oaths. But what of that? By the taking of them I have saved many lives. Which counts the weightiest in the balance of life ? And who is it that sneers at me for my conduct in this regard ? An honest man's criticism I can accept ; but for the judgment of these double-oathed gentlemen who, having first taken the Fenian oath, then rushed to Westminster to swear allegiance to the Crown and Constitution they had aforetime sworn to destroy, I have nothing but contempt and derision. Away with such rubbish and cant as they indulge in to the regions where common-sense finds no place.

I said I have saved lives by my action as a Government agent. I hope I shall have done

more by my appearance in the witness-box. To
me no more satisfactory result could attend my
disclosures than the realisation by the poor deluded
Irish in the States of the way in which they have
been tricked and humbugged in the past years.
For these poor weak people, animated by the
purest, if the most mistaken of patriotic motives,
who give their little all in the hope and trust that
the day will come in their lives when Ireland will
be a land flowing with milk and honey, I have
the deepest and the most sincere sympathy. To
know these people, to come into contact with
them, and to discuss with them the eternal subject of Irish nationality, is to respect their honesty
of purpose, no matter how much we feel called
upon to condemn their methods of procedure.
But, for the blatant loud-voiced agitator, always
bellowing forth his patriotic principles, while
secretly filling his pockets with the bribe or the
consequences of his theft, there can be no other
feeling but that of undisguised loathing.

I speak of what I know from personal experience, when I say there is no greater fraud in this
nineteenth century of ours than the modern Irish
patriotic agitator in America. Gold is his god,
his patriotic principles—save the mark !—his bre-
viary and his beads, holding aloft which he stands
at the corner of the market-place so that he may

be seen of all men, and paid tribute to by some. By jobbery, trickery, treachery, and delusion of the meanest and most despicable type he works his way along, rising higher and higher in the ranks of his fellow-conspirators, till at last, in the position of responsibility and power, he sells the votes he can command, and pockets the funds over which he has control. Brave and blustering in speech, he advocates, in the safety of his American city, three thousand miles from the seat of danger, the most desperate of enterprises; and without the slightest pang of compunction or twinge of conscience he rushes his poor dupes across the water to their fate on the scaffold or the living death of penal servitude; while his lips unctuously mumble of the righteousness of their beloved cause, and his whisky-laden breath blasphemously calls for the blessings of Heaven upon the foul enterprise.

It has been in fighting such scoundrels as these that I have spent the last quarter of a century. From them I would fain deliver their poor dupes ere I completely efface myself from Irish affairs. I have no stronger, no sincerer wish than to see an end put once for all to the delusion which is practised upon thousands of poor Irishmen throughout the States by the men of whom I have written. With the rank and file it has assuredly been a case

of "theirs not to reason why, theirs but to do
and die." I hope it may not be so in the future.
I trust that what I have penned, and what the sad
murder of Cronin has writ large upon the page
of history, may not be without its effect; and that
to-day men may pause ere they continue in such
a way as I have pictured, the mere tools of an
unscrupulous faction, the miserable dupes of a
reckless and improvident executive. Gallahers,
Dalys, and Mackay Lomasneys there always
will be—men inspired with fanatical hatred of
all things English, and ready at all times to risk
freedom and life in working out their designs;
but, apart from them, there are thousands whose
criminality reaches no further point than the
paying of those subscriptions so frequently and
so persistently demanded.

With such men I hope these words of mine
will have weight; and if, awakening to a true
sense of their situation, and realising that their
combination and support help not Ireland but
Ireland's professional mendicants, they turn to a
better path, and a clearer and more honest view
of Irish matters as they really are, then shall I
feel that I have not struggled or written in vain.

APPENDIX.

I.

THE STORY OF THE JUBILEE PLOT.

FULLY two months before the celebration of the Queen's Jubilee in London, reliable intelligence reached the Scotland Yard authorities that a gang of skilful and unscrupulous conspirators in America were devising a plan for carrying out acts of murder and destruction in London. The names of the principal persons engaged for this purpose were known to the police, and the individuals were closely watched even during their voyage across the Atlantic. The headquarters of the organisation were established in Paris, and both there and in Boulogne their movements were under strict observation. The direction of the conspiracy rested with General Millen, a well-known Fenian agent, who, finding the police espionage unbearable, had latterly kept out of England. Had he returned, he would have been immediately arrested. Last Saturday he left Amsterdam for New York, being watched by English detectives down to the time of the vessel sailing. After the Jubilee celebration, some of the gang crossed the Channel and came to London, their plans previous to the Jubilee celebration having been disconcerted. The most prominent of the arrivals in London was the man Melville, said to be the shrewdest of the whole gang. The police do not believe that those conspirators were in communication with O'Donovan Rossa, or acting with his cognisance. Cohen's presence in London was known to the police some time prior to his death. There was only one of the gang of whose presence they were not aware. Strangely enough, the police were on their way to arrest the deceased [Cohen] at the moment of his death, and had they been twenty minutes earlier they would have captured the unknown individual who left the death chamber just previously.

The man Melville came to London as an agent of Millen, and took modest lodgings in Gladstone Street, but at the time was deficient in funds. The police, however, watched him closely, and found that on two occasions he called on Mr. Joseph Nolan, M.P., at the House of Commons. He had for his companion the man Harkins, and both of them were seen in company with the dead man Cohen, upon whom an inquest was held yesterday [26th October 1887]. The police suspicions of Melville's business were confirmed. His assertion, that he represented Mr. Philips, of Philadelphia, proved entirely false. Afterwards Melville went to Paris, and there met a man named Dennehy, who, with a man named Maloney, sailed for America on August 17. Dennehy is a member of the Clan-na-Gael, and his address is known to the police. Melville then returned to London and stayed at the Hotel Métropole with a Miss Kennedy, of 53 Charles Street, Boston, with whom he travelled through Ireland, and afterwards to Paris, where he called upon General Millen at the Hôtel du Palais, and was also seen in a cab with a man remarkably like the deceased man Cohen, who was absent from his lodgings about five weeks ago. He sailed for America from Havre on September 17, and on reaching New York, his companion, Miss Kennedy, was arrested for smuggling a large quantity of valuable goods. Melville's hurried departure upset the plans of the Clan-na-Gael, and closely following this Cohen died. Harkins admitted yesterday that he called at the House of Commons with Melville, and that he had written for money to Burchall. Melville's address in America is known to the police—viz., Mr. J. J. Moroney, 925 Tenth Avenue, New York.—*Daily Press*, 28th October 1887.

THOMAS CALLAN, 46, labourer, and Michael Harkins, 30, grocer, were placed upon their trial at the Central Criminal Court, London, on February 1, 1888, upon an indictment of various counts, charging them with maliciously conspiring with Joseph Melville and Joseph Cohen, and other persons, to cause, by an explosive substance, an explosion in the United Kingdom of a nature likely to endanger life, and to cause serious injury to property, and with having in their possession and under their control an explosive substance with intent by means thereof to endanger life and cause serious injury to property within the United Kingdom, and with having in their possession and under their control an explosive substance in such circumstances as to give rise to a reasonable suspicion that they did not have it in their possession and under their control for a lawful object.

The prisoners were found guilty, and each sentenced to fifteen years' penal servitude.

The SELECT COMMITTEE appointed to consider the regulations applicable to the admission of strangers to the HOUSE OF COMMONS met again on Thursday, the 19th inst., Viscount EBRINGTON presiding.

Mr. JAMES MONRO, Assistant Commissioner of the Metropolitan Police, examined by the Chairman, said:—Melville's real name is Moroney, of Philadelphia, New York, and a member of the Clan-na-Gael. He was sent over here in pursuance of instructions, and for the purpose of committing an outrage in the Jubilee week. He came over with Callan and Harkins in the steamer *City of Chester*. They did not arrive in England until June 21. They had missed the previous steamer, all the berths being engaged, and they did not arrive until the Monday. They came at once here, only to find that General F. F. Millen had been rendered powerless by the operations of the police. Melville was the man who was chief in giving them dynamite, in enabling them to get it in here.

and in giving them instructions how to dispose of it. The dynamite was brought over by other persons to Melville—two men, and also a person of the name of Callan, and another man, I believe. The other man we have not been able to get hold of. But Melville and this fifth man arrived on May 15; so that when Melville and his associates came on June 5, Callan was here to meet them.

The House of Commons was one point in these dynamite operations. One of these men was sent down on two occasions to Windsor Castle to " prospect" the State apartments, taking with him a watch for the purpose of finding out how long it would take him to effect his purpose and get away. On both occasions the State apartments were closed. He did not go back again, because I suppose he thought he would be identified. General Millen was a man known twenty years ago in Fenian matters. He was connected with the Fenians in 1867. He was what was called a military member of the Clan-na-Gael, and he was sent over to this country on a secret mission in 1879. He reported his progress to his associates under the name of Robinson.

He was in communication with Melville. That is to say, he met Melville on one occasion in Paris, not in this country. He met Melville in Paris in September 1887. Melville was sent over. He left in April and arrived in France about the end of April. He was in England before that. He left this country in January 1887, and went to America. He left America and arrived in this country in April. I forget the exact date.

General Millen had no home in England, but he had relatives—his daughters, living in London for a certain time. On August 4, Melville and Harkins came to the House of Commons, and sent up their cards, or rather, Mr. Melville sent up his card to Mr. Joseph Nolan. Mr. Nolan came out to them and saw them in the central lobby. After a little conversation they went away. On the 5th of August the visit was repeated by the same two men. They sent up their card to Mr.

Joseph Nolan. Mr. Nolan came out and disappeared with them ; by that I mean the police did not follow them. He took them, it is believed, to the gallery. Now it is known that he did so, as the entry in the Strangers' Gallery book shows. They were not seen to leave that night by the ordinary entrance. They were for some time on the terrace.

They must have gone down with a member ?—They were accompanied by Mr. Joseph Nolan.

About how long did they remain ?—About twenty minutes or half an hour, as far as I can remember. They were under observation by my men ; they were seen by the House of Commons police. They were under observation outside.

At that time were you aware of any business in which they were engaged in this country ?—We had not identified Harkins at that time, but I knew Melville was a dangerous character. On his visit here my information was that he might be looked for in the House of Commons. That information was received in connection with his relation with Millen. He was met in Paris afterwards, and Melville was actually in Paris in the month of July, but I am not prepared to say he met Millen then, but they were connected. There was another man in Paris in regard to whose movements I was apprised in connection with Millen's relations in Ireland ; and it is also a fact that General Millen was in communication with Mr. Joseph Nolan by means of letters conveyed by Millen's daughters, who were then in London and under observation. One of these letters so conveyed was a letter of introduction to Melville.

Was that prior to the visit to the House of Commons?— That was prior to the visit; that was on the 14th of July, on which date Millen's daughters visited the House of Commons. They saw Mr. Joseph Nolan and repeated the visit on the 15th. Millen is their real name. They had been living here for some time before that.

THE HOME SECRETARY.—Did they visit the House on that occasion, or did they remain in the central hall?—Witness: On the first occasion they were taken by Mr. J. Nolan to the

Ladies' Gallery, and on the second occasion they were taken by Mr. Nolan to the bar of the House of Lords, and after they left they were accompanied by Mr. Nolan some little up the street on both days.

They did not go over the House of Commons?—I cannot say they did. They then left for Paris, where Millen then was, and, as I said before, on the 4th of August Melville then appeared.

Did you follow up this matter by any inquiries of Melville himself?—Melville was traced to his lodgings, and on the 8th of August he was interviewed. After Melville's interview we interviewed Mr. Joseph Nolan on the 16th of August. He was asked whether Melville had visited him and whether he knew him. Mr. Nolan said Melville was a stranger to him, that he had brought no letter of introduction, that he had mentioned the names of several gentlemen known to him (Mr. Nolan) in America, among them a gentleman named Stack, who had been successful in life and was over in England on a trip ; that he (Stack) seemed to be well acquainted with the oil wells and silver mines in the Rocky mountains, that he seemed to be a man well read in history, and altogether was a rather well-informed man; that he had come with this letter of introduction, and that he (Nolan) treated him with the same civility that he would expect in America. We made inquiries, and we came in the Strangers' Gallery book, upon an entry which we believed to be in Mr. Nolan's handwriting. We had the handwriting submitted to an expert, and he said it was the same as that on a remittance sent by Mr. Nolan. We had no doubt on the subject, because when Mr. Nolan was examined he said it was in his handwriting. We made inquiry of Mr. Stack, and had him interviewed on the 26th of January this year. He said he did not remember anything in connection with the registry in the book at the gallery in the House of Commons, and did not remember anything about the man Melville. The writing in the book appeared, he said, to be his own, but he was certain he never gave an order to Mr. Joseph Nolan, M.P.

and Mr. Nolan knew nothing about his signature. It was an understood thing among the Irish party that everything possible was to be done for Americans who might wish to see the House of Commons, and the consequence was that there was scarcely a day passed without application being made for admission to the House by Americans. This matter would stop that kind of thing. If the Irish members were aware of it they would shun an American as they would poison, and it would be detrimental to the party generally.

By Mr. FORREST FULTON.—One of the letters conveyed by the daughter of General Millen to Mr. Joseph Nolan, who was in communication with General Millen, was a letter of introduction of Melville to Mr. Nolan. Millen introduced Melville as a friend.

Is there any statement at all as to what Melville was doing in this country?—No, not so far as I am aware.

THE CHAIRMAN.—I think you spoke of letters passing?—Yes, more than one. This was one of the letters conveyed to Mr. Nolan from General Millen by his daughters.

And these letters passed on various occasions?—Yes, they passed on more than one occasion.

By Mr. FULTON.—Mr. Nolan said he knew nothing at all about Melville, and had not received any letter from him?—Yes.

MR. FULTON.—You say you know where the daughters of General Millen reside. Do you know that they were visited by Mr. Nolan at any time?—Not at the period referred to, so far as I know.

On other occasions?—On a previous occasion they were.

When was that?—In January of the previous year; but I had not commenced observations then.

The Committee adjourned till three o'clock in order to give MR. JOSEPH NOLAN, M.P., an opportunity of replying to the evidence of Mr. Monro.

THE CHAIRMAN communicated to Mr. Nolan the statements made by Mr. Monro. Mr. Nolan said he had no wish to go back upon the evidence he had given in Court in connection with the dynamite trial. He had received no introduction of any one from General Millen.

You visited the House with two daughters of General Millen on the 14th or 15th of July, and showed them over the House, and that one of them gave you a letter from her father introducing a man who would come subsequently—a man named Melville. Is it true that the two daughters of General Millen were there on the 14th or 15th of July, and were shown over the House by you?—It is true that I showed two ladies named Millen over the House.

The daughters of General Millen?—I do not know about that.

Were they strangers to you at that time?—One of them was.

One of them you did know?—Yes.

She was the daughter of General Millen?—That I do not know.

Did you meet her in London?—I met her in London, I think, in 1886. She has been living in London.

Did you know General Millen?—I know him by repute.

As what?—As an officer in the Mexican Army, and as correspondent of the *New York Herald*.

Have you ever met him?—Yes.

When?—In 1886.

In England or abroad?—In England.

Was he a stranger to you then?—He was.

Where did you meet him ; at a private house?—He called upon me at my own house.

Was that the only occasion on which you ever saw him?—Yes.

Mr. Lawson.—Called upon you doubtless as many Americans do?—Yes.

The Chairman.—Is it true that the ladies brought a letter of introduction about Melville? It is not true.

Or a letter of any kind?—No.

The statement was a letter written by the General?—No; not that I remember; in fact there was no necessity for it, because one of the ladies knew me.

It is said they brought a letter to you at the House introducing Melville to you on a future occasion?—That is not so. One of the ladies said she had not seen her father for years, and she believed he was ill at the time in Europe, and that she intended to call upon him.

Have you had any communication with him?—No.

THE HOME SECRETARY.—Are you aware that Melville and Millen had met each other?—No, and I may say that I had never heard that General Millen had any connection whatever with what is known as the dynamite party. It has been stated, I believe, that he has, but I never heard it previous to the recent case. On the contrary, I heard that General Millen as an Irish officer was clearly opposed to the policy of that party.

THE HOME SECRETARY.—That has nothing to do with it. Did Melville come from America; he had been in London for some months?—I did not know that.

Did Melville speak about Millen?—No.

Were you aware that they were acquainted?—No. I knew a number of Irish Americans who have visited me at the House. They asked for admission, and I have been told that he was among the number. I remember that a policeman or gentleman who said that he belonged to the detective force called upon me in the House, and made inquiry about some one or two men who had visited the House. I told them all I knew at the time.

MR. LAWSON.—It is said you did not acknowledge the handwriting on the Speaker's Gallery ticket as yours, and you said it was not your handwriting?—I simply said I could not swear to the writing as being mine.

THE HOME SECRETARY.—Have you any doubt about it?—I rather think it was I who wrote it, but I could not positively swear.—*The Times*, 20 April 1888.

T

THE STORY OF THE CRONIN MURDER.

The Cronin murder trial ended yesterday, after prolonged deliberation on the part of the jury, in the conviction of four of the five prisoners arraigned. By the laws of the State of Illinois the jury not only decide the issues of guilty or not guilty, but also award the punishment of the convicts. To this fact is probably due the long delay in the present case in the announcement of the verdict. The jury have acquitted John F. Beggs. They have awarded imprisonment for life to Daniel Coughlin, Martin Burke, and Patrick O'Sullivan, whom they convict of murder ; and imprisonment for three years to John Kunze, whose offence is reduced to manslaughter, and whose part in the crime was shown to be of a very minor kind.* Now that the case is over, it seems desirable to state in a connected form the theory upon which this remarkable trial was instituted by the State of Illinois.

The prisoners, Daniel Coughlin, Martin Burke, John F. Beggs, Patrick O'Sullivan, and John Kunze, were indicted for the murder of Dr. Patrick Henry Cronin, on May 4, 1889. The case naturally created intense excitement throughout the State, affecting as it did many and complex interests of party, race, and creed. Committees were formed and funds were raised for the prosecution and for the defence, and the prisoners were convicted and acquitted on the platform and in the Press, with that reckless disregard of common decency which dis-

---

* The Coroner's jury brought in a verdict of " wilful murder " against Alex. Sullivan, and he was formally arrested, but subsequently released, for want of sufficient evidence against him

graces the partisan warfare of America. American judicial proceedings are, however, framed to work in a society which habitually indulges itself in debauches of partisan fury, even while prisoners stand at trial for their lives, and accordingly the most elaborate safeguards are employed to secure the impartiality of the jury. The State and the prisoners exercise the right of challenge both peremptorily and for cause, in a degree undreamt of in this country. Each juror, before he is sworn to try the issues, is subjected to the most merciless examination and cross-examination by counsel for the State and for the prisoners, and challenges "for cause" are allowed on grounds which in English eyes appear ludicrously trivial. The prisoners in the Cronin case were, by law, entitled to twenty peremptory challenges apiece, or, as they combined their challenges, to one hundred peremptory challenges in all, and the State was also entitled to one hundred peremptory challenges. The work of impanelling the jury began on August 30, and ended on October 22. Seven full working weeks were spent in this preliminary labour. No fewer than 1115 unfortunate citizens of Cook County were exposed to the rigid scrutiny of counsel for the State and counsel for the defence. Of these, 927 were "excused," to use the American euphemism, for cause, while 78 were peremptorily challenged by the State, and 97 were similarly challenged by the defence. Thus the State had 22 challenges unexhausted, and the defence only three when the tale was completed. At last, on October 24, the State's Attorney "got down to trial" and made his opening speech. The case relied upon and proved by the State depended on the following assertions and inferences.

Dr. Cronin was summoned from his home at half-past seven on the evening of May 4, and never returned. On May 22 his naked body, bearing marks of violence, was found in the catch-basin of a sewer. The theory of the prosecution was that he was murdered in pursuance of a conspiracy, and that the accused, together with other persons not in custody, were members of that conspiracy. The jury by their verdict have declared that Dr. Cronin was so murdered, and that all the prisoners save Beggs did conspire to murder him. This conspiracy arose from a bitter quarrel within the ranks of the United Brotherhood, or Clan-na-Gael. The history of that organisation was sketched by State's Attorney Longenecker in his opening speech. It was founded in 1869, to " free " Ireland by open warfare. Irishmen joined it from " patriotism," Irishmen joined it for the purposes of American political warfare, and others " for the sake of the money that was in it." The organisation grew " until now it stretches from ocean to ocean in our land." It was organised by districts, each with its District Member and District " Camps." Each " Camp " had a public name, by which alone it was known to the general public. Thus, " Camp 20," to which several of the prisoners belonged, was called the " Columbia Club," and other " Camps " were known as " Literary Clubs," and so on. Prior to 1881 the organisation was governed by an Executive Body, which was composed of the District Members. In 1879 this Board consisted of fifteen members.

In 1881 a National Convention of the United Brotherhood was held in Chicago. At that Convention the Executive Body was reduced to five members, and Alexander Sullivan, Feeley, and Boland were appointed thereon. These three men constituted a majority of the new Board, and, in the State's Attorney's phrase, " took charge " of it. " They then adopted," he says, " what is called the dynamite policy. They called it ' active work.' They adopted a policy to blow up property and individuals, and that policy was adopted immediately after they got possession of the Executive Board of the organisation." Moreover, this new Executive Body inserted a provision in the oath of the organisation binding all members to obey the Executive Body without question. " If they directed a man to go and kill another man in England it had to be done, and they had no right to question the order." In 1884 this controlling Board adopted the symbol of the Triangle, and issued orders under that designation. The whole object of this Junta was to steal the funds of the organisation, and the State's Attorney roundly accuses them of endeavouring to effect this object by acts of well-nigh incredible infamy. They pretended to their organisation that great sums were being expended upon "active work." To lend colour to this fiction they procured a certain amount of such work to be done. They sent emissaries to this country. But they failed to provide them with the funds indispensable for their personal safety. The men were referred to an agent of the organisation in England, and when they had reached this side of the Atlantic precautions were taken that they should not too speedily return. When the dynamite emissary landed in the United Kingdom, "I say to you," says the State's Attorney, "that somebody there made known who the man was, and what he was detailed to do, and he was immediately arrested and thrown into prison. To-day the prison doors in England are locked against twenty or more men who were sent there by that Board."

The next trick of the Triangle, to hide their embezzlement of the funds, was to circulate a rumour that English detectives were watching the Order, and to get the biennial Convention postponed upon that plea. A meeting was held of the friends of the Triangle, "and they destroyed every vestige of work they had done. They destroyed their books, and then sent out a circular showing that the Order was indebted to them $13,000, notwithstanding when they took hold of it they had a fund of $250,000 in the treasury." Naturally these proceedings led to great dissension in the Order, and finally to a split in its ranks. To the quarrel that thus arose, Dr. Cronin, on the theory advanced by the prosecution, and accepted by the jury, owed his death. Cronin from the first protested against the action of the Triangle. In 1885 he was tried for treason to the Order. Alexander Sullivan prosecuted, and the convict Daniel Coughlin sat on the Trial Committee. Cronin was convicted and expelled. Thereupon Cronin joined a new organisation formed by the seceding members of the Order, and no further steps were taken until June 1888. In that month a joint convention of the two factions was held in Chicago with a view to reunion. At that convention Cronin charged the old Triangle, which had then ceased to exist, with misappropriation of the funds of the Order, and with misconduct towards their emissaries to Europe. It was resolved that the charges should be investigated, and a Trial Committee of six, three from each faction, was appointed to try Sullivan, Feeley, and Boland. Of that Trial Committee, Cronin was a member. A memorandum in Cronin's handwriting, containing the joint findings of Cronin himself, and one P. M'Cahey, as members of the Trial Committee, and also minutes of the evidence adduced at such trial, were found amongst Cronin's papers, and proved at the coroner's inquest. These documents were, of course, inadmissible at the actual trial, according to a well-known technical rule of evidence, but, as they undoubtedly guided the State's Attorney and his associates in framing the case against the prisoners, and as, moreover, they possess a very special and personal interest for Englishmen, we do not feel constrained to ignore their contents here.

The Trial Committee, it appears, met at Genesee House, Buffalo, on August 20, 1888. Alexander Sullivan objected that "one of the committee was a malignant enemy of his," and he named Cronin as that enemy. Feeley and Boland joined in Sullivan's objection, but Cronin denied that he had any personal enmity to Sullivan and the objection was overruled. Boland then charged the notorious John Devoy, who was a friend of Cronin's, and attended the Trial Committee, presumably in his interest, with being a British spy. Cronin defended Devoy, the committee settled down to work, and the trial proceeded. The minutes of the evidence taken by this committee, and found in Cronin's own handwriting, form one of the most startling documents ever produced in any Court. Four principal witnesses were examined in support of the charges made against the Triangle of neglecting to supply the emissaries actually engaged in dynamiting with funds, and of neglecting the families of those emissaries who had perished by explosions, or had been sent to penal servitude in this country. The first witness was himself one of the London dynamiters. The last was the widow of Mackey Lomasney, who was blown up while attempting to destroy London Bridge. The names of the male witnesses are not given. The first witness swore that after the Boston Convention of 1884, one Donovan, "who acted as agent for the body," and "was then in the employ of General Kerwin," asked him if "he could furnish enough men to accomplish a certain amount of active work." The witness procured one recruit. Donovan and John J. Moroney paid their steerage passage, and gave them $100 each "to carry on work." For further funds they were referred to "the agent on the other side." The two dynamiters crossed to this country, but the funds were not forthcoming. The agent, it is satisfactory to learn, "was sure he had been betrayed by some one," and it is yet more gratifying to know that he "is now in prison." The witness then gives the following account of his exploits in this country, and of the base ingratitude of his employers :—

"At the agent's request, work was delayed six weeks. I at last told him I would do the work. There were four of us. . . . . I finally induced him to give orders to do the work. This was on Thursday. On Saturday we did it. After the work was done I met him the same evening. He remained in capital city seven days afterward. I was so reduced for funds that I prevailed upon him to give me four pounds of the sixteen he had left. On landing in this country had three-and-one-half pounds. . . . . I at once complained to Donovan and Moroney, and through them to the executive, or General Kerwin, of the treatment I had received, and the culpable neglect of the F. C. About the last of February 1885, Donovan furnished me with $10 with which to reach my home.

"*Q.* How many operations did you perform ?—*A.* Three. We always bade each other good-bye after each meeting, thinking it might be our last meeting on earth. I have learned that, in order to get back, the other man who went over with me had to sell his clothes to get passage-money. He came with a sprained ankle. In July or August 1885, he received $7 from Moroney."

Subsequently the witness found that the mother of Cunningham, the dynamiter, was in want. He complained to Moroney and General Kerwin, whereupon Kerwin told him he ought to be expelled. The munificent sum of $100 was finally sent by the "F. C." (Executive Body) to the mother of their dupe Cunningham, now undergoing in this country the just but awful punishment of penal servitude for life. The witness further ascertained that Mrs. Mackey Lomasney, the widow of Captain Mackey Lomasney, who "was killed in London, and was assured, witness was told, that his family would never want," was in great distress. The relatives of Dr. Gallagher, another dynamite convict under a lifelong sentence, were also in want. A hundred dollars was raised for Mrs. Gallagher. Then comes this terrible statement, a statement which should warn the miserable tools of the Clan-na-Gael what kind of succour they may look for from their chiefs when their "heroism" lands them in the dock. "I requested," says this same witness, "that the men on trial on the other side should be defended. General Kerwin said that friendless men were better off in such cases." To the men who have risked their lives at its bidding, the Order, with its ample revenues, grudges the few pounds needed for their legal defence, and coldly abandons them "friendless" to their fate.

The next witness confirms the above statements as to the conduct of the organisation towards Mrs. Cunningham. In July 1885, he succeeded John Moroney as D. M. (District Member), and in October of that year he "went out as an organiser of the National League in the West." "I saw General Kerwin and told him that he should send money to Mrs. Cunningham, that the lady was hurt on the subject of being neglected by us. He said he would send it."

The cross-examination of this witness was directed to show that he entertained animus against Kerwin and Boland for

endeavouring to defeat his candidature for the presidency of
the National League, which candidature, he alleges, had been
officially adopted by the Clan-na-Gael. " The slate," he says,
" was Baldwin, Minton, and Carroll for F. C. (Executive Body),
and myself as President of the League." Boland asked him
why he would not take the secretaryship.

The third witness, "a member since the beginning of the
old organisation," knew Mackey Lomasney, and remembers
his departure for Europe in August 1884, with his brother Jim,
and a third conspirator. The witness describes his efforts to
obtain relief from the organisation for Mackey Lomasney's
widow. In 1885 he went to Newhaven and saw Dr. Wallace
(who was then " D."), Condon, and Boland. Boland "denied
all responsibility," and alleged that Mrs. Mackey Lomasney
had been supplied with plenty of money. The witness called
on Carroll. " He professed utter ignorance of the whole
affair. I said, ' By God, you must see her.' Carroll offered the
witness $100, which he refused. I said, ' You know how to
send this, as you have the others ; if you respect the memory
of the dead, and the widow and the orphan made so by your
act, do your duty by all." The witness further states that Mrs.
Mackey Lomasney continued to be in a poverty-stricken state,
without coal or clothing, until August 1886.

The last witness was Mrs. Susan Mackey Lomasney herself.
Upon Alexander Sullivan's request, made presumably to show
his reliance on the bare word of a dynamiter's wife, she was
not sworn. Mrs. Mackey Lomasney stated that her husband
went away in August 1884, and that since that date she had
received $1000 from the organisation. She called on
Alexander Sullivan in 1885, but did not ask for help. In
August 1886, she again visited Sullivan, explained to him the
state of her affairs, and asked for help. " He asked me for a
schedule of my liabilities—$200. He would attend to the
matter. He gave me no money, nor offered me any." Sullivan
told the witness not to mention his name to any one. She then
called on " James Q.," who "talked to her about Father Dorney."

but gave her no help. The witness was so poor at this time that she borrowed a dress to visit Sullivan. Several weeks after the witness again called on Sullivan and applied for a loan of $100, which she obtained. That was all she ever got from Sullivan. In cross-examination Mrs. Mackey Lomasney admitted that her husband wrote to her from Europe, saying he had received money from Mr. Sullivan. The witness did not know the amount.

"Here," say the minutes, "Mr. S. admitted that (Mackey) Lomasney was sent by the organisation."

The Trial Committee was divided in opinion as to the guilt or innocence of the accused. Four members were for an acquittal. Two, Cronin and M'Cahey, were for a conviction on the principal charges, and, in particular, on the charges of " scandalous and shameful neglect " of " the family of one who lost his life in the service of this Order," and on that of issuing a fraudulent financial report and squandering the funds.

Dr. Cronin's documents illustrate many interesting points. Amongst other things they prove that he, his friends Devoy and M'Cahey and their faction, are to the full as wicked scoundrels as Sullivan, Feeley, Boland, and the party of the Triangle. The minority report does not condemn the Triangle for dynamiting, but for dishonest dynamiting. It does not reprobate the despatch of miscreants like Mackey Lomasney to work slaughter and destruction in the heart of a great city, but the subsequent neglect of the Order to keep faith with their emissary, by providing for his widow. It acquits the Triangle of wilfully omitting to supply the actual authors of the dynamite explosion with funds to fly from the law, but it severely censures their " agent " for the omission. Both wings of the Clan-na-Gael were engaged in the same devilish plots, and while every one must rejoice that the assassins even of a dynamiter should meet their lawful doom, Cronin merits no more sympathy as an individual than " Captain Mackey " himself. He was brutally murdered, while himself engaged in plotting the wholesale murder of others.

On the theory of the State's Attorney, now endorsed by the verdict of the American jury, it was Cronin's persistent efforts to have the evidence taken by the Trial Committee published with the report, that sealed his doom. That committee, as has been seen, sat in August 1888. The report did not appear while Cronin lived. But on the day of his murder the Executive Body of the Clan-na-Gael met, and on the next day, or the next day but one, the report was published to the Order. The evidence was not then issued with the report, but a protest from Alexander Sullivan was annexed thereto, in which he charged Cronin as a perjurer, and a traitor to the Irish cause. All the prisoners except Kunze were members of the Clan-na-Gael. All those members belonged to the same "Camp" of the Order, known in the ranks of the Order as "Camp 20," and in public as the "Columbia Club." The prisoner, John F. Beggs, was "Senior Guardian" of the "Camp," and an intimate friend of Alexander Sullivan's. On February 8, 1889, the "Camp" met, with Beggs in the chair, and from that meeting the prosecution dates the conspiracy to murder Cronin. A member got up and said that they should investigate the affairs of the Triangle, these men who had robbed them of their funds. The prisoner Coughlin and others demanded the speaker's authority for this statement. He replied that he had heard part of the report of the Trial Committee appointed to try the Triangle read in another "Camp." That other "Camp" was Dr. Cronin's. The State alleged that Beggs made a violent speech and declared that he would not have these attacks made upon the Triangle, and that it had to be stopped if it took blood. Coughlin at once moved that a secret committee of three be appointed to investigate. The motion was carried, and the prisoner Beggs, as Senior Guardian, was directed to nominate the committee. All the accused except O'Sullivan and Kunze attended this meeting of "Camp 20." Two days later Beggs wrote to his superior officer, a man named Spellman, and informed him that "it was charged that the S. G. of the Columbia Club at a

recent meeting read to the assembled members the proceedings of the Trial Committee." On February 17, Spellman
disclaimed any jurisdiction "to inflict the penalty" in the
case. On February 18, Beggs replied that the matter had to
be investigated or there would be trouble. The State's
Attorney argued that this secret committee of three was in fact
appointed to try, and did try, the murdered man, and that
Spellman's disclaimer of jurisdiction to inflict "the penalty"
proves that Cronin had been convicted and already stood for
sentence at the bar of the Order.

On February 19, a man giving the name of Simonds, who is
not in custody, took rooms at 117 Clark Street, Chicago,
immediately opposite to Dr. Cronin's office. On the same
day he bought some furniture and a carpet. He asked for
goods of the cheapest quality, and stated that he required
them only for temporary use. He also bought from the same
dealers the largest packing trunk they had, a valise, and a
trunk strap. He told the shopman that the first strap supplied
to him was not large enough, and a larger one was procured.
All these articles were put into the rooms at 117 Clark Street.

On March 20, a man, proved to be the convict Martin
Burke, hired Carlson cottage, under the name of "Frank
Williams," for one month from Mr. Carlson, who himself lives
next door. Burke then went to the prisoner P. O'Sullivan,
whose premises immediately adjoin the Carlson cottage, and
told O'Sullivan that he had taken it. Burke and another man
not in custody next removed all the furniture, the trunk, the
valise, and the carpet from 117 Clark Street into the Carlson
cottage. This removal took place on the evening of March 20,
the day Burke took the cottage.

O'Sullivan is an ice man by trade. On March 29, nine days
after the taking of the cottage, O'Sullivan tried to find one
Justice Mahoney, to come and make a contract between him
and Dr. Cronin. O'Sullivan did not find the justice on March
29, but some time in April they went together to Cronin's
office, and a contract was made between O'Sullivan and

Cronin, whereby Cronin agreed to attend to O'Sullivan's workmen. O'Sullivan then gave Cronin some cards and said, "I may be out of town and my card be presented." O'Sullivan's business was not dangerous. No accident had ever occurred amongst his men. Numbers of doctors lived between O'Sullivan's place of business and Dr. Cronin's office, which is nearly an hour's drive from O'Sullivan's yard. "What," the State asked, "was the object of this contract, made after the discussion in ' Camp 20,' and after Beggs had been directed to appoint the secret committee?"

On April 20, Martin Burke, under the *alias* of "Frank Williams," returned to the Carlson cottage and paid a second month's rent in advance. He had never occupied the cottage. He said his sister was in hospital and could not come to housekeeping. The Carlsons grew uneasy about their tenants. They inquired of their neighbour O'Sullivan about these men, who had taken their house but never moved into it. O'Sullivan said, "You will get your rent; it is all right," and told them he knew one of their tenants. Shortly before May 4 the convict Coughlin was heard to declare in a "saloon" or public bar that a certain north-side man, a leading Catholic, or a leading Irishman, would soon bite the ground, or to use words of the like effect.

On the evening of May 3 there was a meeting of "Camp 20." A member asked if the secret committee appointed in February to inquire into the alleged publication of the report of the Triangle Trial Committee in Cronin's "Camp" had itself reported. The State alleged that Beggs, the Senior Guardian, answered, "That committee is to report to me. The 'Camp' has nothing to do with that."

Between eleven and one o'clock on May 4, the convict Coughlin went to Dinan's livery stable and ordered a horse and buggy to be ready about seven that evening "for a friend." Later he telephoned to the convict O'Sullivan to go out. About 7.15 in the evening Coughlin's friend came and asked for the buggy. The ostler harnessed a white horse. The stranger objected to the colour, but the ostler said it was the only horse he could have. The stranger then drove to Dr. Cronin's. He reached Cronin's home about 7.20, gave him one of O'Sullivan's cards, saying, "O'Sullivan is out of town, and here is his card"—the very words used by O'Sullivan himself when he made his contract with Cronin—and told Cronin that one of O'Sullivan's men had his leg crushed, and that the doctor was wanted immediately. The doctor took his instruments and some cotton with him and drove hastily off in the buggy. He was never seen alive again.

The State allege that the convict Burke was at the Carlson cottage on the night of May 3, together with another man, after the meeting of "Camp 20." On the night of May 4 Burke was also there, and he bade good-night to his landlord and neighbour, old Mr. Carlson, at a late hour that evening. A casual passer-by saw a man whose description answers to that of Cronin get out of a buggy and hastily enter Carlson cottage, and she afterwards heard blows and cries. Between eight and nine that night, two men, whose descriptions answer to those of Coughlin and Kunze, were also seen to drive up to Carlson cottage, and Coughlin was seen to enter it.

On the night of May 4-5 a waggon was seen at three different points by policemen and night-watchmen in the neighbourhood of Lake Michigan. There were three men in the waggon, a driver and two others, who, when the waggon was first observed, sat on a large chest which the policemen took to be a tool-chest. At one in the morning of May 5, the watchman at Edgewater challenged these men in the waggon, and asked them what they were doing. They said they were trying to find the lake shore drive. The drive is not continued up to this point, and the watchman gave them some directions, after which they drove away. They were seen later on in the same waggon, but without the chest. The catch-basin in which Dr. Cronin's body was subsequently found is half a mile from Edgewater. On the morning of May 5, a trunk identical in all respects with that purchased by the tenant of 117 Clark Street,

in February, and afterwards removed by Burke to the Carlson
cottage, was found between this catch-basin and the city,
about three-quarters of a mile from the catch-basin. During
the trial Dr. Cronin's clothes were found in a valise in the se. ?r
about a quarter of a mile further on from the point where the
trunk was found. This valise corresponded in all respects
with that bought by Simonds and delivered to him at 117 Clark
Street, and afterwards removed by Burke from Clark Street to
Carlson cottage. It will be remembered that Cronin took
cotton with him to dress the wounds of his expected patient
on the evening of May 4. Cotton was found in the trunk on
May 5. It was smeared with blood, as also were the sides of
trunk.

On May 6 the convict Martin Burke called at a tinsmith's
shop, and asked the smith to solder up a box for him. The
smith wanted to raise the lid to do his work. Martin Burke
told him not to do so, and made him secure the box by
passing a metal band round it and soldering the band. The
smith had read some report as to the disappearance of Dr.
Cronin two days before. While he was soldering the box he
asked Burke what he thought of the matter. Burke replied
with coarse abuse of Cronin, denounced him as a spy, and
declared he would turn up all right.

On May 13, two men called on old Mrs. Carlson, the wife of
the owner of Carlson cottage, and tendered her another
month's rent. She refused the offer, as she said she wished
the cottage to be occupied, and she added that no rent was
due until May 20. Shortly afterwards the Carlsons received a
letter from their tenants saying that they were sorry to give up
the building, and sorry that they had had to paint the floor,
but that that was done for their sister.

On May 20, the date of the expiry of " Williams'" lease of the
cottage, the Carlsons entered the building by the window.
They found the whole of the house in confusion and signs
that a severe struggle had taken place therein. All the Clark
Street furniture was there, but the trunk was gone, the valise

was gone, and the carpet was gone. The walls and the floor were stained with blood. Paint had been hastily daubed over the floor. The arm of the rocking-chair was wrenched off and a key, which afterwards proved to fit the lock of the blood-stained trunk discovered on May 5 near Edgewater, was found under a bureau, stained with some of the paint which had been applied to the floor.

On May 21, the Carlsons reported the state of their cottage to the police, and on May 22 some men engaged in cleaning the sewers found the naked body of Cronin in the catch-basin. Some cotton similar to that taken away by the doctor on the evening of May 4, and similar to that found in the bloody trunk on May 5, was also found with the body in the catch-basin. The head of the corpse was cut in a dozen different places on the back and temples.

As soon as the body was identified, Martin Burke fled from Chicago. He crossed the Canadian frontier, and was finally traced to Winnipeg, where he was arrested under an assumed name. He had taken a ticket from Winnipeg to Liverpool.

Kunze has rightly escaped with a much less severe sentence than his co-conspirators. The more material of the allegations against him, in addition to the fact mentioned above of his having driven Coughlin to the cottage on the night of the murder, are that he was seen in the rooms hired by Simonds at 117 Clark Street, and that he told a fellow-workman after the murder, but before the discovery of the body, that he knew Cronin was murdered, and that the body would never be found.

The substantive defence appears to have consisted chiefly of a series of *alibis.* They were of the familiar Irish type—a type which in the graphic American tongue is described as "lop-sided."

Full reports of the speeches for the defence and of the concluding arguments for the State have not yet reached this country, and can hardly be expected for some days. But whatever the line taken by counsel for the prisoners may have been, it has failed to prevent a purely American jury of citizens of Cook County from convicting and sentencing to severe punishment four members of as foul and wicked a conspiracy as ever was hatched by Irish brains. That conspiracy, as the evidence shows, was itself the outcome of those intestine quarrels that by a just retribution ever corrode the heart of the Irish-American plots against this country. It was the State's Attorney's cue to paint Dr. Cronin as an innocent and patriotic Irishman, murdered by the hands of villanous rivals. But the true nature of the patriotic society to which Dr. Cronin belonged, and to the hands of whose members he owes his dreadful end, can hardly escape the American public when they come to study the records of the Cronin trial and the verdict of the Chicago jury. Whether that study will nerve the honest citizens of the Republic to rise against the tyranny of Irish machine-men, and purge their name and nation of the stain of harbouring and tolerating such associations, remains to be seen. At any rate, the people of Illinois are to be congratulated on their victory—a victory which, in spite of endless "exceptions" taken on behalf of the prisoners throughout the case, and the endless series of appeals allowed by American law, will hardly be affected in the long run by any fresh proceedings. On the other hand, the convictions may not improbably result in some of the convicts turning informers *more patrio*, and thus bringing the real prime movers in the murder, whose existence is widely believed in in America, in turn to their doom.—*The Times*, 17th December 1889.

WINDES & SULLIVAN,
LAWYERS
702 AND 704 OPERA HOUSE BUILDING
CHICAGO.

THOMAS G. WINDES
ALEXANDER SULLIVAN
—
HENRY BROWNE

TELEPHONE NO. 970.

Aug 30 188 8

My Dear Doctor

Just recd your telegram.
Will you, if the enclosed
are correct, subscribe
to and return them to
me? I am not sure
whether you were in
the '86 convention. Of
course, I know you
were in '84 You can
subscribe before a Notary
or before your J.G. or S.G.
Please fill in the blanks.
On the first line, your name.

WINDES & SULLIVAN
LAWYERS
702 AND 704 OPERA HOUSE BUILDING
CHICAGO

THOMAS G. WINDES
ALEXANDER SULLIVAN
—
HENRY BROWNE

TELEPHONE No. 970.

Z

103

on the 2d. no. of D
an line at end,
sign your name and
write in name of
county at the head
In haste
Sincerely
Alex

NOTE.—The above letter was written to me by Sullivan before the trial of the charges brought against him by Cronin, and refers to evidence being collected by Sullivan to refute those charges. "D." means division, "J. G." and "S. G." mean Junior Guardian and Senior Guardian; and the use of these initials peculiar to the Organization prove Sullivan's continued participation in the Clan-na-gael.

H. le C.

INDEX.

*

THE END.

PRINTED BY BALLANTYNE, HANSON AND CO.
EDINBURGH AND LONDON